ENCHANTED T

A KASTEEL VREDERIC STORYBOOK FOR CHILDREN

"From the library of Kasteel Vrederic, a magical lantern glows and pours its enchanted powers as it brings to life, a charmed diary filled with enchanted tales for the blessed children of the world."

Ann Marie Ruby

Copyright © 2022 Ann Marie Ruby

All rights reserved. No part of this book may be reproduced in any form or stored in any retrieval system without prior written permission from the publisher. Book cover images are composed of stock photos from istockphoto.com, shutterstock.com, and/or specifically illustrated for this book. Interior images are composed of stock photos from istockphoto.com, shutterstock.com, stock photos released under CC0 from Pixabay.com, and/or specifically illustrated for this book.

Disclaimer:

This book ("*Enchanted Tales: A Kasteel Vrederic Storybook For Children*") in no way represents or endorses any religious, philosophical, political, or scientific view. It has been written in good faith for people of all cultures and beliefs. This book has been written in American English. There may be minor variations in the spelling of names and dates due to translations from provincial dialects, regional languages, or minor discrepancies in historical records.

While facts related to the continents, countries, cities, towns, and villages are real as of 2022, references to historical events, real people, or real locations in the tales are used fictitiously. All the tales in this book are a work of fiction. Names, characters, places, and incidents in the tales are the product of the author's imagination or are used fictitiously. Any resemblance to actual persons, living or dead, is purely coincidental.

Published in the United States of America, 2022.

ISBN-13: 979-8-9875085-2-7

DEDICATION

"The largest tree of life grows invisibly upon Mother Earth's chest with new blooms filling in and old ones falling off every hundred years or so. Some leaves fall before their time back onto Mother Earth's chest. Yet all of these leaves are the blessed children of Mother Earth."

ENCHANTED TALES: A KASTEEL VREDERIC STORYBOOK FOR CHILDREN

Love is a school where she holds on to all around her eternally. The one world made from love is a school where we the humans are all her students. With the birth of a child, a story begins to take place. This story is mostly unknown to the world except the few people around the child. Some stories, however, make it to the libraries as they get bounded within a book. Yet some stories never find a page in history. They only find a page in the memories of the beloveds.

As I stood in a very stormy park with a few papers in my hands, I watched the loose papers fly all around me. I saw some children running to catch the papers for me. As they did get them, I told the children these were empty pages of a diary. They could make airplanes or boats with them. The children took the papers and started making airplanes with them.

I wondered if I could have had the stories of these children written on these papers, then I would have sent them all around the globe. I admired the talented children of all different race, color, and religion playing together, trying to help one another. For the children, the parents too gathered and joined in the game. The children held on to love for one another as they created memories together.

Hope, which we hold on to for support, is found within our love for oneself and all others. Above the park appeared an enchanted rainbow which made the children feel they must have created this rainbow through magic. They hoped for a miracle for their loving friends and found the treasure chest at the end of the rainbow. I knew the children's love for one another had created this magical rainbow above the skies as they believed in love and hope.

The musical sounds of nature joined in as the rustling leaves danced with joy. The crowd passing by the delightful children had all smiled back at the children and took positive energy with them. I heard a friend say, even if you can't smile and are forced to smile through some magical dust, it's then the mind, body, and soul awaken with a feeling of completeness. The magical dust I knew then were the children of this world. Their hope and their love awakened my inner faith.

With newly awakened faith, I watched the same park. That's when I watched the tree leaves in the park were all turning orange and I knew they would all fall off soon as it was autumn. Yet in the spring, the magical tree would blossom again with new leaves and new life. New fairy dust would shower upon the trees and new leaves would blossom from love, hope, and faith. The children of the future are the true love, the only hope, and our ultimate faith that shall continue throughout time. The olive tree that stands so tall, did you know its branches are symbols of faith and peace? Oranges symbolize hope. Apples symbolize love. Children are symbols of love, hope, and faith.

So, I knew I would always welcome all race, color, and religion as we are all this everblooming Mother Earth's children. We all come from one tree of life and forever will be one family, the human family. Justly, the children of this world are the true love, true hope, and true faith, we should rejoice with and for.

Today to celebrate this one world, I bring to you my enchanted tales in a storybook for children. Here you will travel around the world and get to know some magical children of this one world. You will get to see the world through my eyes and know beyond your own country and land, this world has so many other countries where we all look different. Yet as we hold on to the hands of our neighboring countries, together we all create the human rainbow.

Open your eyes and just take a look. Know this world is the chest of our Mother Earth. Here we are all the amazing leaves on the one tree of life. The roots of this tree have spread all around the globe and this tree has on its different branches, different race, color, and religion in different countries. If you don't see them, do try to see them as your eyes can only see as far as your hearts shall reach. We all are standing in a closed-door house, where we are able to see what is in our own house, not beyond. Yet if we just walk out of our own home and try to see the other side, we will see all the children of this world, not just our own.

Here within this book, you will travel to the places you may have never visited. Travel through this book, and know this Earth is your open classroom. Hold my hands and see the world as I have weaved enchanted tales from around the globe through the eyes of a child. Through the members of my Kasteel Vrederic family, these tales are retold.

As you travel around the world, you will meet different children from different countries. Each magical child will in his or her voice share his or her tale and seek help from Griet Vrederic van Phillip, the blessed daughter of my *Kasteel Vrederic* series, as children find comfort within one another and trust each other. Through the Kasteel Vrederic family members, we will hear amazing tales.

Dear children of this world, maybe you don't know the members of Kasteel Vrederic as you are young, but your parents have met them through their diaries. You too can read their diaries along with your parents, with your parents' permission.

ENCHANTED TALES: A KASTEEL VREDERIC STORYBOOK FOR CHILDREN

Now our famous doctor and the leading character of my *Kasteel Vrederic* series, Jacobus Vrederic van Phillip, and his family members will share a story each night until we have traveled through the seven continents of this world. We will only hear stories from the countries the Kasteel Vrederic family members have visited. Come on and let's get into the group of children who are all sitting in front of the enchanted lighthouse of Kasteel Vrederic as they are ready for another enchanted tale from Kasteel Vrederic.

Here within the crowd, we all are introduced to the magical goddaughter, blessed granddaughter, and beloved daughter of this castle, Griet Vrederic van Phillip. The beloved magical child is also known to the world as the girl with the lantern. With Griet, you will also meet Rietje Vrederic van Phillip, the brave warrioress, Theunis Peters, the brave soldier, and Alexander van der Bijl, the brave knight.

As we start our journey through this blessed world through the enchanted tales from children who have within their hearts love, hope, and faith, I introduce to you once again the Netherlands as our first stop in the *Enchanted Tales: A Kasteel Vrederic Storybook For Children*.

I dedicate this book to all the children of this world. The children with their pure innocent minds have made my life better and brighter. Just volunteering some quality time with children in schools or libraries or even parks, can make a person feel like they too have given the future generation something to carry into the future with them. Spending some quality time with them and listening to their thoughts, I personally realized how blessed the children of this world are. For every prayer that is answered from above, I believe a little child has asked for that particular prayer to be accepted, and so now the prayer is answered.

Children in my eyes are the magical fairy dust we all search for. Their little hands covered in mud or just clean scents of baby powder, and the pure innocent looks of a child are all the blessings this world needs. A child doesn't have to be your own but can be your friend's child. All children are ours as we all come from the same tree of life.

I pray all the children of this world find loving parents to guide them. Today's children are tomorrow's future. Children are in my eyes the greatest wonder of this world. Their energy and their love for this one world have kept my faith in this one world alive. Somehow, they always brighten the world.

I have met so many children around the globe through my personal journeys. I keep the children, their families, and their friends in my book of memories. I can't travel to see all the children of this world or give them gifts even though my heart wants to send them small gifts which they could keep as treasures.

To all the children of this world and their blessed parents, I have come up with a gift that you can keep forever. Yet this gift you can share with your family and friends. This gift of mine you can actually share with your future generations. This gift of mine we can share with the world citizens and together we can treasure all the children of this world. Through my gift, we can travel around this globe over and over again on many more of our endeavors.

Read around the globe and make this one world your one home. I have written this book for all of you. For all the love and support the world citizens have bestowed upon me from all the corners of this globe throughout my journey as an author, I with all my love and blessings, dedicate this book to all the children of this one world. The children of this world are my love, hope, and faith, as today's children are tomorrow's future.

ENCHANTED TALES: A KASTEEL VREDERIC STORYBOOK FOR CHILDREN

TABLE OF CONTENTS

Dedication	i
Prologue	1
Kasteel Vrederic Family Tree	9
Chapter One: Continent Of Europe	10
The Netherlands	22
Tale: "The Girl With The Lantern"	
Italy	32
Tale: "Twins Of Trevi Fountain"	
Switzerland	43
Tale: "The Chocolate Canoe Of Lake Geneva"	
Greece	53
Tale: "Underwater Miracle Boy"	
United Kingdom	61
Tale: "The Girl Who Fought The Loch Ness Monster"	
Chapter Two: Continent Of Australia And Region Of Oceania	71
Australia	80
Tale: "Willow, Koolewong The Koala, And Joey The Kangaroo Of Queensland"	
New Zealand	89
Tale: "Lake Taupō's Mermaid Mia And Merman Nikau"	
Papua New Guinea	100
Tale: "Samarai Island's Miraculous Triplets"	
Chapter Three: Continent Of Antarctica	111
Snow Hill Island	120
Tale: "The Mystery Penguin Princess Of Snow Hill Island"	
Chapter Four: Continent Of South America	130
Brazil	139

Tale: "The Jaguar Prince Of The Amazon Rainforest"

Chile   148
Tale: "The Magical Star Girl Of The Atacama Desert"

Chapter Five: Continent Of North America   158
United States Of America   168
Tale: "The Magical Eagle Of The USA And His Warriors"

Costa Rica   178
Tale: "The Warrior Monkey Boy, The Turtle Boy, And The Macaws"

Chapter Six: Continent Of Asia   188
India   199
Tale: "The Classical Dancer, The Peacock Prince"

Bangladesh   209
Tale: "Padma River's Youngest Ferry Boy"

Chapter Seven: Continent Of Africa   219
Kenya   232
Tale: "The Mystical Princess And The Rhinos Of Maasai Mara"

Madagascar   242
Tale: "The Lemur Girl Of Madagascar"

Egypt   251
Tale: "The Invisible Boy Of The Nile River"

Conclusion   261

Inhabitants Of Kasteel Vrederic   266

Glossary   269

Answer Key   271

Message From The Author   277

About The Author   283

Books By The Author   286

PROLOGUE:

Kasteel Vrederic
Naarden, The Netherlands

"The world becomes one home as you see all the children of this world through the eyes of a father."

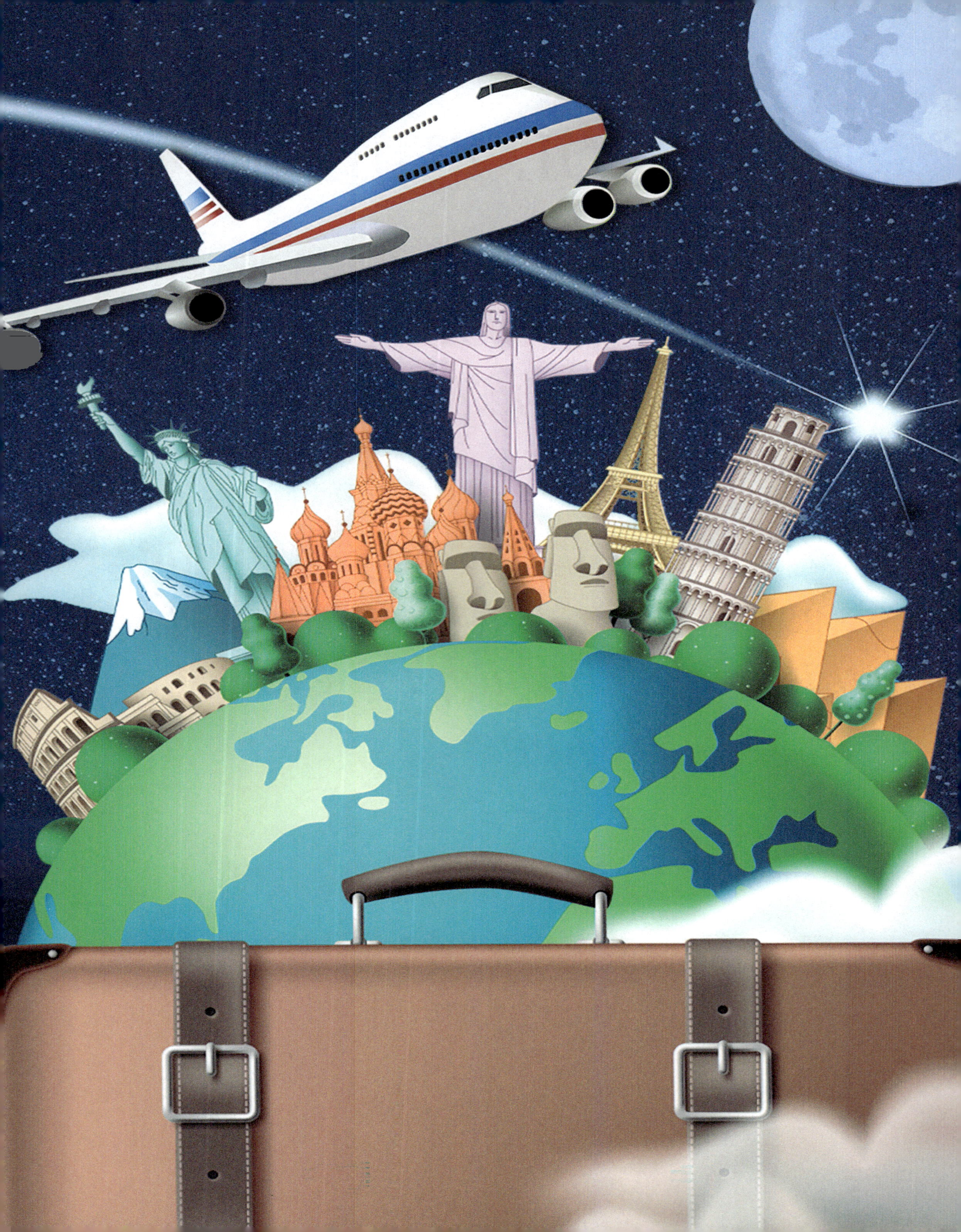

Dear blessed children of this world, welcome to my home. We call her Kasteel Vrederic, named after my ancestors. My home is my haven where miracles are like sprinkles of fairy dust appearing all around us. Within the walls of Kasteel Vrederic, my home, magical stories take birth with every newborn child. I have as my support my family members. Here everything is possible if only you believe.

Throughout our journey of life, we have created infinite and immortal love stories. I hope you all believe in true love as within my castle, twin flames have risen from ashes like the magical phoenix only to unite with one another. Did you know, my ancestors had saved accused witches from the gallows? I also have as my ancestors one of the greatest warriors from the Dutch Eighty Years' War. We have in our household, psychics who can see the future and the past. So, they guide our household members and all visitors who come and visit our home.

In this home, we are not afraid of anything, not even death. We truly believe in reincarnation as we take that route to journey back to our home and family members. We have also through the tunnel of light traveled back in time to the seventeenth century to help our ancestors.

I hear a lot of you don't believe in time traveling. Yet have you not seen your family members who have become twinkling stars of the night in your dreams? You have, right? So, you see then you too have traveled time. Yes, through the door of dreams. My family believes in dreams as one of the greatest miracles in existence. Some dreams we see during our sleep as they come to us through the door of miracles.

Yet dear children, do not take for granted the dreams you see during the daylight hours as for those dreams, we the humans have traveled to the moon and beyond. Through those dreams, we have amongst ourselves great painters, musicians, teachers, and like me, even doctors. Your parents too are magical as through eternal love and uniting after rising like the magical phoenix, they had you, the biggest miracle in this universe.

Now through my diary let us, my family members and me, introduce you to some magical stories. From the voices of my family members and their guidance, you will hear stories of and from the seven continents of this world. These magical stories will be of enchanted magicians, phenomenal wizards, skilled supernatural children, blessed reincarnated children, paranormal dream psychics, mysterious time travelers, and more.

These children have united the world through their amazing gifts. They did not forget their friends of the animal kingdom. For when and where we get into trouble, it is then our animal friends come to our rescue.

They know the complete truth and believe this world is actually a huge tree, one tree from where all of this world's population are from. Yes, we are all from different branches, different leaves, and different fruits, yet we are all from the same tree. Our mother is Mother Earth, and this tree to you and all is known as the tree of life.

So, come on and take a journey through the seven continents of this world through the eyes of young children from around the globe. These amazing gifted and talented children will tell you about their countries and their tales. Through their short tales, you will be introduced to their country, their land, and their people. You will see their rivers, their landmarks, and different wonders of this world.

This enchanted book will be bound with enchanted tales of these magical children. I will place this book in the libraries across this world for you to pick up and enjoy. For after reading this book, you the child, the future of this world, will give your blessed hands to greet and hold on to the blessed hands of your neighboring countries.

Through all of the children's hands spread out to greet and hold on to all the children of this world, we will again have one world and one family. Then you the child will grow up and say we are family. You and I across this globe in union are one family.

Now let us go to the Netherlands first as that's where I am from. I come from Naarden, the Netherlands where we too have in our home a blessed daughter. We call her the girl with the lantern. Why don't you hear her tale now? With her beloved twin flame, the greatest warrior of the sixteenth century, she had guided Kasteel Vrederic for years.

After her journey through the magical tunnel of light, she came back as the girl with the lantern. Her sacrifice became the biggest gift for my family and my home. Now we have her as the blessed daughter of Kasteel Vrederic. Now let us begin the first tale of this book from the Netherlands as we call this story, "The Girl With The Lantern."

I could hear the footsteps of my mother Anadhi Newhouse van Phillip coming into the library. My mother is of half-Indian and half-American heritage. Her dark black hair falls long behind her back. Her olive-colored skin feels soft and like my safe haven. My father who is of Dutch heritage calls her his Indian princess. I call her Mama.

ENCHANTED TALES: A KASTEEL VREDERIC STORYBOOK FOR CHILDREN

My beautiful evergreen mother walked in with a little toddler running in with her. I saw my mother had our blessed daughter, my brother's daughter, Griet Vrederic van Phillip with her. We all call her the girl with the lantern.

Mama said, "Jacobus, what are you doing? We will be late. All the children from the orphanage and schools around here have gathered up in the front courtyard with their own lanterns. They are all ready for the first story of the night."

I watched my father Erasmus van Phillip, six feet tall, a very muscular yet slender-built Dutchman, walk in with my young daughter Rietje. My parents are the joint diarists of *Be My Destiny: Vows From The Beyond*.

Papa then said, "Jacobus, the children are all ready, and so are your brothers. They are all waiting for story time to begin."

I smiled at the two toddlers, my goddaughter and niece Griet and my daughter Rietje as both came and jumped on my lap. I was blessed this night, as I got two huge kisses planted on my two cheeks at once by my favorite girls. These girls first appeared in the famous diaries I had written in my past life as the famous diarist Jacobus van Vrederic.

Rietje appeared in *Eternally Beloved: I Shall Never Let You Go* and *Evermore Beloved: I Shall Never Let You Go*. She reappeared again in *Entranced Beloved: I Shall Never Let You Go*.

That's when I heard my brother Antonius van Phillip, the diarist of *Heart Beats Your Name: Vows From The Beyond*, and his wife Katelijne Snaaijer van Phillip walk in with sweaters for their daughter Griet and my daughter Rietje. They both were very excited for the story time campout as both girls knew story time and loved listening to stories, yet tonight was special as we had so many children, toddlers, and their families come over.

Antonius came over and said, "Big Bro, Alexander and Theunis are ready and have invited Aunt Marinda here for the event. We were not sure where the magical psychic was, so we did not want the boys to get their hopes up. They are as magical as is Aunt Marinda, so she appeared."

My brother came over and hugged me as we always start our days with hugging one another. I hugged him back and rubbed his hair which my very stylish artist brother does not like, yet he only laughed out loud as we both knew the laughter was for Andries who was at the door.

Andries van Phillip, my brother, from his previous life yet my reincarnated nephew in this life is also very magical as he grew before our own eyes and aged within days to a twenty-nine-year-old man. He also appeared in Antonius's diary, *Heart Beats Your Name: Vows From The*

Beyond and *Entranced Beloved: I Shall Never Let You Go,* which Antonius and I co-wrote. His age progression and reappearance, however, occurred in my most recent diary, *Forbidden Daughter Of Kasteel Vrederic: Vows From The Beyond.*

In the same diary, my twin flame also reappeared as Dr. Margriete Achthoven, now Dr. Margriete Achthoven van Phillip. I saw then my wife appeared with the magical boys who had reentered this world not through birth but through the tunnel of light with the very miraculous and magical psychic Aunt Marinda, the time traveler, in my last diary. Margriete came and hugged Mama, Papa, Antonius, Katelijne, and Andries. She came near me as I placed a kiss on her head. I knew she was going to say something.

She said, "Jacobus, the boys have started to glow like light in the dark. I am worried what do we tell everyone if anyone should raise any questions?"

I saw she had with her Alexander the knight who was still a very small child and our sixteenth-century warrior Theunis. Theunis and Griet in union are the spirits of Kasteel Vrederic who appeared in the magical lighthouse that stands on top of our home. Even though both have reappeared as humans on Earth, due to the magical spells of Aunt Marinda, the two still appear in the lighthouse when someone from Kasteel Vrederic needs them.

I told them, "It shall all be all right as it's a magical night. This night shall be filled with enchanted tales from around the globe. We shall all just say to celebrate this magical night, they have appeared like this. Also, we must get the children's parents in our audience ready for the next diary that's coming out. *The Immortality Serum: Vows From The Beyond* is where more of the magical and spiritual miracles await all of us and all of them."

My family members all went outside by the camp as they welcomed the visitors. I introduced ourselves to all the visitors. I am Jacobus Vrederic van Phillip, and my wife is Margriete Achthoven van Phillip. My father is Erasmus van Phillip, my mother is Anadhi Newhouse van Phillip, my brother is Antonius van Phillip, his wife is Katelijne Snaaijer van Phillip, their son and my reincarnated brother is Andries van Phillip, and my home is known to all of you as Kasteel Vrederic.

Before we travel through the seven continents of this world, let me introduce you to the four children who will take us on magical journeys through enchanted tales. Griet Vrederic van Phillip is the girl with the lantern, who had guided all the inhabitants of Kasteel Vrederic from the magical lighthouse. She has returned in her reincarnated form. With her lantern, she travels to guide and help everyone. Rietje Vrederic van Phillip the warrioress is back in the twenty-first century. Born in the sixteenth century, the warrioress had fought and won back Kasteel Vrederic in the seventeenth century for her family with a horse and her sword. The Kasteel Vrederic lineage continued through her. Now her horse and sword travel time and come to her when she needs them.

Theunis Peters was a soldier in the sixteenth century and had married Griet in his previous life. He has returned and his sword too comes to him from the sixteenth century when he calls upon it. Alexander van der Bijl was an honorable knight of the seventeenth century and husband of Rietje. He stood by Rietje and her family members as he fought and protected Kasteel Vrederic from invaders. He has traveled time and has been reborn again to be with the family. His sword from the seventeenth century travels time and comes to him even today to help him in his time of need.

If you all are a bit confused about my family tree, don't worry as I have added my family tree for all of you. As you are going through the enchanted tales, you can quickly glance through my family tree to understand who is taking you through each night's tales.

We will all take turns to retell blessed stories to all of you as we retell these stories to Griet, Rietje, Theunis, and Alexander, the children of Kasteel Vrederic and all of the visiting children of this world. So now I would like to say on behalf of my entire family, some of whom you can see and maybe some of whom you can't, welcome to our home, Kasteel Vrederic.

We will start this book with my home and my country, the Netherlands. Let's visit the Netherlands in the continent of Europe. We will in this diary learn and visit the seven continents of this world through geographical maps, some of the countries from each continent, and the wonders of this world. Yet remember we will mostly listen to some enchanted tales from each continent through the eyes of enchanted children who reside in the seven continents.

It's a good idea to know where your little friends are from, before you head into their homes. Remember if you are visiting a friend tonight to have a sleepover, you need to get your parents' permission to go there. Before you head over, why don't you try to see and learn a little about their culture and their heritage?

Let's first learn the names of the seven continents before we learn about them in detail as we read each enchanted tale from the seven continents. The seven continents of this world are as follows:

1. Asia
2. Antarctica

3. Australia/Oceania
4. South America
5. Europe
6. North America
7. Africa

The world we live in also has Seven Modern Wonders. When traveling through this world, you might not be able to see all of the wonders of this world but maybe you can see some or get introduced to them through this book. The Seven Modern Wonders are as follows:

1. Great Wall of China
2. Machu Picchu
3. City of Petra
4. Chichen Itza
5. Christ the Redeemer
6. Colosseum
7. Taj Mahal

Now let us travel through the seven continents of this world through the pages of,

Enchanted Tales:
A Kasteel Vrederic Storybook For Children.

ENCHANTED TALES: A KASTEEL VREDERIC STORYBOOK FOR CHILDREN

Family Tree Of Kasteel Vrederic

Johannes van Vrederic ♥ Mahalt

Jacobus van Vrederic ♥ Margriete van Wijck

Theunis Peters ♥ Griet van Jacobus

Alexander van der Bijl ♥ Margriete "Rietje" Jacobus Peters

- Anadhi van der Bijl
- Margriete van der Bijl
- Griet van der Bijl

Vincent van Phillip ♥ Greta van Phillip

Hieronymus van Phillip ♥ Grietje van Phillip

Hendrick van Phillip ♥ Griete van Phillip

Erasmus van Phillip ♥ Anadhi Newhouse van Phillip

Petrus van Phillip ♥ Giada Berlusconi van Phillip

Matthias van Phillip

Jacobus Vrederic van Phillip ♥ Margriete van Achthoven

Andries van Phillip

Antonius van Phillip ♥ Katelijne Snaaijer van Phillip

Rietje Vrederic van Phillip

Andries van Phillip

Griet Vrederic van Phillip

Vows From The Beyond · I Shall Never Let You Go

9

CHAPTER ONE:

CONTINENT OF EUROPE

Storyteller:
Andries van Phillip

"I am the second-smallest continent in the world. Did you know I also have the smallest country known to you as the Vatican City, within my chest? I am known to this world as the continent, Europe."

ENCHANTED TALES: A KASTEEL VREDERIC STORYBOOK FOR CHILDREN

Welcome to the world of *Enchanted Tales: A Kasteel Vrederic Storybook For Children*. Weaving a story through the minds of children and for children is what will happen here. I am Andries van Phillip of Kasteel Vrederic. It is true our family has psychics, dreamers, time travelers, authors, diarists, pianists, soldiers, knights, painters, warriors, famous models, and doctors like the famous doctor, Jacobus, who was there in the sixteenth century for all who needed him. He is here again in the twenty-first century for us, and for all of you in the future. He taught us through the journey of his life, to be there for all race, color, and religion, anywhere, anytime.

Before we start sharing with you the enchanted magical stories, let's talk about the continents these stories will come from. This night we are in Europe as you can see on the globe where we are tonight. Remember we will circle the world through seven nights.

Europe is the second-smallest continent among the seven continents in this world. It is located in the westernmost part of the Eurasian landmass. There are forty-four countries in Europe. Europe is bordered by the Mediterranean Sea in the south, the Arctic Ocean in the north, the Atlantic Ocean in the west, and the continent of Asia in the east. Here in Europe, we are rich in our diversity as two hundred different languages are spoken in this continent. From these, however, only twenty-four are official languages. Just think how rich and diverse these countries are. Also try to think how many languages you might be able to speak just from Europe if only you try.

We will have a few children from each of these continents meet up for a story and dinner. Every night as we visit each continent, we will get to try different items from different continents for dinner, arranged by my family members representing each continent for all of you. So, all of you here and all who are reading this book, please do come over and get to know Kasteel Vrederic and my family members as we take you around the globe. Also, if you are reading, then why don't you ask your parents to maybe make a dish from each continent through the seven nights and enjoy it as you read through these chapters? Tonight, we will travel through Europe.

SOME OF EUROPE'S FAMOUS FOODS

Let's get introduced to some of Europe's famous foods. The famous couple Anadhi and Erasmus from *Be My Destiny: Vows From The Beyond* are my adoptive parents from my last life. I call them Big Mama and Big Papa. My family members love Indian food as my adoptive mother Anadhi, whom I still call Big Mama, is half-Indian and half-American. My adoptive father

Erasmus, whom I still call Big Papa, is Dutch. Big Mama's faith brought me back as she believes in love and miracles.

In this life, my biological mother Katelijne, whom I call Mama, is of Italian heritage and my father Antonius, whom I call Buddy, is half-Italian and half-Dutch, raised by the same mother I shared with him in my previous life. Oh yes, maybe your parents have read all about my rebirth in *Forbidden Daughter Of Kasteel Vrederic: Vows From The Beyond*. They could share with you my life story maybe another day.

International cuisine is something I have grown up with. All food made in my home has a little bit of international spices added to them. My family members are all very good cooks as we realized through our travels. Trying new food and sharing food around a table can unite all different countries and citizens. So, my dear children, here are some of the famous European foods for you to try out.

Pasta – *Italy* *Spain* – **Paella**
Sernik – *Poland* *Iceland* – **Kleinur**
Moussaka – *Greece* *Sweden* – **Köttbullar**
Currywurst – *Germany* *Denmark* – **Wienerbrød**
Fish and Chips – *England* *Portugal* – **Pastel de Nata**
La Cuchaule – *Switzerland* *Belgium* – **Belgian Pralines**
Poffertjes – *the Netherlands* *France* – **Gratin Dauphinois**
Viennese Apfelstrudel – *Austria*

· Menu ·

COUNTRIES OF EUROPE

Now let's learn to say the names of the countries in Europe, so when you get to see a child from Europe, you will know where exactly your friend is from. Here are the names of the forty-four countries from the continent we all know as Europe. Even though we will stop over in only a few countries, it is nice to get ourselves introduced to all of the countries in Europe as miraculous stories are hidden within all of the countries. Here are the names of these magical lands.

Albania

Andorra

Austria

Belarus

Belgium

Bosnia and Herzegovina

Bulgaria

Croatia

Czech Republic (Czechia)

Denmark

Estonia

Finland

France

ENCHANTED TALES: A KASTEEL VREDERIC STORYBOOK FOR CHILDREN

Germany

Greece

Holy See

Hungary

Iceland

Ireland

Italy

Latvia

Liechtenstein

Lithuania

Luxembourg

Malta

Moldova

Monaco

Montenegro

Netherlands

North Macedonia

Norway

Portugal

Russia

Serbia

Slovenia

Sweden

Ukraine

Poland

Romania

San Marino

Slovakia

Spain

Switzerland

United Kingdom

LANDMARK QUIZ

Which landmark is this and where is it located?

A. Eiffel Tower, France
B. Belém Tower, Portugal
C. Leaning Tower of Pisa, Italy
D. Parthenon, Greece

SOME OF EUROPE'S LANDMARKS

When you visit Europe, do stop by some of these amazing landmarks. Remember all you have to do is open a book to travel through them.

Landmarks

Eiffel Tower – *France*
Colosseum – *Italy*
Parthenon – *Greece*
La Sagrada Familia – *Spain*
Stonehenge – *England*
Leaning Tower of Pisa – *Italy*
Binnenhof – *the Netherlands*
Brandenburg Gate – *Germany*
Blue Lagoon – *Iceland*
Belém Tower – *Portugal*

STORY TIME WITH ANDRIES VAN PHILLIP

I do hope you all are now a little more familiar with the continent Kasteel Vrederic is in. Now let's hear some stories from this continent. I am Andries van Phillip, a son of the famous Kasteel Vrederic, and I will take you through the stories of Europe. You will meet my family members one at a time as we will all guide you across this one home, we all call Earth, through *Enchanted Tales: A Kasteel Vrederic Storybook For Children.*

THE NETHERLANDS

The Girl With The Lantern

"Throughout the day, you all have the bright sun guiding you, yet my beloved family and friends, throughout the dark moonless or moonlit night, you will be guided and have an extra protection, from the girl with the lantern."

ENCHANTED TALES: A KASTEEL VREDERIC STORYBOOK FOR CHILDREN

Netherlands

The Kingdom of the Netherlands is a parliamentary constitutional monarchy. The Kingdom includes the Netherlands in Western Europe, and Aruba, Sint Maarten, and Curaçao in the Caribbean. Each country is a constituent sovereign state. Here though we will only visit the Netherlands, a country in northwestern Europe. The language spoken in this country is Dutch.

King Willem-Alexander of this country is a very humble man and is often seen riding on his bicycle with his wife, Queen Máxima, and the Princess of Orange, Princess Catharina-Amalia. They are loved by the citizens as they too love the citizens like their own family members. Did you know the Netherlands is connected to France, Germany, Sweden, Norway, Belgium, and Denmark through the North Sea? The capital city is very famous and is called Amsterdam. This place was also home to the admirable diarist Anne Frank. The Netherlands has twelve provinces and two of the provinces are called North and South Holland.

Do visit the Netherlands and maybe you can dance like the tulips in the magical tulip fields of Zaanse Schans, where the musical windmills will join in with your musical dancing group. You can stop by the political capital, The Hague, and watch the politicians work in the oldest parliamentary building still in use. Who knows, you might be lucky and get to see our famous longest-serving Prime Minister, Mark Rutte, of the Netherlands during your visit as he constantly bikes within the citizens of this country.

Did you know a fun fact about my own country is the Dutchmen are supposedly the tallest men in the world? I really don't think I made the list though. It is also said the Dutch children are the happiest children in the world. I want this happiness to spread all around the world like the tulips of the Netherlands have spread all around the globe. These famous tulips, however, were brought to the Netherlands from the Ottoman Empire.

Another fun fact is the telescope and the microscope were both Dutch inventions. We are proud of our inventions and how we fought and befriended our worst enemy, the water, as one-third of my homeland is under water. Yet we fought and have become victorious against the waterwolf, a monster that had tried to swallow up our land.

Do you enjoy painting? Buddy and Big Papa are both famous painters as they wanted to follow the footsteps of some of the world's greatest painters including Rembrandt Harmenszoon van Rijn, Vincent van Gogh, Johannes Vermeer, and Hendrik Willem Mesdag.

ENCHANTED TALES: A KASTEEL VREDERIC STORYBOOK FOR CHILDREN

Now let's go to Naarden and visit the famous home known to all of us as Kasteel Vrederic to listen to our first enchanted tale of this night. The enchanted musical sound of the piano playing in the background relaxes my enchanting little sister Griet. She is a miracle child I am blessed to be related to. In this life, I am her big brother. I am the miracle child who was born with complete memories of my past life. Yet I grew older within a couple years of my birth in this life. Miraculous phenomena are not particularly strangers within our home, known to all of you as the mystical Kasteel Vrederic.

In my past life, I was a famous pianist. Strangely the world does not know I have traveled through the door of reincarnation and am back home again, as the same pianist. So, I tell my toddler sister Griet, who is two years old and our cousin Rietje who is almost two, not to fear anything in life. Where and when you just want a sprinkle of magical dust in your life, you should close your eyes and make a wish upon the starry night's skies.

I am Andries van Phillip and tonight let me start the campfire as I retell a true story about my sister. You see before her birth, she was known to all of this world as the girl with the lantern. She was also known for more than four hundred years as the famous spirit of Kasteel Vrederic as she had guided this home with her husband the great warrior Theunis Peters for centuries. Now after her birth in this lifetime, she is known to all of this world as Griet Vrederic van Phillip.

Tonight, as you all get comfortable under this open tent in your very comfortable sleeping bags, let me take you on a journey through the past. This is a magical story of my blessed sister Griet. I call this enchanted tale, "The Girl With The Lantern."

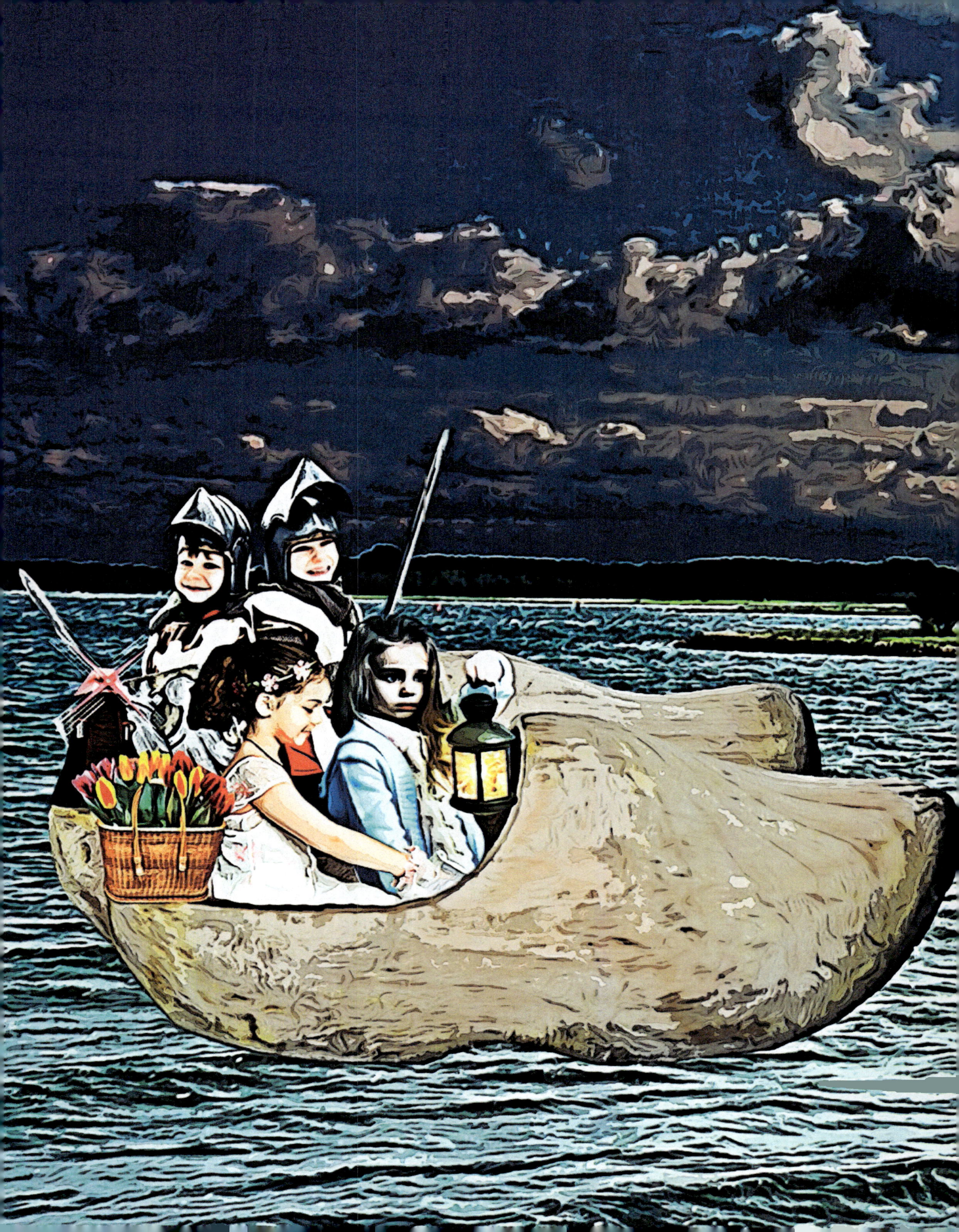

THE GIRL WITH THE LANTERN

It was a starless, stormy night, where the glorious light of the glowing moon was missing. The furious thunders roared above the dark night's skies. Angry bolts of lightning flashed all around the dark North Sea as the only string of lights visible. The fury of the night was heard through the very angry songs of the howling winds. This night, the hooting owls stayed away in their trees, as did the singing nightingales. All the children and their parents stayed home on this night.

On a stormy night like this, children are told about famous mischievous tales of knights and soldiers who roam around like floating ghosts and goblins to maybe create some mischief. Yet there are some knights and soldiers, warriors, time travelers, and miraculous children who roam around the dark nights to help and guide the helpless.

I was watching the stormy night while I knew my baby sister was sleeping like a princess in her princess bed. I fell asleep by the lake behind my home on our family boat. I felt very sleepy as I had yearned to see the ferocious storm firsthand and waited for the thunder and lightning to get even more ferocious.

There in front of me I saw my baby sister Griet. A five-year-old girl was standing and glowing like the miraculous night's star. As all the inhabitants of Kasteel Vrederic were used to seeing Griet at the time of need, I knew my sister was here because someone in trouble had called upon the girl with the lantern.

I jumped up at the sight of her and asked, "Griet, is everything all right? How did you come here? I know I had left you in your bed."

She watched me and spoke in sweet musical tunes as she said, "Big Bro, there are some forty boats with fish and forty fishermen who are stranded in the North Sea, by the Fisherman Village in Scheveningen. Their families are waiting for them, but they will be lost in the rough sea because there is no one to guide them back onto the right course. They will all vanish and never be found as the evil sea monster is waiting for them with his mouth open. He will gobble them up in one go and they will be lost forever."

I heard her worries and told her, "I am confused as these days we have patrol boats who will guide them back to shore."

My sister watched me and said, "Big Bro, always remember with all the technologies in the world, there are still the lost and stranded boats and ships that go missing and are never found.

There are no reasons found when miracles do occur or do not occur. I must help the fishermen of Scheveningen as there are so many children who are waiting for their fathers to come back home."

That's when I saw our home's famous seventeenth-century knight, Alexander, appear as an eight-year-old child in front of me. With him came along the brave warrior from the sixteenth century, Theunis, as an eight-year-old child. I tried to see what was happening when I saw the famous sixteenth century's diarist Jacobus van Vrederic's beloved granddaughter Rietje appear as a five-year-old child, on her horse with a sword in her hand.

I knew if the four miraculous children have traveled miraculously and come over to help someone or something, then the situation must be serious. They were all here to prevent a devastation from becoming a reality. It was then I saw our family time traveler whom some called a witch, and some now call a psychic, appear in front of me with her ever-glowing gray hair.

Aunt Marinda told the four children, "Come on everyone, we don't have all night. Get in the boat and let's get going."

I wondered what boat they were getting into as my small boat only could fit one person. That's when Aunt Marinda took off her wooden clogs and placed them in the lake that connects to the North Sea. In front of my eyes, the clogs became a twin boat that looked like two attached gondolas.

Then Aunt Marinda said, "Andries, we don't have all night, so close your mouth and hand me the bucket of tulips I left on the dock. Also get in the boat everyone and Andries please bring the windmill that I left next to the bucket as you get into the boat."

I did as I was asked. I watched how the four kids got in the boat. Rietje's horse became a seahorse, became huge, went into the water, and held the double gondola on her shoulders. All of these magical events were taking place as Aunt Marinda placed magical dust from her hands around the night's skies. At that moment, I watched our girl with the lantern sit on the nose of the gondola so bravely with her little lantern in her hands.

The lake and the dark night glowed ever so brightly as if the moon in her true glory just came and placed herself on my little sister's hands. I was a proud brother who forgot all the danger of the rough sea as I admired my sister for her bravery and dedication to save all who need her.

Griet said, "The blessed tulips of the Netherlands and the blessed windmill who accompany us on this frightful night, won't you become our eyes and ears?"

ENCHANTED TALES: A KASTEEL VREDERIC STORYBOOK FOR CHILDREN

The bucket of tulips became little fairies who flew with us, guiding our gondola. The single windmill became the voice as it converted to become a man and told all he will be the skipper of the gondola.

I watched a magical clog gondola, with a windmill gondolier, and tulip fairies all guide us, led by the girl with the lantern. We knew there in the dark sea was hiding a sea monster who only fed on humans as his prey. Yet tonight, the monster would learn a lesson. When and where people unite, even children who unite for the better of this world, no one or nothing could come in between them, their destiny, their destination, or their achievement.

I sat next to my sister who sat at the front of the gondola, on the tip of the gondola. She had a lantern in her hand and at all times as she kept an eye on the rough and scary sea. I saw she had her eyes out for the lost fishermen of the sea. As we floated along the cold and dark sea, we saw how quiet everything looked. There were no boats nor were there any fishermen to be seen miles ahead of us. The only light guiding our gondola was the magical lantern my sister with her very steady hands held all along.

That's when Griet said, "Aunt Marinda, I hear them. They are calling me through the dark waves. I know they are all imprisoned behind a huge boulder near a bend in the sea."

In the dark night, I watched Alexander, the brave knight, and Theunis, the brave soldier, stand in front of Griet as she stayed still at her seat without moving or bending. The children did not whisper or say anything yet somehow spoke mind-to-mind with one another. It was then I saw for the first time in my life, a real-life sea monster. The monster looked like a huge crocodile but somehow it had a human-looking head and it had feet like humans too.

The sea monster was floating in the water as its feet and tail blocked forty fishermen and forty boats filled with fish. All were returning home to their families and villages to feed their own families. The sea monster blocked them with its tail and feet as it tried to look at us with its huge eyes.

It was then I saw Rietje's seahorse that was pulling our gondola take upon her our little Rietje. At that time, Rietje, the warrioress, flew from behind me as she threw her magical sword into the monster. Griet held her magical lantern as its light glowed on the monster. I saw the magical tulip fairies started to sing sweet songs of the sea. The sea monster was afraid of the enchanting sounds of the tulip fairies.

The windmill gondolier started to sing along with the tulip fairies as the song began to hurt the sea monster. He was becoming weak and started to let go of the fishermen and their boats, one by one.

Like the magical fairy dust, the huge sea monster too became dust and flew on top of the skies. Aunt Marinda watched the skies as the moon appeared with its glorious glow and swallowed the huge sea monster. My four little brave warriors all danced with joy at that time.

The tulip fairies and the windmill gondolier kept on singing with joy, as the magical clog gondola guided all the lost and stranded fishermen back to the fisherman village in Scheveningen. I watched all the fishermen walk out of their boats in a daze as if they were all confused. They started to talk amongst themselves and asked one another what had just happened. It was then I saw the tulip leaves from the tulip fairies fly on top of them.

Griet said, "Big Bro, they will now forget everything they had witnessed. The magical tulips will become fairy dust and erase their memories. They will forget the sea monster, and about all of us. It's for their own good. Sometimes humans can't take miracles from the beyond as anything normal. So tonight, for their own good, they will forget everything that had occurred to them or around them. They all have returned to their families safely and unharmed."

Aunt Marinda said, "Yet they will know somehow remember there in the dark and vast sea, forty fishermen and forty fishing boats with fish returned home safely because they were all guided by a brave girl and her magical lantern."

I watched my sister, the girl with the lantern, still kept a strong grip on her lantern as she told the glorious moon, "Dear moon and the bright night stars who are ever so bright and always guiding the lost and stranded throughout the dark nights, if ever you do take a break and must hide behind a dark cloud, it is then and there I will appear as your little helper. Forever and always, I am known as the girl with the lantern."

That night when I returned home, I placed my little sister in bed. I knew I would be there for her as she is and shall be there for all who need her. For the inhabitants of Kasteel Vrederic, she was and is known as the spirit in the lighthouse of the castle. Throughout centuries from the magical lighthouse, she watched over my family members. Yet as she entered this Earth as my sister, she will watch over all who call upon her. She is known to all as the girl with the lantern.

ENCHANTED TALES: A KASTEEL VREDERIC STORYBOOK FOR CHILDREN

Netherlands Trivia Time

What is the language spoken in this country?

What is the political capital of the Netherlands?

What sea connects the Netherlands to France, Germany, Sweden, Norway, Belgium, and Denmark?

31

ITALY

Twins Of Trevi Fountain

"Legend has it couples place coins in the magical fountain so that they could be granted a wish, a wish to find one another. Yet what happens when children place a coin and wish to find their parents?"

ENCHANTED TALES: A KASTEEL VREDERIC STORYBOOK FOR CHILDREN

Italy

33

Welcome to Italy. Italians call their country Italia and the nickname is Bel Paese, which means beautiful country. This amazingly beautiful country is situated in South-Central Europe. Some of my ancestors came from this land. This country is a unitary parliamentary republic.

The famous city Rome is its capital city. Italy has various charming sceneries and is known for its beautiful landscapes. Because of its shape like a boot, Italy is also famously nicknamed Lo Stivale which means the boot. The language spoken in this country is Italian. Did you know this language is also known as a Romance language?

I have visited Italy a few times, in this life and my past life. I do have memories of both lives. You see, I too am a magical son brought back to this world through the magical wishes of my adoptive mother, Big Mama. Once upon a time, she too sat under the bright starry nights and made a wish when she saw the first twinkling star of the night. Her wish was granted as I, the miracle boy, came back to Big Mama's home. Some might say now I am her grandson, yet I still call her by the name I always did, Big Mama.

A tour guide told us Italy is the fifth most visited country in the world. The Italian culture is rich in art, music, food, and architecture. Did you know thirteen out of thirty-eight of William Shakespeare's plays were based in Italy? It's an amazing and miraculous place where you too could write plays and let your imagination go wild. Have any one of you seen an active volcano? If not, then you should look up Italy as in this country, there are all three of Europe's active volcanos.

My family's favorite part of visiting Italy is having pizza in Naples. Since it is not possible to visit the country continuously, we brought their pizza and pasta recipes into our home. Why don't you try to make some Italian pasta or pizza tonight? The Italians have made and had pasta since the fourth century B.C., and yes, that's even before my Big Bro Jacobus was born. If you all have met him, you should know he is the same sixteenth-century diarist. In this life, he is the famous doctor.

Maybe as you are listening to this story, you could try baking a fresh Italian pizza or maybe make some authentic Italian pasta. Before we go and listen to another enchanted tale, I want you all to remember when you go to school tomorrow, ask your teachers if they knew Italy was also the home to the famous legendary Roman Empire. Additionally, famous painters like Michelangelo di Lodovico Buonarroti Simoni, commonly known as Michelangelo, and Leonardo di ser Piero da Vinci, commonly known as Leonardo da Vinci, called this place their home. Now when you are taught about them in school, you can tell your classmates you have already heard about them.

Tonight, let us visit the Trevi fountain as that's where we shall find a set of twins. These twins are a boy named Giovanni and his twin sister named Fiorentina. The famous Trevi Fountain is visited yearly by millions of tourists from all over the world. Everyone hopes this magical fountain might grant them with magical wishes. In the Trevi fountain each year, visitors throw over one million euros.

Each person who throws a coin into the fountain makes a wish. It is said where there is hope and where wishes are made from the heart, they do come true. Tonight, let me take you on a journey through the past. I am Andries van Phillip a son of Kasteel Vrederic and this is the story of Giovani and his twin sister Fiorentina. I call this enchanted tale, "Twins Of Trevi Fountain."

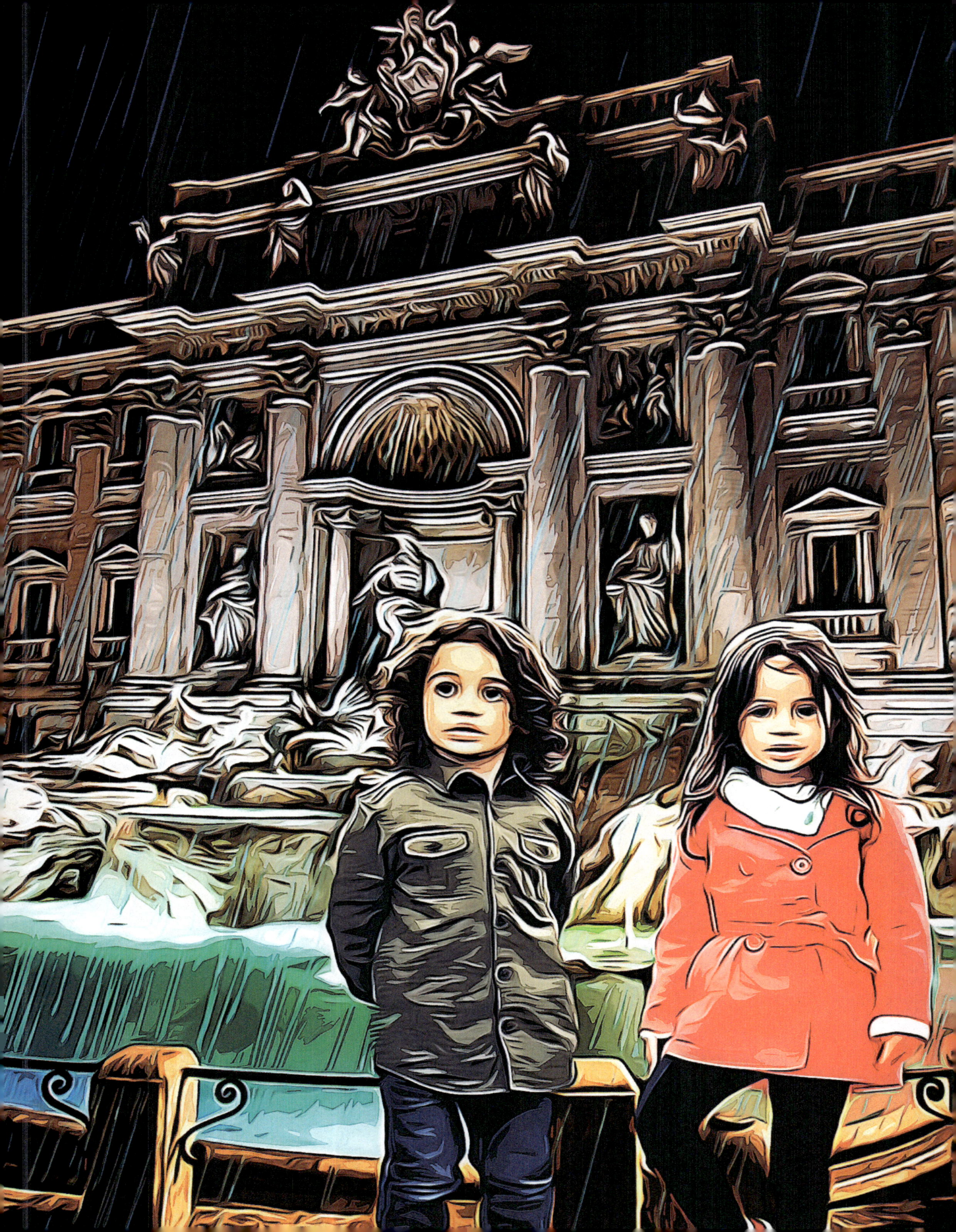

TWINS OF TREVI FOUNTAIN

On a very sunny and hot summer day, I was in Rome, Italy with my family. My job was to babysit my sister Griet and my brother Jacobus's daughter, my niece Rietje. I was also responsible for the two miraculous boys Alexander and Theunis whom Aunt Marinda had adopted and live with us as our family members. It might sound strange, but Big Mama has made it a rule that our family members live in the same home, and we vacation together too.

We have our very busy lives as individually we all travel a lot for our job requirements. I will share with you the truth is we love being together as much as we can. No one could separate my family members from one another, not even death as I proved it, by returning from the beyond. You can call our family the united family members, of Kasteel Vrederic.

Abruptly during a very hot summer day, we saw a forceful summer storm come over Rome. It was unusual but it does happen in Rome. The tour guide told us the storms come down very hard, yet they would be over soon. It was strange as I called Big Bro, Jacobus, and he said where he was, there were no rain showers. But his colleague had called and where his colleague was, there an accident had happened because of the heavy rainfall.

I knew wherever my Big Bro was, everyone would be all right as he is the doctor with magical hands. So, I assumed all the storms of this life would be over soon. Little did I know there would be another kind of storm that would be visiting us soon.

I could see the magical Trevi Fountain from my hotel room. It looked amazing as the rain poured from the skies ferociously. Everyone who had been waiting around the fountain to make a wish left, leaving the fountain completely empty. Then I saw on the television, the news was reporting the unusual weather storms had caused major flooding in central Italy. It was so strange as I thought now, we have a flood to deal with on our short trip. I remembered from my history lessons that the Trevi Fountain used to be the oldest water source for Italy.

From the corner of my eyes, in the midst of the heavy storm, I saw them through the windows of my room. The two unknown children were getting soaked in the very violent summer storm. I saw lightning bolts sparked all around and my inner soul cried out for the unknown boy and girl who were just standing in front of the Trevi Fountain. My family members were all out that day as it was my turn to babysit the Kasteel Vrederic family children.

I watched Griet stand up as she was sleeping next to Rietje in the same toddler bed the hotel provided us with. I called Big Bro Jacobus and heard Buddy, my father Antonius, answer the phone.

He asked, "Andries, are you okay? Are the children okay? Why aren't you saying anything? Hey Buddy, is everything, all right? Now answer me or I will fly through your phone to your room. Buddy, your mother is running now, and she is screaming for her son. Okay, you not talking got Big Mama running with her."

I smiled to myself as I knew he had Big Bro's phone. He is my biological father, yet I still called him Buddy. I told him, "Everything is all right. The children are all here. The girls are here with me, and the boys are with Aunt Marinda. By the way, what are you doing with Big Bro's phone? I was wondering if he could look into something for me. I called him because I know you would panic thinking the children sneezed."

Buddy answered, "Andries, he is helping with some medical emergencies. Both Jacobus and Margriete are giving a helping hand as this surprising summer storm has a lot of injuries. Jacobus's Italian colleague asked him for some help. So, I have his phone as Margriete and Jacobus are together, and they have her phone."

That's when I heard my mother Katelijne say out of worry, "Andries, are you okay? Are the girls okay? Big Mama and Big Papa are here with us. We will be there in a few minutes."

I could not even tell them I was all right as I watched Mama and Big Mama storm into my room with Buddy and Big Papa. Aunt Marinda ran in with the boys. Yet she was calm as if she already knew everyone was coming. I will tell you, if you all have a time traveling psychic in your home, be careful as they see everything.

I told everyone, "I am fine. I just wanted to ask if you all could find out why those kids were getting drenched in this torrential rainstorm. Maybe one of you could bring them inside, until the storm fades away. I just didn't want to go out in this storm with the children."

I knew Big Mama was there and she saw the two kids were in need, so the whole family geared up to go outside in the heavy summer storm. We all geared up in our rain gear and we had taken extra rain gear for the unknown children. We had decided not to take the little kids, but I don't know why Aunt Marinda had brought the four kids with us. We said nothing to her as we knew when Aunt Marinda does something, there is always a reason.

The scenery in front of us shook us more than words could have explained. There in front of us were two little children who were around five years old. They watched us and were very frightened. I watched Aunt Marinda tell my family members to stay behind and not to get too close to the children. That's when I saw our brave little girls. My baby sister, also known as the girl with the lantern, just became big like a five-year-old child, as did Rietje. Rietje's magical horse from the seventeenth century appeared from somewhere behind the clouds.

The two little boys Theunis and Alexander became eight-year-old boys and had on soldier and knight's attires. I knew as did my family members to stay behind the children and let the children deal with the situation. We would be there for them if they needed us or when they needed us. Big Papa was trying to get his two granddaughters in his arms but was forced by Aunt Marinda to stay back.

Griet asked the children, "Are you both lost in the spiritual world? What is it that you require? Please trust us and do share your thoughts. We will try to help you if we can. I know you are not born yet, nor are you dead, so is it that you are floating in between?"

I then saw the two children turn around and they were crying and shivering, not from the cold pouring summer storm but from fear. That's when I saw they looked almost humanlike yet somehow, they were transparent. They were miraculously completely dry as if the rain could not touch them. I felt neither could the sun touch them. They almost glowed like glitter.

The children saw Griet and her magical lantern and said, "We are lost, or will be lost very soon."

They were crying but when their tears touched their cheeks, their tears became like paint and looked like magical rainbows. I saw two very cute children standing in front of us. I thought both of them looked very frightened, yet they held on to one another. The boy had brown hair and olive-colored skin with huge brown eyes. The girl had black hair with the same brown eyes. I knew they were of Italian heritage.

Griet told them, "I am Griet and this is my family. What are your names?"

The girl spoke as she said, "My name is Fiorentina, and my twin brother's name is Giovanni. We missed the flying boat that picks up all children to be born. The captain of the boat is the person who drops all the children onto this Earth and leaves them in the houses they are to be born in. The flying boat has left without us a few times. The captain of the flying boat said our parents did not find one another as of yet. You see, if they don't find one another and fall in love and get married before the next flying boat's arrival time, we shall become a part of the rainbow and then fly into the night's skies. We then shall become the night stars in the skies above."

It was then Giovanni who said, "So we wait here to throw coins in the magical Trevi Fountain. We heard people come here and throw coins to fall in love and get married. Since our parents could not come over, we came over and thought maybe if we could throw coins for them and wish for them, we will be born. Yet we have no coins, and no one can see us who could give us two coins."

I was so shocked as never did I think children too pick their own parents. I had picked Big Mama over and over again. I watched Big Mama cry as she too knew I was thinking about her. She came near me and held me in her arms. That's when we saw Griet and Rietje smile and hold hands with Alexander the knight and Theunis the soldier. I knew if Griet was smiling, then there was more magic that shall be in motion tonight.

As our miraculous four held hands in front of us, there in the sky appeared a rainbow out of Griet's magical lantern. The horse of Rietje had grown wings and from her wings, I saw two adults appear in the mist. The rainbow then poured magical gold coins into the hands of our brave soldier and our knight. The two boys only took two coins out of thousands of coins that was being poured yet disappearing as they were dropped. Theunis and Alexander gave the two coins to the two miraculous children who were fading away.

Theunis said, "Only two coins, you shall take from the pot of gold which the rainbow has brought to you. Remember always, never in your life shall you take more than what you shall need. For if you always follow the right path, you shall end up in your parents' home. This journey will be easy as you will be with your parents very soon and it will feel like you have just awakened after a nice sleep. Just go and throw the coins and make a wish."

Giovani and Fiorentina ran with the two gold coins and threw them into the magical fountain.

They said, "Dear Trevi Fountain of Rome, we come here with our wish to be born into the home of our parents. We know people wish upon the night's stars, yet we wish upon the magical fountain and hope our parents find one another tonight."

They threw the coins into the fountain as the summer storm halted and there from Griet's magical lantern, a rainbow appeared in front of us. The two humans who were standing on the wings of Rietje's horse were now standing in front of the magical fountain. The man had dark black hair like the girl and the woman had brown hair like the boy.

It was then I saw the children flew into the magical flying boat and the captain of the boat told them, "You two made it onto the boat. I guess you found out the Trevi fountain is magical, and it even unites parents with their children. Sometimes parents wish to find one another yet sometimes the unborn children too wish upon the magical fountain to unite with their parents. I see you have met up with Griet, the girl with the lantern, as it is then your wish too has come true."

So, my message to all of you tonight is don't be a skeptic and do make a wish. Remember to do so even if you don't have a coin as a coin will be provided magically when you visit the Trevi Fountain. To this day, this magical fountain is visited by people from around the globe to make a wish.

That night, we all came back to the hotel and knew to make a wish in the magical fountain for all who can't come but want to make a wish. In front of our eyes, we saw two magical children had made a wish and had united with their family. I asked Griet how the children were, as she went to bed as a very cute and adorable two-year-old toddler.

Griet watched me and said, "They shall live happily ever after, the twins of Trevi Fountain."

Italy Trivia Time

What is Italy nicknamed because of its shape?

Where in Italy is the famous Trevi fountain located?

Who are the two famous Italian painters mentioned in this story?

SWITZERLAND

The Chocolate Canoe Of Lake Geneva

"Grandchildren and grandparents unite through the canoe of miracles even if that means this magical canoe must be built miraculously."

Switzerland

ENCHANTED TALES: A KASTEEL VREDERIC STORYBOOK FOR CHILDREN

Come with me and let's travel to another country within Western, Central, and Southern Europe. This land to all is known as Switzerland. This country is officially known as the Swiss Confederation. The capital city of Switzerland is Bern. One thing that fascinates me is in this country, there are four official languages which are German, French, Italian, and Romansh. Over sixty percent of the Swiss people speak German or Swiss-German which is a dialect of German spoken in Switzerland.

When my family told me we were going on a trip to Switzerland, my mind went into thinking ski trip and lots of chocolates. I love cheese and boating in their lakes. We can swim or boat in one of their lakes as Switzerland has thousands of lakes. I wanted to see Lake Geneva as aside from its amazing crescent shape, it is also the second-largest freshwater lake in Central Europe.

With a horse-drawn carriage, we finally got into our magical cottage near Lake Geneva. Aside from Switzerland, Lake Geneva also enters France. My family including my Big Bro Jacobus and his wife Margriete, my father Antonius whom I call Buddy and my Mama Katelijne, Big Mama Anadhi and Big Papa Erasmus, and I had all traveled together. We brought the love of our life, the four young children of Kasteel Vrederic, along with us.

It is in Big Mama's belief system that she can only breathe when they are all with her and she knows for sure with her own two eyes they are all sleeping in their beds comfortably and safely. That night was no different as we let the kids sleep in their beds. We finally took out all the tour books and started to vote for which places we would visit. My vote was we must first try cheese fondue and Swiss chocolate first.

After we entered our very small stone cottage, we were told by the caretaker that Lake Geneva had frozen, and it was normal, but a lot of visiting families were stranded. If we are only going to ski, everything would be fine. We were worried as the caretaker told us all transportation to this village has been disconnected and therefore, we should keep an eye out for when everything will open again.

My family told him we would enjoy our time in the cottage, locked in due to the snowstorm. My family members love spending time together in different parts of the world. Most of the time when any member of the family has work conferences around the globe, we all travel along if and when we are free.

Yet like always, I had a cold shivering feeling somewhere something was wrong. I just hoped this was a feeling that was not true. Now let me take you on a journey through the magical resort near Lake Geneva in Switzerland. I am Andries van Phillip and this is a magical story of Elias and Elijah, two brothers who will show you family comes first. I call this enchanted tale, "The Chocolate Canoe Of Lake Geneva."

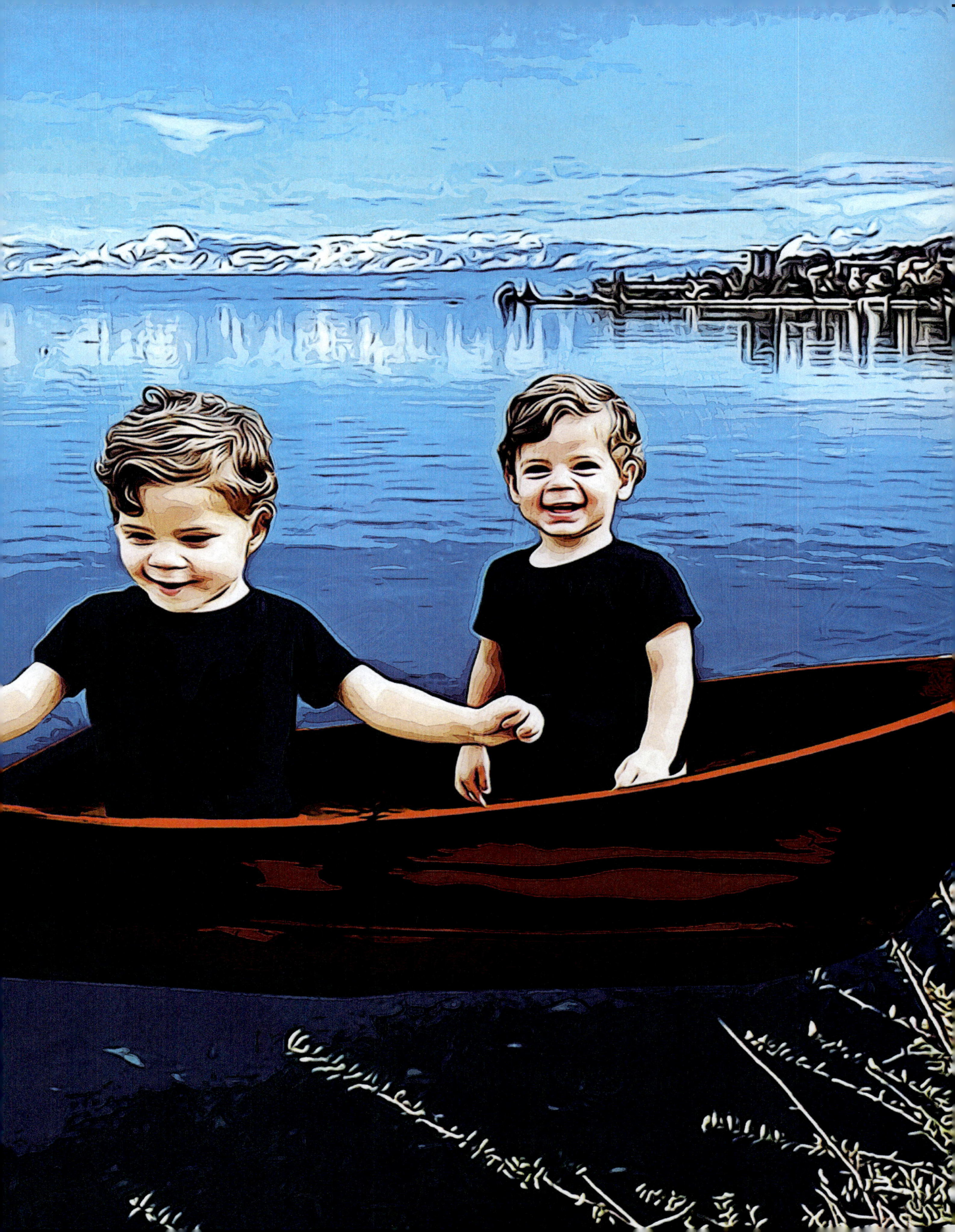

THE CHOCOLATE CANOE OF LAKE GENEVA

The skies around our small stone cottage looked clear. There was a crescent moon out which shined its glorious light onto the crescent-shaped Lake Geneva or as it is also known by the name Lac Léman. I wondered if the moon and lake were creating a moonbow. Our cottage had a fire going on as we all sat by the fireplace trying to watch the television which was out due to the heavy snowfalls.

I heard my baby sister Griet was crying and making unusual sounds. I watched Big Bro, also her godfather, and his wife Margriete both run in and take her. The whole family gathered in the small bedroom where we had placed the four children in for the night. It was so strange as the four miraculous kids all started to cry one by one. After Griet, we saw Rietje, Theunis, and Alexander join the crying musical band.

Big Mama took Griet on her lap as Big Bro told everyone, "Weird as I checked every single one of them and there doesn't seem to be anything physically wrong with them."

He then asked his wife Margriete, who is a pediatric cardiovascular surgeon, to check the children again.

He said, "I know I am a doctor, but when these children are involved, I am worried sick for no reason. Please check them Margriete."

She was my doctor, and I know she has a magical touch. As she touched me, I had healed magically. She is Rietje's biological mother and Griet's godmother. She just smiled and did check them all, one by one.

She then said, "My babies are all healthy and happy. There is nothing to worry about as they will feel better after they get some food in their cute bellies."

No one said anything as we all knew Big Mama, the dream psychic, knew more than she was sharing with any one of us. That's when we all heard Griet cry loudly and in her baby voice she talked aloud.

She said, "Papa, Big Papa, Opa, Big Bro, help the boys! They will be injured if they don't get help!"

That's when we watched our four little babies change shape and become five- and eight-year-old children. They all walked outside in the freezing snow as they wanted us to follow them.

We all walked into a van that was snow proof and followed the kids to Lake Geneva in the cold, shivering, and snow-filled night. I held on to my sister Griet close to my chest as she led the way. Then she began to cry, pointing her finger toward the cold freezing lake. There in the middle of the freezing lake we saw were two little boys with brown hair, one a little chubbier than the other, otherwise they both looked identical. They were trying to swim and float in the lake without any water-resistant clothing. I knew proper water-resistant clothing would have helped them float longer.

Big Bro and Buddy ran toward them as Big Papa parked the van. I held on to my sister Griet as Mama, Margriete, and Big Mama held on to the other three children. As we went closer to the lake we had to let go of the children as they all took their magical forms.

I watched as Griet became the girl with the lantern, Rietje sat on her magical horse with her sword, Theunis became the brave soldier, and Alexander was in his knight form holding on to his shining and blazing sword.

The kids went close to the boys as Big Bro scooped up the drenched and freezing boys in his arms and brought them to our van. I watched Griet kept on shining her lantern across the lake as I knew something was not right.

I asked the two boys, "Who are you? What are you two doing in the middle of the night in the frozen lake? You are old enough to know it is risky to be here without your parents and this lake is frozen. You should never ice skate on a frozen lake anyway."

They both watched Griet and smiled and said, "Hi girl with the lantern. We knew you would come and help us. We saw you in our dreams. You said you would help all who love their families more than they love themselves."

Griet watched them and said, "Yes I will, but one must be safe first to help others. If something happens to you two, then who would help your family?"

I was confused as were my family members, yet no one said anything as we watched the story take place in front of our eyes. We knew we just had to trust the girl with the lantern and the kids.

One of the boys then said, "We are orphans and I, the handsome and chubby one, am Elias, and my brother is Elijah. We live with our uncle who is known very famously in our village as Uncle Greedy. Our uncle was eating in a food festival, where he ate so much and got sick. He is sleeping in his cabin, and he is too sick to travel. Our grandparents had called a long time ago and said their house had collapsed. They need help. They are poor and don't have much."

They began to cry as then I saw Griet say, "They are somewhere in Lake Geneva. If we don't rescue them quickly, they will become night stars. They need our help. They tried to get out of their house, but the evil river otter got to them. He is also known as the evil weasel of Lake Geneva."

That's when I saw our brave warrioress Rietje fly into the lake on her magical horse with Theunis and Alexander. All the time, Griet walked by the lake with her lantern.

She stopped along the way and screamed, "There! Over there!"

We saw there holding on to a river raft, an elderly couple was floating. Next to them was a huge, larger-than-life otter. The animal looked more like a monster and was trying to push the elderly couple off of their small raft. The animal was making sounds and laughing as it was all a joke for him. The monster otter watched our warriors and flew off into the night sky. I wondered where he went.

Griet said, "He left and won't return again anytime soon. Maybe on another night when the moon will appear in the shape of a crescent over the crescent-shaped Lake Geneva, he might return if the lake freezes again. Yet now, we must save them."

That's when I saw Elias and Elijah both gave Griet a chocolate bar. They gave the four kids four Swiss chocolate bars.

They said, "We are not greedy as we won these bars at the food festival. We were saving them for our grandparents as they are poor, and no one wants to take care of them. We will take care of them when we are all grown up."

I watched Rietje take the four bars as she laid them on top of the frozen lake. Then she placed her sword on top of them. She asked the brave knight and the brave warrior soldier to touch them with their swords. It was then Griet placed her magical lantern on top of the chocolate bars. Like a miracle in the cold frozen night, I watched the chocolate bars turn into a chocolate canoe. The two boys jumped onto the canoe and all by themselves rescued their grandparents.

Griet then told them, "Never shall you or any one of your family go hungry or be poor, as all the people throughout time shall know both of you as the brave boys who rescued their grandparents selflessly with the chocolate canoe of Lake Geneva."

Remember everyone always to be selfless, yet remember safely, for your grandparents might need you but they want you to be safe first. You don't know when you are trying to help someone selflessly, then and there you too might see the girl with the lantern appear. Elias and

Elijah found out because of their all-embracing love for their grandparents, the girl with the lantern gifted them for eternal sustenance, the chocolate canoe of Lake Geneva.

Switzerland Trivia Time

What shape is Lake Geneva?

What is Lake Geneva also known as?

What are the four official languages in Switzerland?

GREECE

Underwater Miracle Boy

"Hope is the first part of the magic and believing in it will complete the journey as you will then see you have just completed another miracle all by believing."

Greece

ENCHANTED TALES: A KASTEEL VREDERIC STORYBOOK FOR CHILDREN

Sailing through the Mediterranean Sea was Big Mama's dream yet it became a reality as Big Papa had a traveling art exhibition through the world. My father, the famous painter who was taught to paint by Big Papa, too had traveling art exhibitions as both of them co-participate in the same exhibitions.

The Kasteel Vrederic family members joined them as we all decided to go on the tour with them. I had a few piano concerts I participated in. My famous Big Bro doctor and the rest of the family members took this trip as a vacation of a lifetime.

Have you been to Greece? If not, let's travel together. We will all go on a cruise in our cruise ship rented by Big Bro as he said this would be a unique sailing experience for our family members. We will get to see Greece's thousands of years of history as we travel through the Mediterranean Sea.

Greece is located in Southeastern Europe. The capital city is Athens. People here mostly speak in Greek. We will be visiting the Parthenon, an ancient temple in Athens, Greece on the Acropolis. This temple was built in the fifth century B.C. and was dedicated to the famous Greek goddess Athena. Did you know in Greek mythology, they have twelve main gods and goddesses? Some famous names you may know are Zeus, Hera, Dionysus, Athena, Apollo, Hermes, Artemis, Hephaestus, Aphrodite, Ares, Demeter, and Poseidon.

Some of the famous temples everyone likes to visit are the Temple of Apollo in Delphi and the Temple of Poseidon in Cape Sounion. Greece is known as the cradle of western civilization and the birthplace of democracy. Also, if you guys are into the Olympics, then for your information, Greece is also the birthplace of the Olympic games.

I love to get some inspiration from this land as aside from the famous gods, this land is also known to have given birth to some of the world's famous philosophers including Socrates, Plato, Aristotle, and Pythagoras. I also love to try some of the famous Greek dishes. If Mama and Big Mama had permitted, I would have loved to have gone snorkeling in the Mediterranean Sea. Ahh but little did we know, my wishes would come true in a very short time, even if Mama didn't want me to go snorkeling.

I could just see if and when this dream came true, Big Mama would knock on my head saying, "Be careful what you wish for Andries."

Tonight, come on board our cruise ship as I, Andries van Phillip, take you on a journey through the Mediterranean Sea. I call this enchanted tale, "Underwater Miracle Boy."

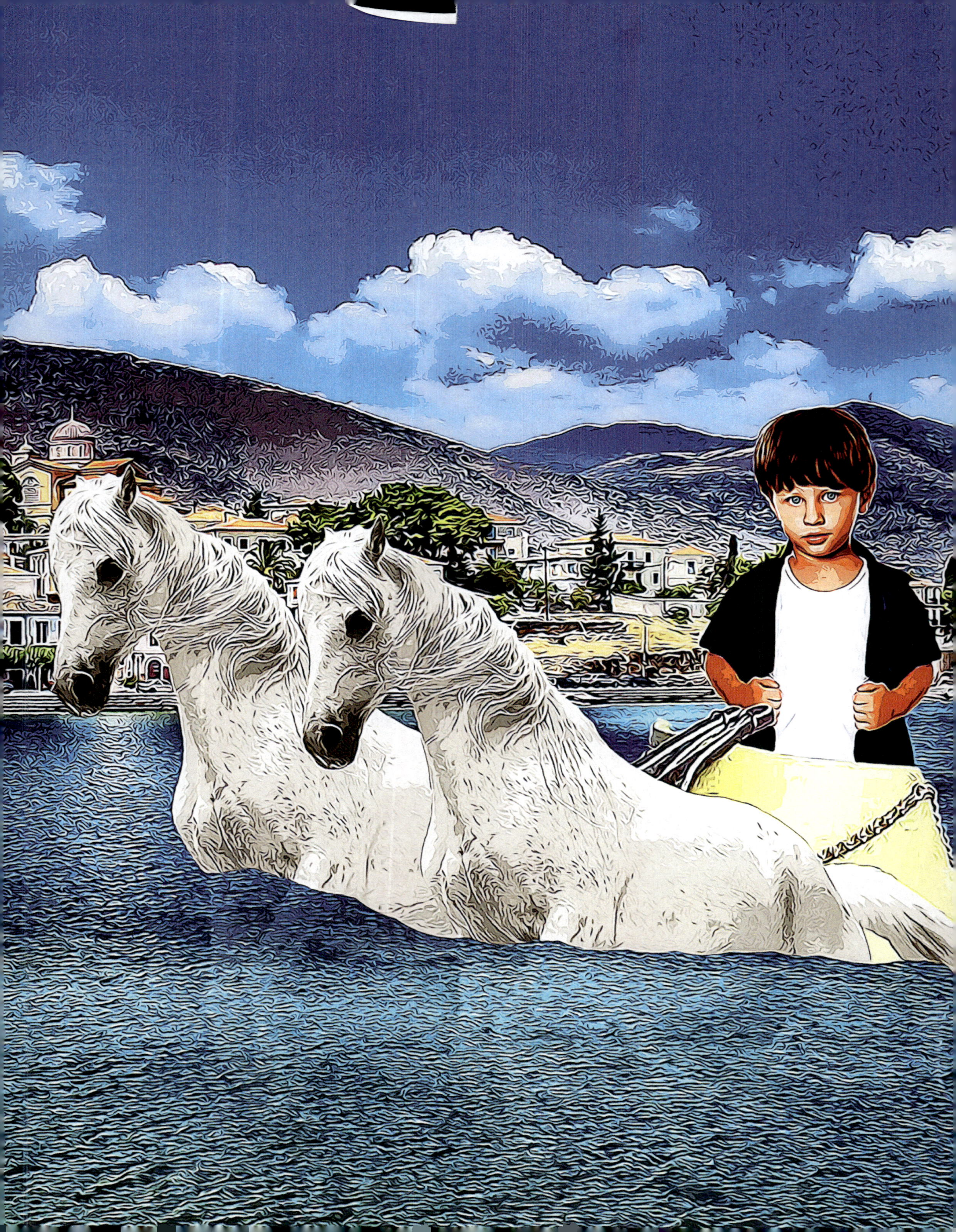

UNDERWATER MIRACLE BOY

The Mediterranean Sea touches twenty-one countries as it flows through three different continents of this world. We were cruising through Greece and enjoying the ever-blue waters of the sea. It was a very clear day where the sun was shining ever so bright upon the blue skies. The seawater felt warm and just right to take a swim in. I wondered if by swimming in this vast sea, I could maybe touch the hands of the past travelers of this sea.

Suddenly I saw Mama and she looked distraught and restless. She was walking back and forth with my little sister Griet.

I asked her, "Mama, are you all right? Why are you so restless? Is Griet okay? Maybe I can walk with her if she is seasick."

I watched my whole family run out to the dock of the ship as everyone heard and assumed our little princess was seasick. Big Bro ran out to the dock and scooped up Griet as I watched my parents just watch them. We all knew when it was Griet, Big Bro was emotional and as her godfather, he kept her near his heart.

He asked her, "Little precious one, what bothers you today? Are you feeling sick or are you frightened by something you see but we cannot?"

Big Papa came and held Big Bro and said, "Jacobus, little Rietje, Alexander, and Theunis are all trembling as if in fear. I wonder if we should ask the captain to slow down or maybe keep an eye out for something out of the blue."

That's when we saw there on a clear and sunny day, a dark cloud had appeared out of the blue. The sun was totally covered like an eclipse, yet there was no eclipse that day. The skies became so dark as if it was nighttime. It looked like a moonless night during the daylight hours. We couldn't see anything as our ship's lights were not working, neither was the brand-new cruise ship which we rented moving. The crew members were trying to get everything fixed and tried to calm us down.

The captain of the ship came out and said, "Please remain calm as we get everything under control."

Big Mama never stops from saying what's in her mind and said, "We are all calm, yet it seems you and your crew members are not. So, I recommend you go and see what is wrong first. That way we can be back on our route. Please go and fix your cruise ship and don't worry about our family members. Whatever the situation may be, I am not worried because my babies and grandbabies are all with me."

As the captain tried to talk with us, we saw in front of us there was a huge cruise ship that seemed to be floating upside down. I saw Griet was standing in front of us with a lantern in her hand. She again became a five-year-old child instead of a two-year-old toddler.

She had the only visible light around us in the vast Mediterranean Sea. Then I saw Rietje turn five years old as she called upon her horse to appear. Theunis and Alexander too became eight-year-old boys. Theunis had on his soldier attire as Alexander had on his knight attire.

It was then through Griet's magical lantern we saw the cruise ship ahead of us that flipped over in the sea was filled with school-going children. We could hear faint sounds of the children crying in fear as they were all drowning. My family members and the crew members of our ship all tried to get into the now cold and dark seawater.

We tried to do something but watched Griet as she said to all of us, "Move back up into the ship or he will not come. He can only come if a pure and innocent soul calls upon him from the other ship. I am here because I too heard her calls."

That's when we saw in front of us there in the window of the ship was a child, barely ten years old who was praying with her hands together in a praying gesture. She was trying to help the other children who we assumed were her classmates or friends.

Griet also placed her hands together as she held the lantern with both hands and said, "Dear Poseidon, god of the sea, please send someone if you cannot come as I, the girl with the lantern, ask for your help. May you not let innocent children be hurt as you are the protector of the sea, earthquakes, and horses."

I watched the four brave children then float in the cold and dark Mediterranean Sea as in front of our eyes there was a tidal wave. From the water, there appeared a tunnel and like a burst of lightning we saw a boy of about ten years old appeared. With brown hair and modern-day clothing, he appeared on a horse-drawn carriage that floated on the water.

He smiled and told Griet, "Dear Griet, I am Poseidon the child, who Poseidon the god of the sea has sent to help you. Now some of you also know me as the underwater miracle boy. I come to you Griet as I know you are the girl with the lantern, and if you have called, then there must be something terribly wrong."

I saw Griet then waved her lantern and Poseidon just smiled and said, "That's just enough light for me to see. If only I had a horse and a rider to help me pull the ship out. I will need two brave warriors to help me with this."

I watched Rietje, Alexander, and Theunis get into the cold sea as Griet kept her lantern steady all the time for everyone to see. In front of our eyes, we watched another chariot appear from beneath the sea. Suddenly there appeared Poseidon the child's magical chariot.

I watched Rietje's magical horse fly in front of Poseidon and his chariot as Theunis and Alexander helped pull the ship. Somehow in front of all the adults who watched tonight's event, a few magical children pulled the ship full of children over to safety in the blink of an eye.

It was then we saw Poseidon come over to Griet and say, "Dear Griet, girl with the lantern, I thank you for calling on me. For you today the children sailing in my sea are safe. Please let all know if they ever need me anywhere, anytime to call upon me as I am also known as Poseidon, the underwater miracle boy."

The dark clouds disappeared as then the police boats had appeared, and all the children were taken to safety. We continued sailing through the Mediterranean Sea on our cruise as we knew everyone would remember the children of the boat and how they were rescued by my family. Just like miracles are secrets that happen when you believe but the magical details are not to be shared, I knew everyone would forget about the girl with the lantern and the underwater miracle boy.

Greece Trivia Time

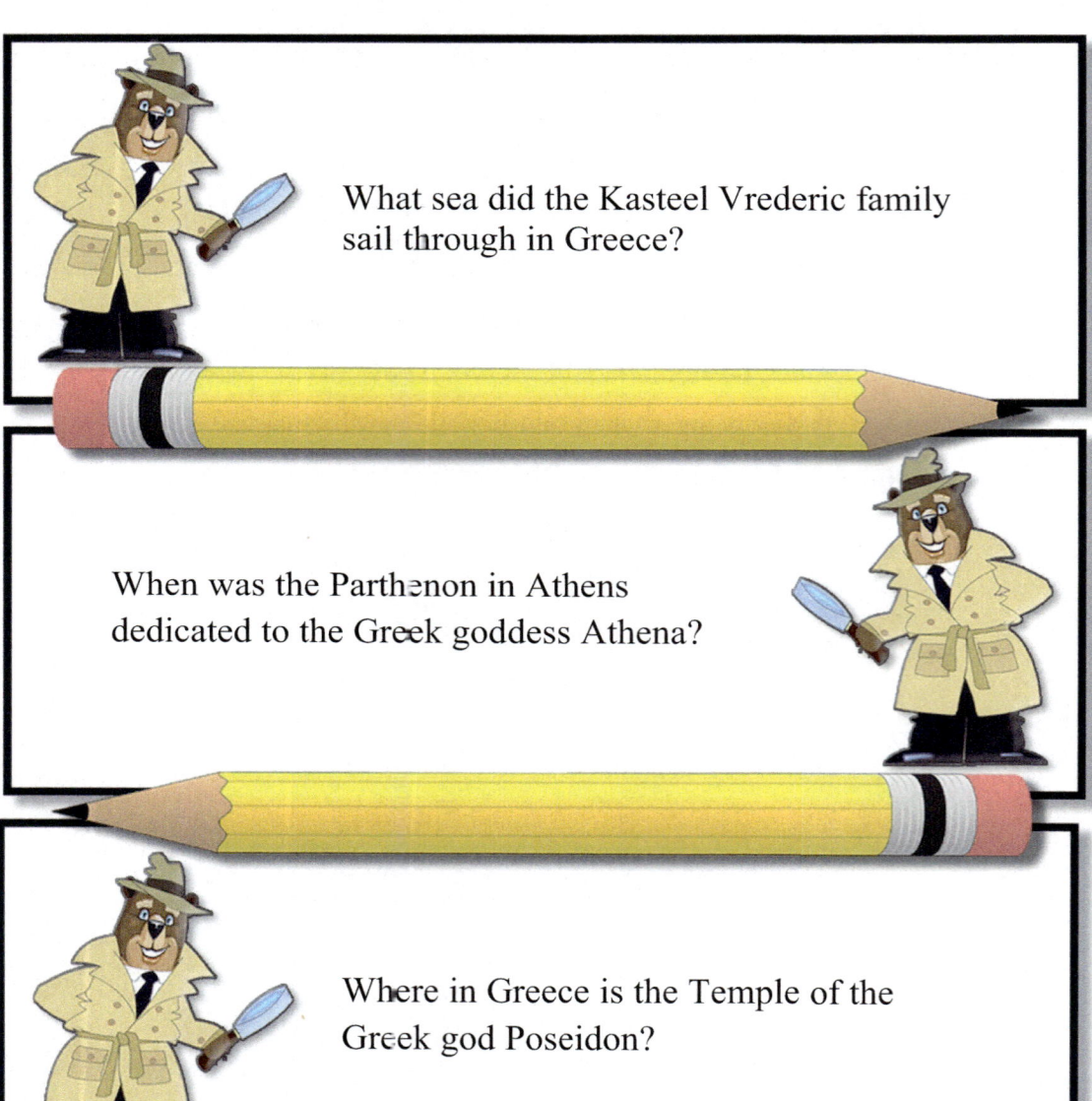

What sea did the Kasteel Vrederic family sail through in Greece?

When was the Parthenon in Athens dedicated to the Greek goddess Athena?

Where in Greece is the Temple of the Greek god Poseidon?

UNITED KINGDOM

The Girl Who Fought The Loch Ness Monster

"Dear all, don't fear the unknown or unseen monsters of the night, for remember they only want to frighten you as they are afraid of you the warrior."

United Kingdom

The United Kingdom is a sovereign state. The capital of the United Kingdom is London. It is a monarchy, and the current monarch is King Charles III, who ascended to the throne on September 8, 2022, after the death of his mother, the beloved Queen Elizabeth II. The system in this kingdom is a constitutional monarchy with a parliamentary government. The primary language spoken is English.

Did you know the United Kingdom was formed slowly? The Act of Union of 1536 united Wales and England. The Acts of Union of 1706 and 1707 united England and Scotland. Ireland was not brought into the union until the Act of Union in 1801. England, Scotland, Wales, and Northern Ireland, which are all individual countries, in union make the United Kingdom. Tonight, however, we will only travel through England and Scotland.

When you all get some time to travel to England, keep an eye out for the green grass all around this country as this country enjoys green grass all year round. Also, when you travel through the United Kingdom, you must try all of their national foods. If you are in England, you will find fish and chips and chicken tikka masala are considered to be this country's national foods.

In Northern Ireland, you will find Irish stew. Once you land in Scotland, you will see haggis is this country's national or as some say favorite food. If your journey takes you to Wales, you will see cawl is considered this country's traditional food.

Here is an interesting fact you can share with your classmates. The first king of England, King William I, enforced a curfew law prohibiting everyone from going outside after 8 p.m. The United Kingdom is a very diverse country where all of you will find something similar to you. Here the people are very different from each other as are their foods, yet uniting through their differences, they live in their individual countries peacefully.

We traveled through the United Kingdom where Big Mama had a book signing in London. Afterward, we toured through some small villages in Scotland. My family members love to travel through small villages and live and be with the locals as we travel around the globe.

I looked forward to being in Scotland as I had never been there, and I felt pulled toward the magical land. Maybe someone or something would be waiting for us there.

So now let me take you on a journey through Scotland. After finishing our tour through England, we were on our way to a small village near the Loch Ness, a lake, in Scotland. I am Andries van Phillip and this is a magical story of Ailish, a very brave girl from Scotland. I call this enchanted tale, "The Girl Who Fought The Loch Ness Monster."

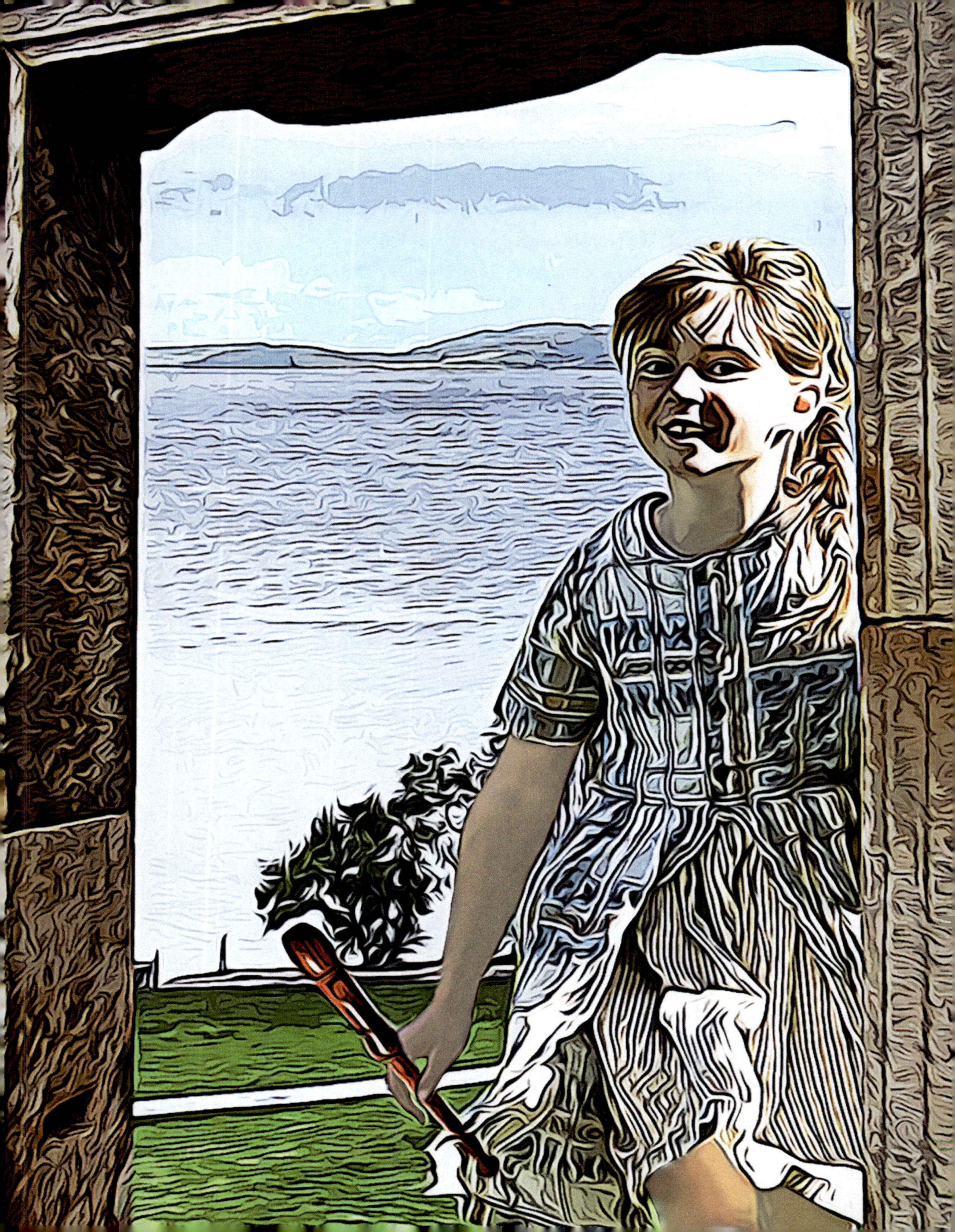

THE GIRL WHO FOUGHT THE LOCH NESS MONSTER

Loch Ness is a beautiful lake and is in the Scottish Highlands in Scotland. We rented a small stone cabin near the lake, and it actually felt like a magical kingdom. Our small magical cabin had a stone fireplace which we could make soup in.

Papa, whom I call Buddy and whom you know as the famous painter Antonius van Phillip told Big Papa, the world-renowned painter Erasmus van Phillip, "Big Papa, let's do another joint painting of this amazing lake and the stone cottage. I could do the house and the lake, and you could do the imaginary Loch Ness monster in it."

Big Mama, our dream psychic, was annoyed as she said, "Don't ask for trouble you guys. We are here for a peaceful break. Don't start calling on monsters, be it a myth or truth."

For some reason, I was shocked at Big Mama's sudden fear as I held her in my arms and told her, "Big Mama, I will save you from all the monsters on this Earth. For now, however, I can only play some sweet music on the family room piano."

She kissed me as I saw there in the family room was a very old and out-of-tune piano all covered in dust. I took some time as I started to play the piano. My family members sat on the floor, all of them holding on to one another. I realized how much we loved one another as we sat there for a long time.

It was the musical sound of a flute that woke all of us out of the dreamy musical event. I loved to play as much as Big Mama loved to listen to my musical notes. Yet the very out-of-tune musical flute awakened all of us. I wondered if it was a small child who was trying to play the flute he or she did not know how to play yet.

I wondered how hard the child was trying and felt a twinge of love for the child in my heart. I wished I could have had a few lessons with her so I could teach her the right way to do it. I don't know why I thought the child was a girl but, in my heart, I somehow knew she was a girl.

Just then I saw Griet walk to her father and said in her baby voice, "Papa, up. Griet now must go and help girl. She calls out to me for help."

It was then Big Mama, the one who wanted to avoid all troubles on this vacation, opened the door of the cottage. There from the cottage, we had an amazing view of the beautiful Loch Ness, one of the most beautiful lakes of Scotland. Yet within this beauty, we all knew was hiding something very eerie.

As my family members made it to the lakeshore, we saw nothing but a very cold and dark lake. All we could see was the beautiful lake. No humans could be seen anywhere around the lake. I knew there were small villages around the lake which were all covered within the trees. For some reason, a fog appeared in front of us, and it was spinning in circles.

As I watched Griet, Rietje, Alexander and Theunis take their older forms, I knew we were all being prepped for yet another night where we would see the children of Kasteel Vrederic in action, this time in Scotland. From nowhere, a girl appeared and walked barefoot on the green grass by the lake. Big Bro and his wife Margriete ran toward her as the doctors in them knew they must help the child who was bleeding. They both picked up the child and started to immediately give her medical attention.

She said in her soft voice, "I am Ailish and I am only ten years old. I will save my village any way, by any means. Yet I am scared as the monster has bitten me. Now I will become like him. Please, I need Griet. She is the only one who could help me. You see my grandmother is a psychic and she told me that the girl with the lantern who is also known as Griet will be here soon. That's when I will be safe and so will my village as the Loch Ness monster everyone thinks is a myth is back. He is hunting our small village and he said he will take everyone from our village."

I watched our little girl Griet stand by the injured child. As she placed her lantern on top of the child, the light pouring out of the magical lantern healed the young child. The healing dust spread like a rainbow from the child's feet to the lake.

Griet said to everyone, "Must follow the magical dust that shines from her feet to the lake. We must do it before dawn for at the first sign of dawn, the magical rainbow will be gone. If we can't take care of the monster by then, this girl too will be ill again. She will be healed completely as soon as we get rid of the monster."

It was then on a cold starless night, we all walked toward the mist that showed us at the other end of the magical rainbow was hiding the Loch Ness monster.

In the moonless dark night, I watched our children walk toward the danger, not away from it. Rietje got on top of her horse who then became big and carried all four children and Ailish.

Griet ever so steadily held on to her lantern as we saw in front of us appeared a huge monster bigger than anything I saw in my life. He looked like a dragon or a crocodile who had feet like a frog. His skin looked slimy and green. His eyes were like two huge holes, dark and never ending.

Big Bro wanted to follow our children as he tried to jump into the mist.

We saw there in the mist appeared Aunt Marinda and she said in a clear voice, "Move back Jacobus, Antonius, Andries, and Erasmus because you will break the magical spells of Griet if you enter the mist. Have faith in the girl with the lantern. It's her destiny to save the children of the world as she saved the inhabitants of Kasteel Vrederic as a spirit. Now she saves the world as a child. She is blessed as she has the other three miraculous children with her. Jacobus, let them do their job."

We knew at that time Aunt Marinda was watching over the children. I held on to Mama, Big Mama, and Margriete as Buddy, Big Bro, and Big Papa held on to one another. The scariest monster everyone knew as a myth was standing in front of us. It was then I saw Griet point her lantern toward the monster.

Rietje, Alexander, and Theunis were ready with their swords as they were nearing the monster. The rainbow created out of the wound of the girl and the monster's face was shining so brightly, I saw the monster was trembling in fear.

It was then Griet told the three children, "Now place your swords in the rainbow and just watch."

As the three swords were placed in the rainbow and the lantern touched the rainbow, the monster became dust. It burned down to ashes. It was then I watched Griet say something in Ailish's ears.

Ailish said, "Beware today's monster and tomorrow's ones. Ailish, the daughter of this land, will protect my village and my land from all monsters eternally. From this day on forward, all of you dark monsters will remember me as the girl who fought the Loch Ness monster."

The monster screamed in fear as it became ashes and turned into nothingness. Where the monster was, appeared a beautiful moonbow as we saw the moon open his mouth and swallow the ghostly monster in one gulp. The night ended with musical notes, as I did happen to squeeze in some musical lessons.

I loved watching how the amazing child who was so brave and fought the Loch Ness monster all by herself now was learning to play her amazing flute. I knew these musical notes would keep the child and her village safe from all monsters all around. After I gave her the required lessons, like a magical dust, Griet had removed all the memories of our meetings from the child's memories.

She will not remember us, yet her village will remember her as the girl who fought the Loch Ness monster.

ENCHANTED TALES: A KASTEEL VREDERIC STORYBOOK FOR CHILDREN

United Kingdom Trivia Time

What four individual countries are included in the United Kingdom?

Where is the famous Loch Ness located?

Who enforced the curfew law prohibiting everyone from going outside after 8 p.m.?

MESSAGE FROM ANDRIES VAN PHILLIP

I hope you all enjoyed visiting some countries in Europe through these enchanted tales. The message from all of these stories is the same. Believe in yourself and know around the globe, there are children like yourself, who are our heroes. You the one reading these enchanted tales are my heroes.

Now I want you all to be ready as tomorrow night, Buddy, the famous painter named Antonius van Phillip, will take you through another area of this world known as Australia and Oceania.

CHAPTER TWO:

CONTINENT OF AUSTRALIA AND REGION OF OCEANIA

Storyteller:
Antonius van Phillip

"I am a small area within the Pacific Ocean. Did you know within my chest, I have only islands and the continent of Australia? I am known as the region of Oceania."

Oceania

Welcome back everyone for the second night of our enchanted tales campout. Last night, we had all enjoyed some of Europe's favorite cuisines. My son Andries had taken us through the continent of Europe and a few of its countries. I really enjoyed the tales as I remember taking the trips together with my family.

Through Andries's storytelling, you too have traveled with us through Europe. Forever now you can share these stories with your family members and your future generations, for then they too would be traveling through these continents through the pages of this book. Now I will take you all on another adventurous journey through Australia and Oceania.

Australia is both a country and a continent. Some people interchange the names Australia and Oceania for the name of the continent. The continent of Australia, however, is located within the geographical region of Oceania in the Pacific Ocean. Oceania consists of fourteen independent countries including Australia. Did you know Oceania got its name because it is linked to other countries in its continent through the ocean, and not by land like other continents?

When I travel to a new place, I try out their food first. It's my family's first stop. As Big Mama always says, food unites family and friends at one table around the globe. So, let's see what foods are specially associated to this continent even though these days we the world citizens have picked up different foods and made them our own. So, I invite all of you here to go ahead and try some food made by my family that are specially served in Oceania, that have been made just for you.

Also, all of you who are at home, take some time and go ahead and make some of these foods with your family members. After you have made them and had a bite to eat, hurry back and then we can go through this continent together.

SOME OF OCEANIA'S FAMOUS FOODS

Let's get introduced to some of Oceania's famous foods. So, my dear children here are some of the famous Oceanian foods for you to try out. Make sure you ask your parents if it is all right for you to have them before you go ahead and try them.

Lū Sipi – *Tonga* *Tuvalu* – **Pulaka**
Meat Pie – *Australia* *Vanuatu* – **Laplap**
Chiko Roll – *Australia* *Samoa* – **Pani Popo**
Faikakai Topai – *Tonga* *Fiji* – **Fijian Kokoda**
Mumu – *Papua New Guinea* *Solomon Islands* – **Poi**
Whitebait Fritters – *New Zealand*
Chukuchuk – *Marshall Islands*

Menu

COUNTRIES OF OCEANIA

Now let's learn to say the names of the countries in Oceania. So, when you get to see a child from Oceania you would know where exactly your friend is from. Here are the names of the fourteen countries from the region we all know as Oceania.

Oceania

Australia

Fiji

Kiribati

Marshall Islands

Micronesia

Nauru

New Zealand

Palau

Papua New Guinea

Samoa

Solomon Islands

Tonga

Tuvalu

Vanuatu

ENCHANTED TALES: A KASTEEL VREDERIC STORYBOOK FOR CHILDREN

LANDMARK QUIZ

Which landmark is this and where is it located?

A. Sydney Opera House, Australia
B. Te Puia, New Zealand
C. Queen Victoria Building, Australia
D. Echo Point Lookout, Australia

SOME OF OCEANIA'S LANDMARKS

When you do visit one of these countries in Oceania do stop by some of the amazing and famous landmarks of Oceania.

Landmarks

Australian War Memorial – *Australia*

Echo Point Lookout – *Australia*

Bungle Bungle – *Australia*

Great Barrier Reef – *Australia*

Melbourne Cricket Ground – *Australia*

Port Arthur – *Australia*

Queen Victoria Building – *Australia*

Sydney Opera House – *Australia*

Wave Rock – *Australia*

Te Puia – *New Zealand*

Tenaru Falls – *Solomon Islands*

Kangaroos and Koalas – *Australia*

STORY TIME WITH ANTONIUS VAN PHILLIP

I hope when you have some time to visit Oceania, do look up some of these places and maybe you could visit some of them. Remember though, you can always visit any of these places through a great book. That way, you don't have to leave your home but can be at different places at the same time. That would be magic like my precious little girl Griet, who is my own magical adventure. So now everyone, come with us and let's see where Griet takes us through Oceania.

Let's go and hear some stories from this continent. I am Antonius van Phillip, a son of the famous Kasteel Vrederic, and I will take you through the stories of Oceania. You will meet my family members one at a time as we will all guide you through some enchanted stories through this one home, we all call Earth.

You have already met Andries van Phillip, the world-renowned pianist. We are proud of Andries as he is a magical journey whom we had introduced to you in our *Kasteel Vrederic* series. Now let me take you through Australia and Oceania. I will introduce you to this region through *Enchanted Tales: A Kasteel Vrederic Storybook For Children*.

AUSTRALIA

Willow, Koolewong The Koala, And Joey The Kangaroo Of Queensland

"Koalas and kangaroos are cute yet dangerous and aggressive. Do not touch them, unless you are Willow, the famous boy who rides on top of his kangaroo with his koala on his shoulders."

Australia

Australia is the largest country in Oceania. It is the sixth-largest country in the world. The capital city of this amazing country is Canberra. There are eight states in Australia which include Queensland, New South Wales, Victoria, Australian Capital Territory, Western Australia, South Australia, Tasmania, and Northern Territory. Did you know Australia is the smallest continent in the world in terms of area?

We had traveled through New South Wales and Queensland. Sydney is in New South Wales, where Andries had a concert at the Sydney Opera House. Our family members all had come with Andries on his tour as we are all proud of our famous boy and never would have missed this opportunity to see him perform live in this amazing place.

Big Papa had reserved a vacation spot in the Gold Coast, in the state of Queensland. We were going to head over to our Gold Coast beach resort there after the concert. On the way, however, we planned to stop over in Brisbane, the capital city of Queensland for a few hours as Big Mama, Margriete, and Katelijne wanted to see Brisbane on their way to the Gold Coast.

So, on this trip we wanted to go around two states. We hoped we would get to see some of Australia's famous animals such as kangaroos, koalas, echidnas, dingoes, wallabies, platypuses, wombats, and maybe more. Did you know in Australia, there are more kangaroos than there are humans?

Aside from the cute animals, Australia is also known for its tropical beaches, marine reserves, lush rainforests, and its Aboriginal culture. For all of you interested in the laughing bird kookaburra, yes, it is a native bird of Australia and New Guinea. Also, their famous laughs are actually callings to warn others of their enemies, or to warn others to stay away.

On this trip, you will meet an Aboriginal boy who is the hero of this story along with his koala and his famous kangaroo. You might be thinking who is an Aboriginal person? Actually, an Aboriginal person is a descendant of the indigenous inhabitants of Australia, the members of the Aboriginal race of Australia, similar to how I am an inhabitant of the famous Kasteel Vrederic as I am a son of the Kasteel Vrederic family.

So tonight, let me take you on a journey through the famous beach of Australia known to all as the Gold Coast. I am Antonius van Phillip, and this is the story of Willow, an Aboriginal boy, his famous koala named Koolewong, and his magical kangaroo named Joey. I call this enchanted tale, "Willow, Koolewong The Koala, And Joey The Kangaroo Of Queensland."

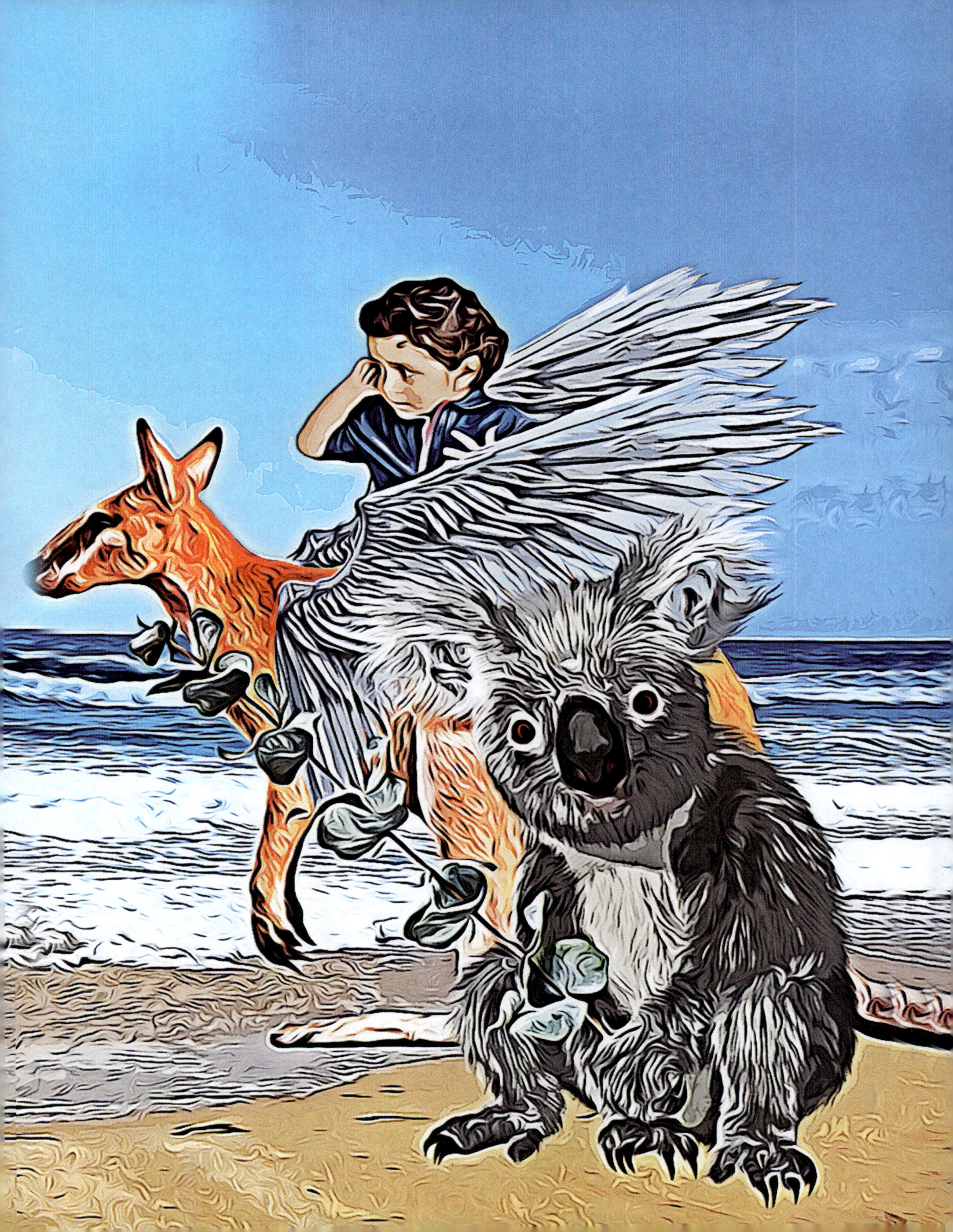

WILLOW, KOOLEWONG THE KOALA, AND JOEY THE KANGAROO OF QUEENSLAND

Summer in Australia starts in December. We had a very hot summer Christmas during our stay on the Gold Coast in Australia. The skies were as bright as the blue ocean waves. There were waves perfect for surfing. Surfers crowded the beach paradise. The skies above told us Santa Claus was getting ready to have his big day for here Santa Claus comes riding a boat. I knew my family would have our kids waiting for him when he comes to visit the Gold Coast on Christmas Day.

We had a wonderful trip through Sydney and Brisbane as we finally arrived on the Gold Coast a day before Christmas Eve. Like many families, Australians too spend Christmas Eve and Christmas Day with their families. So, the beach was visibly empty. Yet I knew all the hotels and resorts around us were booked by tourists from around the globe.

My parents wanted to go around Australia within a caravan. So instead of staying at a hotel, Big Papa booked a campground and parked our caravan inside one of the Gold Coast's famous campgrounds by the beach. Camping in Australia was actually Big Papa's dream.

It was dark by the time we parked our caravan and got dinner ready for the family. Big Papa and I create a painting everywhere we go as a father and son team. Big Papa and I started our painting as we sat outside watching the huge waves. Andries slept on the garden lounge chair after his long concert tour.

My big brother Jacobus tried to scribble with us on the canvas as Big Papa said to him, "Dear Son, stick to your day job. You are an amazing doctor, and a painter maybe in another time."

Suddenly we heard roaring sounds coming from the woods behind our caravan. We paid no attention as we were told at times there are koalas and kangaroos sighted here. We were told not to pat them as they could be very dangerous. The sounds, however, continued and all the guests around the campgrounds and on the beach did not seem to notice or be bothered by the sounds.

The sounds became louder and louder like angry furious screams. It was then we saw our little princess walk out of the caravan and look upon the dark seawaters of the Gold Coast. The waves were now calm and there was no sign of people anywhere. We knew the camp was full and so were the hotels all around us. Yet we could not see anyone around us.

I watched Rietje come stand next to Griet as she asked Griet, "Should I call my flying buddy now? Is it time yet? Do you see anyone out there?"

I saw in front of me, little children were talking to one another. Theunis and Alexander came and stood next to them as did my entire family. We all knew if Griet was upset, then there was some kind of mischief brewing in the air, water, or land around us.

It was then we saw in the dark night, from beneath the very dark sea rose a huge monster. The monster was neither a crocodile nor a dragon but some kind of a reptile. It looked like a snake who had a humanlike head with eyes, a nose, and a mouth. The snake had hair on its head that looked like it was in braids. I almost thought it was Medusa in a snake form. It opened its mouth and blue smoke came out of its mouth.

My little princess said, "Papa, now ask everyone to place their hands on their ears. The sea serpent will put everyone to sleep through his creepy sounds. We must wait until Willow appears in his own time."

I watched Jacobus ask Griet, "Dear beloved child, who is Willow, and where will he come from?"

She watched Jacobus and said, "Papa Jacobus, he will come as I believe in him, so should all of you. Just know when and where we need him, he will come."

Then we saw the sea serpent blew fire out of his mouth as he spread the fire around the coast. I knew every single tourist around here was asleep and needed someone or some kind of miracle to save them.

It was then we saw behind us from the wild bushes jumped out a kangaroo. On his back was a little Aboriginal boy who had on his shoulders a koala.

He stood in front of us and said, "Dear girl with the lantern, I am Willow. These are my friends, Koolewong the koala and Joey the kangaroo. Would you please be my guide as I help save my ancestral land, her citizens, and all visiting guests from this sea serpent?"

Griet told him, "Yes, dear boy of good and kind heart, as you have only wanted to protect and save your ancestral land people and friends, I, your dear friend, will help you with my family."

Then in front of us we watched our little princess turn five years old as did Rietje. The boys also became older. I watched Rietje call her flying buddy. The magical horse appeared in front of her and carried the warrioress, the knight, the soldier, and the girl with the lantern on her back.

Then I watched Australia's magical kangaroo Joey grow wings. On his shoulders, he carried Willow and Koolewong right into the mystical seawater. They went flying into the danger and did not even wait to think about the danger looming in front of them.

Griet held her lantern as I saw Rietje, Alexander, and Theunis hold out their magical swords, pointing toward the sea serpent. That was when we all saw a magical returning boomerang, fly toward the sea serpent. Koolewong the koala became huge and had in his hand a eucalyptus tree branch which he threw like a sword into the serpent's mouth. The branch stopped the fire from spreading as Joey kept flying over the serpent. The returning boomerang cut the sea serpent in half. All along, Griet and her team watched and flew over the sea serpent as the brave boy fought for his land.

Katelijne, Big Mama, and Margriete were holding hands and praying by the seashore. Jacobus, Andries, Big Papa, and I stood in the seawater, dipping our feet as we tried to go near the children who were in the middle of the starless dark night's cold seawaters.

It was then we saw the swords of Rietje, Alexander, and Theunis fly into the serpent as the magical light from the lantern burned the serpent into ashes. Then the moon came out from beneath the clouds as the waves calmed down. Any proof of the dangerous battle of the night was erased from the world.

I went and held Willow's hand as he said to us, especially Griet, "Dear friends of the night, I am Willow and these two are my buddies. We try to be of help to anyone who calls us. I thank you for being here today as I had called upon Griet through my dreams. I am a seer and I see dreams that guide me when and where I need to be. So as my dreams guided me, I knew you would be here to help me protect my land and people."

Griet said, "Like my Grandfather, whom we in Dutch call Opa, would say, 'anywhere, anytime.'"

The night ended as Christmas Day approached us. Afterward as dawn came upon us, we celebrated a magical Christmas on the Gold Coast in Australia with Santa Claus, Willow, and his family which included his friends Joey and Koolewong.

Unlike other tales, as we had left our friends back in Australia, we did not have to erase Willow or his kangaroo or koala's memories. Actually, this time we had shared the story with Santa Claus who was coming on a sailboat in the middle of the night and had seen everything that had happened. He was the one who had with his magical dust erased the memories so Willow too could go on helping everyone without ever wondering if Griet was in his dreams or just a name he remembered. This time, we left that part of the job in Santa Claus's hands.

ENCHANTED TALES: A KASTEEL VREDERIC STORYBOOK FOR CHILDREN

If you are on your way to Australia or maybe you will be in the future, do say hello to all the kangaroos and koalas of this country from far away as they like to see you from far away and don't want to be touched. Just like always watching over you the visitors of this land, and all of her citizens are always, Willow, Koolewong the koala, and Joey the kangaroo of Queensland.

Australia Trivia Time

When does summer start in Australia?

What indigenous group of people does Willow belong to?

What state is the Gold Coast in?

NEW ZEALAND

Lake Taupō's Mermaid Mia And Merman Nikau

"Even though you don't see them, they still protect you from even under the sea, as they are your neighbors."

New Zealand

Aotearoa, or the land of the long white cloud, is the Māori name for New Zealand. Situated within the southwestern Pacific Ocean, New Zealand is the sixth-largest island country by area. The capital city is Wellington.

In 1893, this land gave women the right to vote, which made it the first country to ever grant women this right. The Māori language of the indigenous Māori people became New Zealand's first official language in 1987. In 2006, New Zealand Sign Language became New Zealand's second official language. However, English is the most widely spoken language and de facto official language.

After our long Christmas vacation in Australia, Andries, my big brother Jacobus, and Big Papa, whom you all know as the famous painter Erasmus van Phillip, brought us to New Zealand. They refused to leave without visiting their magical world New Zealand as they are all huge fans of the movies *The Lord of the Rings* and *The Hobbit* trilogy which were filmed in New Zealand. New Zealand's magical sceneries, enchanting landscapes, and mystical mountains were the magical backdrop for the magical and fictional world of Middle-earth.

I know you all are wondering why I was not a fan of *The Lord of the Rings*? You see, I was born blind and then through the miraculous hands of my brother Jacobus and my miracle son's birth, I had gained my eyesight. So, I actually never knew how beautiful this country is or for that matter, how beautiful this world is. Yet now I do see how beautiful this Earth really is. Oh please everyone, don't feel bad for me as I had seen all of this before through Big Mama's eyes and her amazing voice. I am blessed to have her as my mother.

Big Mama had read all these geographical details like a story, out to all of us, her sons, every day and every night. Do you want to know a secret? She still reads everything out loud, as it has become her habit and we all love her for it. It is still a practice in our household that even our children now participate in.

New Zealand, I discovered, is really magical in reality as it is in the amazing movies. Also did you know this was the last country in the world to be inhabited by us the humans? The famous Māori tribe of New Zealand was the first to arrive in this country.

An interesting fact you can retell your friends is, this country has a hill with the longest place name in the world, "Taumatawhakatangihangakoauauotamateaturipukakapikimaungaho ronukupokaiwhenuakitanatahu." This in English translates to, "The place where Tamatea, the man with the big knees, who slid, climbed and swallowed mountains, known as land eater, played his flute to his loved one." I love this fact and the amazing name.

When you are traveling through this amazing country, remember to use the word kiwi carefully. We all are familiar with the fruit kiwi, but in New Zealand, a dry Kiwi refers to a person born in this country, and there is a kiwi bird which is their national symbol. Don't forget to try the amazing fruit kiwi, as this fruit is available all around the world.

So tonight, let me take you on a journey through the past as I had visited Lake Taupō with my family. Lake Taupō is a large crater lake by the Taupō volcano, named after the town Taupō. Did you know Lake Taupō was created about twenty-seven thousand years ago when the volcano had erupted? This was the world's largest eruption. Today, the lake is said to be about the size of Singapore.

I am Antonius van Phillip, and this is the story of a magical set of twins of the famous Lake Taupō. I call this enchanted tale, "Lake Taupō's Mermaid Mia And Merman Nikau."

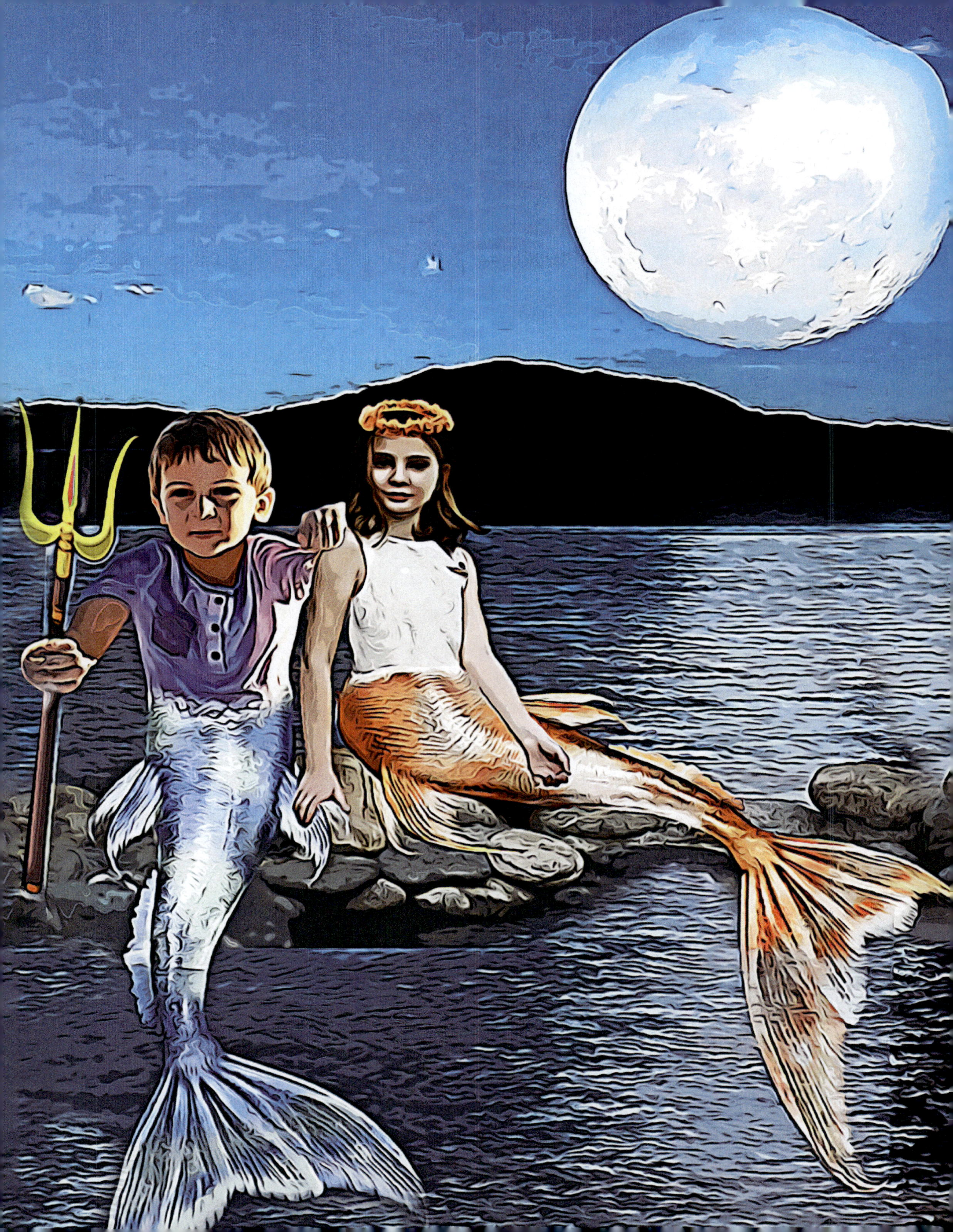

LAKE TAUPO'S MERMAID MIA AND MERMAN NIKAU

Warm, sunny, and comfortable January weather greeted us at Lake Taupō in New Zealand. Yet tourists were missing from the bush-clad mountains, the beautiful lake, and the amazing healing hot springs. The day was bright and peaceful. Although the day was perfect for surfing or boating, it was as if we just walked into a ghost town where the vacation cottages were beautifully decorated. The hotels and restaurants were very welcoming yet again the picture was the same, there were no signs of any humans anywhere.

Jacobus asked me aloud, "Antonius, is it just me or did we just step into a ghost town? When we boarded our flight from Auckland to Taupō Airport, it was crowded. As we rented the van and started to drive to our cabin, I felt like we walked into a déjà vu, or a movie set where we are the town's only inhabitants."

I watched Big Mama and she knew I was wondering if she knew something. Yet I watched how she kept herself busy with Griet and Rietje as the girls were being fussy, and it seemed like they did not have any appetite. We all know if Big Mama is taking care of the children, even my doctor brother or doctor sister-in-law do not dare say anything.

Big Mama gives them her famous stare and says, "I don't need a doctor."

I started to laugh out loud, then realized everyone was watching over me.

No one said anything, yet Big Mama said, "Stop it Antonius. I am your mother so I can read your mind."

We all settled into our cabin that we had rented for our stay. The keys and all things needed for the cabin were left with a note saying, "Dear Guests, please enjoy your stay. As per your request, the cabin was cleaned before your arrival and will be cleaned afterward. The emergency numbers are left on the kitchen counter if you need anything."

It was so strange as no one was here to introduce us to the city or the tourist attractions.

Big Mama said, "We will go boating, and absolutely see the giant Māori rock carvings at Mine Bay. You all know the carvings rise I believe almost forty-six feet above Lake Taupō and this is only reachable through the water. I love this volcanic terrain. We will visit this lake and the carvings first. I don't know why I feel like there is some kind of a miracle waiting for us over there."

Andries asked, "Okay Big Mama, if you mean another scary adventure, then can we just see it from afar and go to the next destination?"

Big Mama walked into the cabin and said nothing as she seemed worried and was busy in her own thoughts. Yet it was Griet who did talk as we all know if something is amiss, either Big Mama or Griet will speak when the time is right.

Griet went to her Papa's lap, not her birth father but her other father whom she calls Papa Jacobus. We all know she is attached to him as he is to her.

He cuddled her on his lap and kissed her head as he said, "Papa Jacobus loves you baby. What is it that is bothering you my dear child?"

Griet watched all of us and said, "No swimming. Be careful when boating. There is a monster shark in the water of Lake Taupō. He has been attacking humans. Everyone thinks he is just a shark, but actually he is a shark monster with a humanlike head. He wants to gobble up the mermaid and merman who live in the lake."

I watched Big Mama and asked her, "Big Mama, what is going on? Where are we? And why are there no humans visible anywhere around us?"

Big Mama said, "I am not sure, but I feel like we entered a magical realm or something. We are at Lake Taupō, so we are actually in our cabin. Yet someone towed us or rather Griet and her group into their world. It's like a parallel world where we are in our own world yet are not, as we somehow traveled into a whirlwind tunnel. I am worried because I know Griet can see them as they can see her too. The rest of us can't see them, but they can see all of us. We must wait until they feel comfortable enough to let us see them too."

It was so strange as our cabin was full of groceries and fresh baked bread and fresh churned butter. The beds were all made. The windows were open where white curtains blew in the fresh wind that was coming into the cabin. It felt like we were in our own time in the twenty-first century, yet I wondered where we were.

Griet stood up and in front of us became older like a five-year-old child as did Rietje. Theunis and Alexander looked a little older too. There in Griet's hands appeared her magical lantern. Rietje's magical horse appeared as did her sword and the magical swords of Alexander and Theunis.

Big Papa stood up as he said, "I don't know what is going on but if my grandchildren are going anywhere, I am going with them. Somehow I know if my wife is this quiet, then something is wrong."

Griet smiled and said, "Opa up."

I want you all to know Opa is grandfather in Dutch. I watched Big Papa carry his granddaughter and kiss her head.

Griet kissed his two cheeks as she said, "It's all right, Opa. We will see Mia and Nikau soon. They will explain to us what they need from us."

I knew soon meant late in the night as I watched the day become dusk and in front of us there was a full moon. We walked over to the amazingly beautiful lake that hid all the mysteries we so urgently needed right know. Yet I knew in my family we had to fight the worst enemy, time, for everything. The night stars appeared in the bright skies. I could see all the hotels, restaurants, and tourist attractions were empty.

It was so strange as Jacobus who never showed any emotion said, "I just feel like we will see something or someone we in reality never would have expected or dreamed about seeing."

Andries said, "If this is a dream, then maybe we will see a real-life mermaid. Hey Big Mama, Mama, or Margriete, do you all think I am a prince and maybe there is a mermaid waiting for me in the blue waters of the lake?"

They all said in union, "No, you're not a prince."

That's when I saw Griet giggle and say, "Big Brother, she is not your princess as you are not a merman. But he is a merman, and they are siblings, like you and me silly."

In front of our eyes appeared not a boat, nor a canoe, nor a shark, but a real-life mermaid and merman. They jumped in and out of the water like they were swimming and having fun. Yet soon I realized looks could be deceiving as these siblings were not having fun but fighting for their world and ours.

The siblings came close to us as we saw the magical creations, we knew to be mythical, in front of our eyes. They came close to us as the mermaid spoke first.

She said, "Dear girl with the lantern, I am Mia, and this is my brother Nikau. We need your help on this dark night. Very soon, the shark that has been attacking humans will become a lake monster as the full moon glows and reflects onto the lake. He will with his mouth set fire and deliberately activate Lake Taupō's supervolcano. Remember about 1,800 to around 2,000 years ago, this volcano had erupted causing great harm worldwide."

I watched Mia, the mermaid, with beautiful flowers on her beautiful black hair glowing in the dark. The mermaid looked like a ten-year-old girl and Nikau, the merman, looked like a twelve-year-old boy. It was so amazing to see even the underwater creations wanting to give us a helping hand as neighbors do for one another.

Nikau then said, "We don't have much time. I need someone to cover up the moon from shining in the water. We will then go and remove the shark monster from here and trick him into the volcano, so he can never be back. Otherwise, he will keep on attacking humans and underwater creations alike."

It was then we saw Rietje talk to her magical horse as she said, "Dear precious one, are you ready, for tonight's adventure? You don't have to jump over the moon like the famous poem but maybe cover it up until the time passes by."

We watched the horse disappear as did the glowing moon. Then I saw in front of us appeared larger-than-life shark that had a human head. He jumped up on top of the lake showing himself.

Griet's lantern glowed as she jumped on top of Nikau. Rietje, Alexander, and Theunis all jumped on top of Mia. They all swam after the shark not away from him. We walked by the shore praying for our gifted children.

In front of our eyes, I watched Andries jump into the water as he saw his sister Griet was having trouble. The shark was coming after her first. I believe the shark knew if he could get to Griet, then he could win the battle.

Andries, a magical child himself who had in about two years become an adult, too had some of his own magical powers hidden within himself. He had the love of a brother that carried him swiftly to his sister. It was then I saw Jacobus and my whole family jump in as did I, without even thinking if we would be of help or a distraction.

Like a wall in front of us appeared Aunt Marinda as she said, "No, you all must not get involved in this magical war. Andries is different and it's all right if he gets involved but I must ask you all to go back to the shore and be there for the children if and when they do need you all."

Like a magical push, we were all back on the lakefront.

We heard Andries say, "Mia and Nikau hold on to my legs. I will swim with all of you toward the volcano. Griet, take over from there."

I watched Andries as did my family with tears in our eyes hoping this miracle too ends in happily ever after.

It was then I saw Griet was smiling and knew all would be all right. Her big brother was there for her, like their Opa says, "anywhere, anytime." Griet had her lantern shining directly on top of the shark monster as the shark then magically flew into the mouth of the volcano. The volcano was still very active. We only saw smoke come out from the volcano and then all was quiet.

Rietje's magical horse came back and carried the four children to the mouth of the volcano. We all saw a light come out from the volcano as the children threw their magical swords into the volcano. Then we saw the swords came flying back to their respective owners.

The children came in front of us and Griet told Mia and Nikau, "All is well, no human, nor any mermaid, nor any merman will ever be harmed by Lake Taupō's shark monster. For now, I promise you two can return to your home safely."

Mia smiled and said, "As soon as we leave, the mystical wall we had placed to keep all humans away from here, and the magical whirlwind created from the magical Lake Taupō we have placed you within, will be lifted. You will be in your cottage with all your memories as we know we can always trust the girl with the lantern and her family, the members of Kasteel Vrederic."

After that, we did go back to our cabin and saw the town was now full of tourists and vacationers everywhere. My family members and I agreed we like to have a quiet time when we are on vacation. This time, we all agreed it really felt good to have people all around us.

It was then in our cabin within a fog, appeared Nikau who said, "Dear friends, don't forget the enchanted tale of this magical night. You shall always know if you ever need anything where to find us for we are the Lake Taupō's mermaid Mia and merman Nikau."

ENCHANTED TALES: A KASTEEL VREDERIC STORYBOOK FOR CHILDREN

New Zealand Trivia Time

What is the Māori name for New Zealand?

What are two famous movies that were filmed in New Zealand?

What fruit shares the same name as the people born in New Zealand?

PAPUA NEW GUINEA

Samarai Island's Miraculous Triplets

"Do you wish upon the stars above in the skies only, or do you also wish upon the stars of the sea?"

ENCHANTED TALES: A KASTEEL VREDERIC STORYBOOK FOR CHILDREN

Papua New Guinea

Independent state of Papua New Guinea is the official name of the country Papua New Guinea. The capital city is Port Moresby. This country is located in southwestern region of the Pacific Ocean. It embraces the eastern half of the island of New Guinea. The early inhabitants of Papua New Guinea possibly arrived there from Southeast Asia about 60,000 years ago. On September 16, 1975, Papua New Guinea proclaimed its independence from Australia. Sir Michael Thomas Somare became the independent country's first prime minister. He is also known as the Father of the Nation.

Papua New Guinea is a very diverse country with over 800 languages and more than 1,000 different ethnic groups. This diverse country also has the world's third-largest rainforest. I have heard Papua New Guinea also has the world's largest butterfly. Yet beware when you go birdwatching in this country as you might get to see the world's first known poisonous bird named pitohui. Scientists, however, have said since the discovery of the pitohui that there may be more rare poisonous birds around the globe.

This country is filled with beautiful beaches and corals reefs. The highest peak is Mount Wilhelm. This country's topography has made it very hard to have roads and bridges or substructures everywhere. So, a lot of the times, airplanes are used as the only mode of transportation.

Did you ever have boiled mangoes, or fried plantains? If not, then you could try it when you visit this amazing country. While swimming in the beaches, keep an eye out for their national animal called dugong. The dugong is a marine mammal which has a tail like a dolphin.

We had to go to Papua New Guinea not just for a vacation but because some children needed medical help from Dr. Jacobus Vrederic van Phillip, my brother. Jacobus and my sister-in-law Margriete, who is a famous doctor herself, travel around the globe giving people free medical assistance if they ask for it or need it.

This was one such occasion where their help was required if they could make it to the island with their own expenses. So, Big Papa volunteered to fly them in his private jet and pay for our hotel and stay. I am proud I have a brother and sister-in-law who donate their time and expertise, yet I am so much prouder of my father who can afford to do this and also who donates his money and time to help people around the globe.

Tonight, let me take you on a journey through Papua New Guinea. I am Antonius van Phillip, and this is a magical story about a set of very special triplets. I call this enchanted tale, "Samarai Island's Miraculous Triplets."

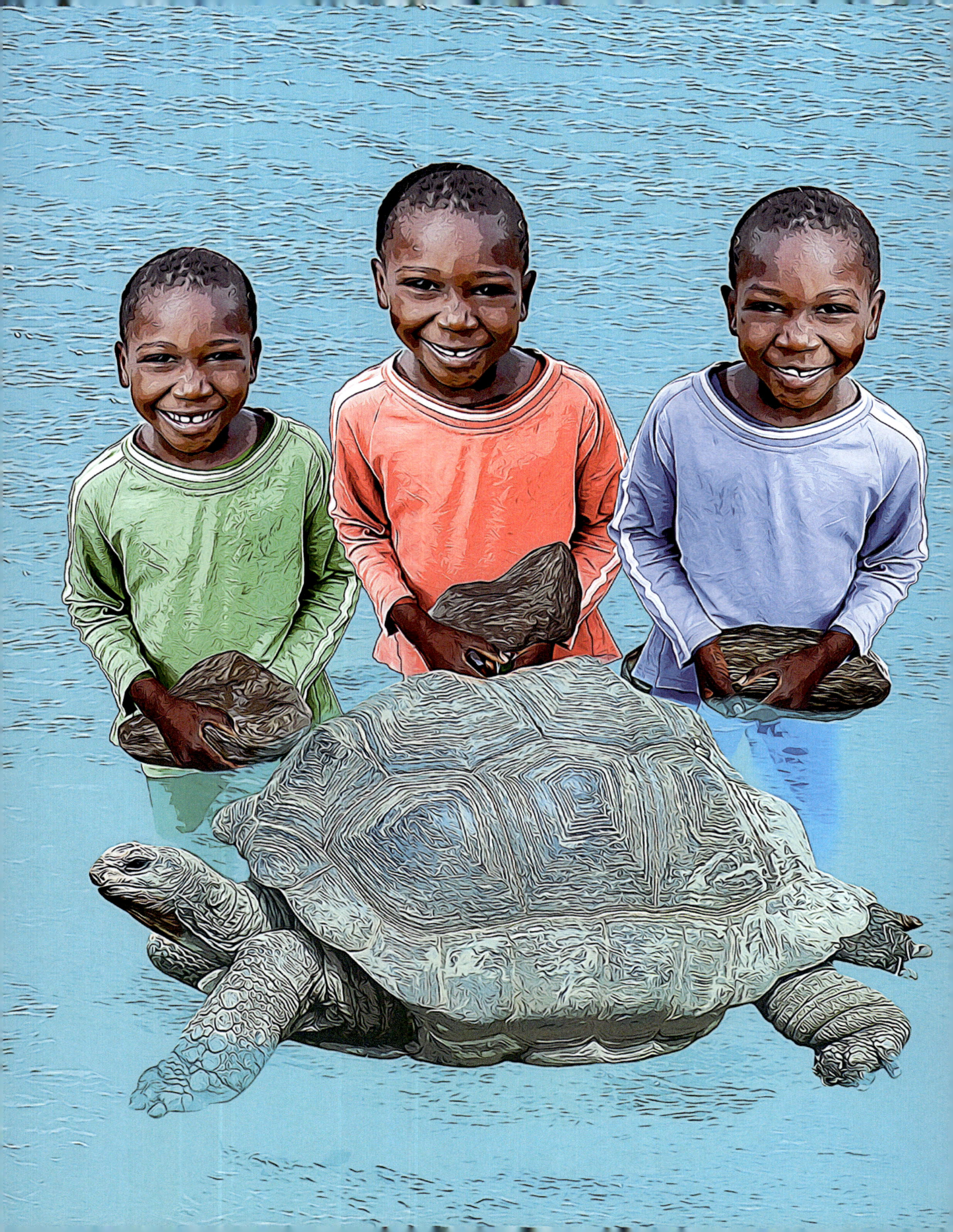

SAMARAI ISLAND'S MIRACULOUS TRIPLETS

Samarai Island is one of Papua New Guinea's islands in the Milne Bay. My family and I had landed at the Gurney Airport in the Milne Bay Province in Papua New Guinea. We had reserved our vacation cabin on Samarai Island, about thirty-one miles away from the airport. We would be going there in about a week.

We got ourselves a private plane ride to this land as we joined Jacobus and Margriete on their medical volunteer trip to provide medical assistance. Our plane went through weather-related turbulence on this trip. A brutally devastating cyclone was heading toward Papua New Guinea.

This country had come face-to-face with a couple of cyclones recently. On top of all of this, Papua New Guinea is very vulnerable to droughts, earthquakes, tsunamis, rising sea levels, floods, and more. After a weeklong of walking with Jacobus and Margriete, and trying to give them a helping hand, our family members finally arrived at our vacation cabin.

It was then Big Mama said to all of us, "We were all very lucky to have a pilot as experienced as Erasmus flying us through this cyclone. We would have all been gone case otherwise."

She hugged Big Papa and I watched how much my parents loved one another. I knew their bond was what kept my family members in a strong union which has lasted quite a lot of generations. The rough weather above us had all of us worried yet we decided not to let it bother us. We just wanted to have a quiet vacation, relaxing by the clear blue waters and the sandy beaches.

I knew this wish of mine was thought of in my mind too early as I saw my little princess Griet was very unsettled. She was being rocked by her Mama Margriete as well as her Papa Jacobus. The love of my life, Katelijne, was trying to help put Jacobus's daughter, little Rietje, to sleep yet had no success.

Big Mama and Big Papa came outside to the courtyard, which had a huge mango tree in the middle with a wraparound veranda watching over the rough Pacific Ocean. You could hear the wind and the ocean waves were getting rough. I wondered if the cyclone had ended or was still out there with a force. We were told the cyclone changed its course, so we got the wind but missed the major damages.

It was then we heard the crying and whimpering of young children coming from the rough waters of the Pacific Ocean. With the sounds of whimpering cries, Griet and Rietje too started to cry. For some reason because of Griet's past-life memories, she prefers to go to Jacobus when she is scared.

Jacobus held her in his chest and said, "Sweet baby, I shall never let you go as you are our blessed daughter. You are completely safe within my chest."

That's when Griet said, "They need our help. They want to go back to their papa, like I am back with you. Their papa and mama can't find them and think they are lost in the ocean. They will leave and go back to their country soon, without the three girls, the triplets who were lost in the ocean."

I stood near my daughter as she was shaking in fear. Big Papa came and held her from one side as I did from the other, yet she hid her head in Jacobus's chest and refused to come out.

I watched our brave girl Rietje walk over to Griet and say in her baby voice, "It's all right. I will help you. We will fight together like always."

Andries came over and said, "Come to Big Brother, princess. Remember I will swim with you in the deep scary ocean, or the frightful sea, or I will jump into a live volcano only for you. Never will you be separated from me, ever. You see brave one, you were separated from Papa Jacobus because Big Brother wasn't there with you. Hey, look at me. I am right here. So never fear as Big Brother is here."

I watched my brave princess laugh at Andries and as she kissed her Papa Jacobus and wiped his tears off his face, she jumped into her brother's embrace and kissed him on his cheeks.

She said, "I don't fear as Big Brother is here."

In front of me, my two-year-old baby girl became a five-year-old girl as did Rietje. The two brave boys who were gifted to us by Aunt Marinda as the protectors of Kasteel Vrederic also became older. Rietje's magical horse too appeared in front of us. We wondered what we were fighting this time.

That's when we saw there in our courtyard stood three ten-year-old boys. They all stood in front of Griet and said, "Dear girl with the lantern, won't you be so kind and help guide three lost girls back to their parents? We are the snorkeling triplets of Samarai Island, Papua New Guinea."

Griet only nodded as she said, "We will help you but who are you three? And where did you come from?"

They said, "We are triplets. Our names are Kentiga, Koina, and Kwimbe. We went swimming into the ocean during tropical Cyclone Rewa, which had come across the Pacific Ocean in December 1993 to January 1994. We promised if we did survive, we would never go swimming in the ocean during a storm."

Kentiga was talking as he continued, "Yet if we didn't survive, then we asked to become the protectors of our homeland and the ocean that flows by our land and save all who need us. So, the miracle continues. We have become immortal as we live under the ocean. People only see us when they make a wish in the ocean where we have found our kingdom within the coral reef beneath the ocean. It's actually amazing and the best part is we get to help everyone who makes a wish."

He continued as he said, "There is a set of triplets, but we don't know their names as we didn't get to talk to them. They had fallen off their boat while they were with their parents. At least that's what everyone thinks. I believe they are about two years old. The truth is their boat had accidently stumbled upon the great green sea turtle named Chelonia Mydas. He is a very bad magician turtle who takes things and steals them. He wanted children for himself, so he stole the three girls and now they have been his prisoners for at least two weeks. If not saved within the next few hours, the three girls will become stony corals within the coral reef which look like turtles under the sea."

It was then Griet who said, "Follow me and as I shine my lantern, the evil turtle will come out to hunt me down. You all must then take him away from the ocean and place him on the land. Without any water, he will become a part of the mountain, and he shall never be able to hunt down anyone again."

We walked with the children and stood by the ocean shore. I watched our four children fly on top of Rietje's horse as the three boys jumped into the cold ocean water. Griet placed her lantern shining toward the water. The magical lantern glowed into the deep ocean water. Suddenly, there was a tsunami of some kind in the water. In front of us, a huge turtle bigger than a dragon appeared. I watched Rietje throw her sword into the turtle as did Theunis and Alexander.

Then Griet asked the triplets to hold on to the magical string that appeared from the lantern to the sword. Like magic, a string appeared and tied the huge monstrous turtle. As the turtle was being pulled to the shore and had been placed on the ground, it then magically flew to the mountain range and became a part of the mountain.

It was then I saw the triplet boys brought near Griet from under the ocean three huge rocks. Each boy carried one rock very gently as if they were holding on to three babies. It was then like a miracle, the three rocks turned into three two-year-old girls.

A gondola appeared from nowhere, and the three miraculous girls were given to the police in the gondola. The police were called as they knew this miracle was the act of the triplets of Samarai Island. Everyone from the vacation town gathered around the ocean shore as all saw three boys had appeared and like magical dolphins, these very human boys disappeared into the great blue Pacific Ocean.

Everyone watching repeated that was Samarai Island's miraculous triplets. Everyone knew and talked about the triplets who keep an eye out for all the inhabitants of Papua New Guinea and her visitors alike. Griet watched the people celebrating from her Papa Jacobus's chest as I held on to my niece Rietje in my chest. The boys, Alexander and Theunis, walked like big boys with Andries and Big Papa. Yet no one knew or will ever know about the girl with the lantern and her team for that's what we had wanted as we left the amazing country and Samarai Island's miraculous triplets.

Papua New Guinea Trivia Time

What is the capital city of Papua New Guinea?

What is the world's first known poisonous bird?

What island did the snorkeling triplets come from?

MESSAGE FROM ANTONIUS VAN PHILLIP

I hope you all enjoyed your enchanted journey through Oceania. You can always find a fruit or a typical food from this continent in your grocery stores. We have started to eat vegemite on top of a slice of toast with cream cheese. It's now one of my favorite breakfast items.

I would love to revisit the kangaroos, the koalas, and all of our newly found friends. I know I can keep this book and all the memories of these places alive. You too can now revisit through the pages of this enchanted book.

Yet before you visit Oceania all over again, I would want you to go ahead and get acquainted with the continent of Antarctica, through the eyes of my beloved wife, the mother of Griet and Andries, and the beloved daughter of my parents, not daughter-in-law as Big Mama says in this home all daughters-in-law are just beloved daughters. Her name is Katelijne Snaaijer van Phillip.

CHAPTER THREE:

CONTINENT OF ANTARCTICA

*Storyteller:
Katelijne Snaaijer van Phillip*

"I have no countries within my chest, as I am entirely roofed by a vast ice sheet. Yet I am the driest, iciest, windiest, and coldest continent. You know me as the continent of Antarctica."

Antarctica

ENCHANTED TALES: A KASTEEL VREDERIC STORYBOOK FOR CHILDREN

Tonight I will take you through a mysterious land, where there are more penguins then humans as no humans live there on a permanent basis. I was captivated and charmed to be on this enchanted land. My family members and I only went there as we accompanied my brother-in-law, the famous world-renowned physician, who was going there on a lifesaving medical journey.

He had actually accepted me, his sister-in-law, as his own sister. So, I call him my brother, not brother-in-law. Did you know I am alive today because of his miraculous hands and devotion to give me a second chance in life? He is a medical genius, who has devoted his life to humans and humanity. Within his hands, I found my second life. Tonight, I will share an enchanted tale of how my brother Jacobus had taken us on a scientific tour through the continent of Antarctica.

Antarctica is a continent which is covered with dense ice in the Southern Ocean. It is mostly covered by the Antarctic ice sheet. This continent is also home of the South Pole. I welcome you to this continent that is virtually uninhabited by humans. Visitors who stop by this continent do so by ship or plane mostly through South America. This continent has no capital city, as this continent has no countries, but does have a collection of international claims.

Did you know this continent found its name from the Greek language? It is derived from the Greek word Antarktikos which literally means opposite to the Arctic. If you are researching for your school, you will learn this continent is one of the fastest warming places on Earth. Also, if you walk around this continent with a compass, all directions will point north.

Although no one lives on Antarctica permanently, this continent did have at least eleven lucky children who were born there. Antarctica has no permanent citizens, yet a lot of scientists and support staff live there on a short-term basis. The scientists go to Antarctica from around the globe to study the weather pattern, geology, and wildlife on the continent. This way, they can help overcome our global climate crisis and prevent disasters from happening.

We too went there for a very short visit as my brother Jacobus had to perform an emergency surgery on one of the scientists who could not be flown back but needed a doctor to go there on an emergency basis. Because of the rough weather, no one was available to take him on an emergency medical flight. Big Papa, an accomplished pilot and owner of a private plane, had flown our whole family over there. Our family members accompanied Jacobus as our family members always stick together, in good times and bad.

SOME OF ANTARCTICA'S FAMOUS FOODS

Cooking in the harshest environment is hard yet did you know chefs from around the globe visit the research stations on a temporary basis to give back to their society? Skilled cooks are responsible for cooking, catering, and everyone's food safety. They are very skilled and serve the researchers five-star cuisines with whatever they can gather. Let's get introduced to some of Antarctica's famous foods.

We know McDonald's has a restaurant in all the continents of this planet excluding Antarctica. Yet wherever we the humans end up, even for a short while, we can cook and make our own food. Although there is no national food of Antarctica, here are some dishes that are found in Antarctica.

ENCHANTED TALES: A KASTEEL VREDERIC STORYBOOK FOR CHILDREN

Seafood
Sledging Biscuits
Pemmican
Hoosh
Duck

· Menu ·

COUNTRIES OF ANTARCTICA

There are no countries in Antarctica as it does not belong to anyone. Antarctica is actually governed internationally as agreed upon in a unique international partnership. The Antarctic Treaty was signed in Washington, D.C. on December 1, 1959 initially by twelve countries. These twelve countries were Argentina, Australia, Belgium, Chile, France, Great Britain, Japan, New Zealand, Norway, South Africa, the United States of America, and the Union of Soviet Socialist Republics.

There are now over fifty countries that have signed the Antarctic Treaty of which twenty-nine countries are involved in decision-making. Did you know there is no military activity in the continent of Antarctica? Countries that have signed the Antarctic Treaty have agreed to dedicate the continent to science and peace.

ENCHANTED TALES: A KASTEEL VREDERIC STORYBOOK FOR CHILDREN

LANDMARK QUIZ

Which landmark is this and where is it located?

A. Mount Erebus, Ross Island
B. Cierva Cove, Antarctic Peninsula
C. Vernadsky Research Base, Galindez Island
D. Emperor Penguins, Snow Hill Island

SOME OF ANTARCTICA'S LANDMARKS

When you visit Antarctica, do stop by some of the amazing and famous places in the continent.

Landmarks

Vernadsky Research Base – *Galindez Island*

Deception Island – *South Shetland Islands*

Amundsen-Scott South Pole Station – *Geographic South Pole*

Cierva Cove – *Antarctic Peninsula*

Wilhelmina Bay – *Antarctic Peninsula*

Robert Falcon Scott's Discovery Hut – *Ross Island*

Emperor Penguins – *Snow Hill Island*

Mount Erebus – *Ross Island*

Blood Falls – *Victoria Land*

Airdevronsix Icefalls – *Victoria Land*

STORY TIME WITH KATELIJNE SNAAIJER VAN PHILLIP

Now that you have learned some information on the enchanted and mystical continent of Antarctica, let's hear one enchanted tale from this continent. As there are no countries in the snow-covered Antarctica, I will share one story. Maybe the original and the current permanent inhabitants will share their miracles with us.

I am Katelijne Snaaijer van Phillip, wife of Antonius van Phillip, mother of Griet and Andries, and a very beloved daughter of the famous Kasteel Vrederic. It is now my turn to take you through the continent with no native human inhabitants and retell an enchanted tale. You will meet some of the original inhabitants of this continent as they too live and share this one home, we all call Earth, our home under the one roof which we all call the vast skies.

So, come now and travel with my family and me, as I take you to Antarctica through my eyes and my enchanted daughter's magical adventures in *Enchanted Tales: A Kasteel Vrederic Storybook For Children*.

SNOW HILL ISLAND

The Mystery Penguin Princess Of Snow Hill Island

"If only we could go back and trace the inhabitants of this continent, we would see penguins arrived before humans, and to this day they still exist as the inhabitants of this continent are still the penguins, the whales, the seals, and other sea birds."

ENCHANTED TALES: A KASTEEL VREDERIC STORYBOOK FOR CHILDREN

Antarctica

During a very dark day, we landed in Antarctica. We were very lucky as our pilot was the only person other than a very beloved doctor brother with whom I would trust our lives on a harsh winter's stormy flight. Big Papa, Erasmus van Phillip, was our pilot. I realized during Antarctica's winter months, the continent plunges into months of darkness. This was one such day where we landed upon a mystical continent which greeted us with complete darkness. No other pilot or plane could have flown us over there but the blessed hands of a very blessed father.

The white continent and its mythical beauty welcomed us with a big hug on a cold and very dark winter morning. Jacobus and Margriete directly went to their patient. We all kept ourselves busy as they were busy for two whole days. After the second day, Jacobus and Margriete came out with a huge success story. Their patient had actually broken his legs and had a heart condition, but nothing serious and was healed.

Griet started to cry as she asked Jacobus, "Papa Jacobus, what happened with the man? Is he hurt? Will he be all right?"

Margriete ran to Griet and hugged her from the other side. The readers of the *Kasteel Vrederic* series know Margriete was the mother of Griet in her previous life. I believe it was Margriete's faith that had brought Griet back to us. Margriete had kept saying, "I love you so much my precious child that I set you free so you can come home to your blessed mother and father as you have chosen."

She did set Griet free, so Griet came back as a daughter of Kasteel Vrederic to Antonius and me. Yet she is a miracle child who now has more than one set of parents. She has the whole Vrederic household raising her. She is our blessed child, the girl with the lantern.

Jacobus told her, "It was easy as we just placed a bandage on his boo-boo, and your Mama Margriete kissed all the pain away. He is completely healed and has a glow-in-the-dark penguin bandage on him now."

Griet said, "Oma gives me glow-in-the-dark bandages and kisses my boo-boo away."

Griet calls her grandmother, Anadhi Newhouse van Phillip, my Big Mama, "Oma" which is Dutch for grandmother. After a long day, we traveled to Snow Hill Island. As it was getting late, we all planned to get into bed early. We had camped in a safe place created by the scientists at Snow Hill Island. Yet remember not everything in life goes accordingly to our plans. That night, we found out someone else was calling our girl with the lantern.

Tonight, come and travel with me as I take you on a journey to Snow Hill Island. I am Katelijne Snaaijer van Phillip, and this is a magical story of a very special princess. I call this enchanted tale, "The Mystery Penguin Princess Of Snow Hill Island."

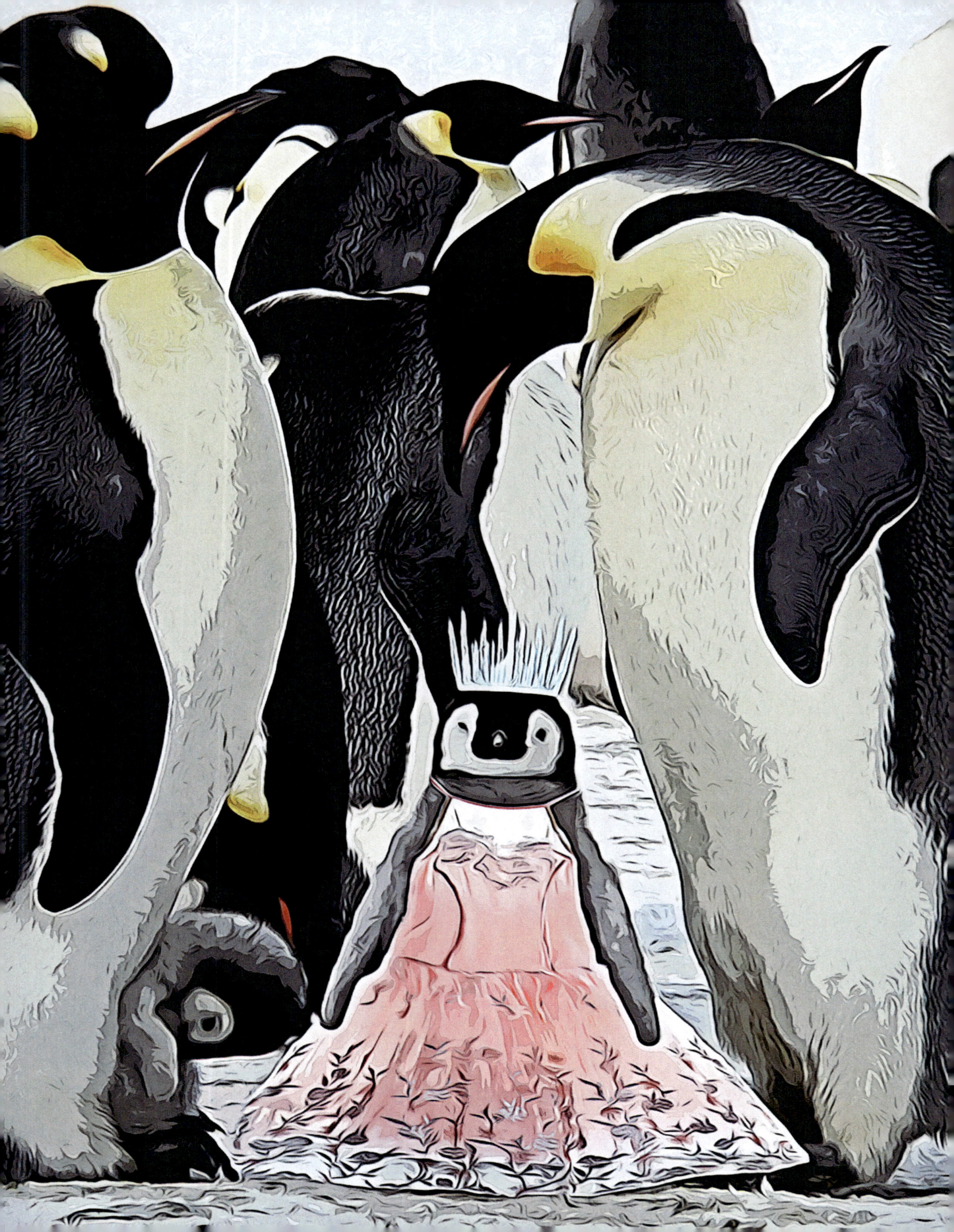

THE MYSTERY PENGUIN PRINCESS OF SNOW HILL ISLAND

We had made it to Snow Hill Island by plane and then walked to the shore where we could see the emperor penguins of Snow Hill Island. It was strange as the winter months brought cold and dark days and nights to the magical land. We were lucky as we got to camp by the shore and had a lot of help from the scientists staying here. Yet as everyone started to relax and enjoy the wonderous and amazing white snow-covered magical land at night, my daughter Griet started to cry.

I watched my daughter as she ran to her big brother and asked him for help. She said, "Big Brother, will you come with me to the end of this Earth to save someone who needs my help? Even if the person is not a person but maybe a little different?"

Andries held her in his arms, and he said, "Anywhere, anytime. Remember, promises are made to be kept in the Vrederic household. We make promises and always keep them."

That's when we saw in front of us, there were a lot of penguins standing and just watching us. Amongst them, we saw a small penguin who was dressed up in royal attire. She was holding hands with a whale boy, a seal girl, and some huge birds who come in front of us. The penguin had a crown on her head that was made out of icicles. If only I could tell the penguin's age, I would think she was like my Griet's age.

Then we saw in front of everyone, my little Griet, baby Rietje, and big boys Alexander and Theunis all become older. They were five-year-old and eight-year-old children.

Griet came in front of the little penguin girl and asked, "How could we help you all in your time of need?"

The penguin girl to everyone's bewilderment said, "Dear girl with the lantern, I know you go around the globe helping humans with their needs. Would you in our time of need please help a penguin girl, a whale boy, a baby seal, and the birds? We are the inhabitants of this continent. I am known as the Penguin Princess, as my parents are the King and Queen of all the inhabitants of Antarctica. We the penguins, the whales, the seals, the birds, and all others have lived here peacefully for years."

She then stopped as we heard a strange sound coming from somewhere. It sounded like a shriek of some kind. All of Griet's guests came closer to us as if they were frightened by the sounds.

The brave Penguin Princess then said, "Griet, there is a monster called the melting iceberg monster. He has taken the form of a huge monster and he is made out of the melting icebergs of Antarctica. He has been hunting down all of our families. He has imprisoned my parents under his home. Please help us rescue my parents and get rid of the monster forever. This monster will eventually destroy human civilizations if not handled now."

I watched Griet ask her brother for his permission as she said, "Big Brother, will you help us? May we go and help this family in their time of need?"

Andries told Griet, "We must help them Griet, as that must be the reason we came here. Jacobus would have come alone like he always does. Since we are here, let's see what we can do unitedly as a family."

It was then we saw in front of us stood a huge gorilla-type monster. The monster was made out of icicles, and he had sharp teeth which were also made out of icicles. He stomped his feet as he was walking slowly, yet with such force that his footsteps were melting the snow in Antarctica. We knew this was not good for the melting continent could endanger all of the population on Earth. The melting of Antarctica is something the scientists too are trying to prevent.

Then like a miracle, the flying horse of Rietje appeared and the four kids jumped on top of the horse. Then I watched the kids fly toward the glaciers and the icebergs of Antarctica. I clenched my fists in fear as every time I watch my little girl go on another adventure saving lives, she takes my life with her. Margriete and Big Mama held on to me like a support, as they too clenched their fists.

We walked with the penguins, the whales, the seals, and the birds that came along with the Penguin Princess. We watched the melting iceberg monster follow Griet's magical lantern. My brave little girl held on to her lantern as she sat on top of the horse with her team members.

Andries called her from the ground and said, "Griet! Now fly over the glaciers so he will jump into the icebergs and become one and freeze inside it."

Griet followed his instructions as I watched Rietje, Alexander, and Theunis throw their boomerang swords toward the monster. Through the power of the swords, and Griet's lantern's forceful glow, the monster was forced to fall into the icebergs of Antarctica and become one.

In front of us, the imprisoned penguins, whales, seals, and huge birds, came out, one by one. We watched the Penguin Princess go to her parents and hug them. She then faced Griet and came closer to us.

She said, "I, the crowned Penguin Princess of Antarctica from Snow Hill Island, thank you and your family for helping us."

It was then we watched the sun was appearing and dawn broke open. The penguins, the whales, the seals, and the birds all disappeared, and the monster too was frozen within the icebergs of Antarctica.

I watched my baby girl come to me and say, "Mama, let's go home. Griet wants to nap now."

Big Mama and Big Papa took the rest of the kids as I carried my little girl back to our camp. Throughout time, we all thought how we forget not only humans need help from one another, yet at times even animals need help from the humans. Yet do remember, they can't say or speak to us, so they need little girls like the brave Penguin Princess, and our girl with the lantern to help and communicate with one another.

In a land far away from our own, I watched Jacobus and Margriete help a scientist in his time of need. Big Papa helped fly an emergency medical plane. Similarly, I watched how my little girl with the lantern had helped the Penguin Princess of Antarctica's Snow Hill Island.

Everyone reading or listening to this enchanted tale, do come and visit this great continent when you can. For now, it's not only the scientists or researchers or doctors but everyone who can take a trip to this great continent. If you can't make it over to Antarctica any time soon, don't worry as you can with this book. Through the pages of this book, you can visit all the continents of this world. Remember through this enchanted tale, you can always visit the mystery Penguin Princess of Snow Hill Island.

Antarctica Trivia Time

What months are months of darkness in Antarctica?

When was the Antarctic Treaty originally signed?

What continent do most people travel through to reach Antarctica?

MESSAGE FROM KATELIJNE SNAAIJER VAN PHILLIP

I hope you all had a very nice time traveling through the continent of Antarctica. This continent contains ninety percent of the world's ice. Remember if this ice ever melts, the rising sea level will become a global crisis. We need to support our scientific scholars so that they find a solution for this.

We the humans and the animals need to work for one another. All need to live under the one sky and above the one Earth in harmony. So, you the child and the adult after this story, keep your thoughts out for the scientific scholars of this Earth. Be there for them as they are doing this for you.

As I leave you tonight, I would like to invite you to try out the biscuits of Antarctica with your parents. I am having one here back in our home, Kasteel Vrederic. Big Mama made them for all of us.

Tonight, we have so many children from around the globe who have come over to our home. They are all trying the delicious biscuits after listening to the enchanted tale of the Penguin Princess and her friends. As now you too have heard this tale, go and share the tale and the tasty biscuits you too could make with an adult and a friend.

Don't leave yet, as tomorrow night's storyteller is Big Papa, Erasmus van Phillip. The famous painter will take you through another magical continent. So, come back tomorrow night and enjoy the *Enchanted Tales: A Kasteel Vrederic Storybook For Children* with Erasmus van Phillip as he takes you on an adventurous trip through the continent of South America.

CHAPTER FOUR:

CONTINENT OF SOUTH AMERICA

*Storyteller:
Erasmus van Phillip*

"I am the world's fourth-largest continent. The world's largest river by volume, the Amazon, flows within my chest. The world's driest place, the Atacama Desert, also calls me home. I am the continent of South America."

ENCHANTED TALES: A KASTEEL VREDERIC STORYBOOK FOR CHILDREN

South America

South America is a continent in the Western Hemisphere. Most of the continent is in the Southern Hemisphere with a small section in the Northern Hemisphere. South America is the world's fourth largest continent with the world's largest river by volume, the Amazon, flowing through her. This land also is a miracle as she holds within her chest the world's driest desert called the Atacama Desert. We will visit both of these places on top of other ones through our journey across this continent.

The continent has twelve countries within her. Coffee lovers like myself appreciate Brazil, the world's largest coffee producer and the biggest country in South America. Also, children, did you know Brazil is the seventh-largest cocoa producer in the world? If you all are going to share some facts with your friends then tell them, the Amazon Rainforest does produce some amount of the world's oxygen. How much oxygen of the world produced there is debatable, maybe six to twenty percent, however, we need to keep on planting trees around the globe. Now let's take a look at some of South America's famous foods.

SOME OF SOUTH AMERICA'S FAMOUS FOODS

South America's cuisine has taken over the whole world. At least once a week, my family members try one of these items listed below. Go ahead and pick out one of the food items from the list and maybe you can make it with your parents.

So, my dear children here are some of the famous South American foods for you to try out, from your own kitchen.

ENCHANTED TALES: A KASTEEL VREDERIC STORYBOOK FOR CHILDREN

Salteñas – *Bolivia* *Suriname* – **Pom**
Chivito – *Uruguay* *Venezuela* – **Arepas**
Brigadeiros – *Brazil* *Guyana* – **Pepperpot**
Encebollado – *Ecuador* *Chile* – **Cazuela Chilena**
Empanadas – *Argentina* *Peru* – **Ceviche Peruano**
Bandeja Paisa – *Colombia* *Amazon Rainforest* – **Arazá**
Mote de Queso – *Colombia* *Paraguay* – **Sopa Paraguaya**

· Menu ·

COUNTRIES OF SOUTH AMERICA

Now let's learn to say the names of the countries in South America. We will visit only a few yet here is the list of them all. Why don't you now go through all of the names of all of the countries in this continent? Do share the names with your friends. These are the twelve sovereign countries of the continent we all know as South America.

ENCHANTED TALES: A KASTEEL VREDERIC STORYBOOK FOR CHILDREN

South America

Argentina

Bolivia

Brazil

Chile

Colombia

Ecuador

Guyana

Paraguay

Peru

Suriname

Uruguay

Venezuela

LANDMARK QUIZ

Which landmark is this and where is it located?

A. Angel Falls, Venezuela
B. Christ the Redeemer, Brazil
C. Machu Picchu, Peru
D. Atacama Desert, Chile

SOME OF SOUTH AMERICA'S LANDMARKS

When you do visit one of these countries, do stop by some of the amazing and famous landmarks of South America.

Landmarks

Machu Picchu – *Peru*

Christ the Redeemer – *Brazil*

Galápagos Islands – *Ecuador*

Amazon Rainforest – *Brazil, Bolivia, Colombia, Ecuador, French Guiana, Guyana, Peru, Suriname, and Venezuela*

Patagonia – *Chile/Argentina*

Laguna Colorada – *Bolivia*

Angel Falls – *Venezuela*

Las Lajas Sanctuary – *Colombia*

Iguazú Falls – *Argentina/Brazil*

Kaieteur Falls – *Guyana*

Atacama Desert – *Chile*

STORY TIME WITH ERASMUS VAN PHILLIP

A South American art convention was something I was looking forward to. I would be going through a few of the South American countries as I had an art exhibition jointly with my son. I am a proud father of three sons, Jacobus Vrederic van Phillip, Antonius van Phillip, and Andries van Phillip, the famous pianist who had been taken away from us yet is now back home with us through the door of miracles as my grandson. Yet I see him still as my son as after a lot of wishes made upon the stars, we got him back.

On this trip, I traveled with my whole family. I had with me, my wife Anadhi Newhouse van Phillip, and my two daughters-in-law whom I see as my daughters, Margriete and Katelijne. I also had with me, my beloved grandbabies, Griet Vrederic van Phillip and Rietje Vrederic van Phillip, and our house's protectors whom I keep close to my heart as our home's beloved grandkids, Theunis Peters and Alexander van der Bijl.

Our family traveled through the continent of South America. It is so much easier to travel because I take my own plane. To tell you the truth, I love flying it in the skies as I get a firsthand aerial view. Because we have our own plane, we are able to travel as a family throughout the world. Maybe when you grow up, you can become a pilot or an artist who can paint all the countries of this world through your canvas.

Now let's go and hear some stories from the continent we call South America. I am Erasmus van Phillip, a son of the famous Kasteel Vrederic, and I will take you through the stories of South America. Through my eyes, you will see this continent yet through my grandchildren's adventures, you will meet and greet some new friends from South America. Remember to take a peek and look at the map of this continent before you head over there. All the places we have visited in the stories are highlighted on the map. Let's now travel over to South America through the pages of *Enchanted Tales: A Kasteel Vrederic Storybook For Children*.

BRAZIL

The Jaguar Prince Of The Amazon Rainforest

"What happens when you fear the guardians as the huntsmen? It's then you become the brave warrior."

Brazil

Brazil is officially known as the Federative Republic of Brazil and is the largest country in South America. The capital city is Brasília. The language spoken here is Portuguese. Brazil is home to more animal and plant species than any other country on this Earth. This amazing and naturally beautiful country is also home to sixty percent of the Amazon Rainforest. We will be visiting the Amazon Rainforest as we travel through Brazil.

The Amazon Rainforest extends through Brazil, Bolivia, Peru, Ecuador, Colombia, Venezuela, Guyana, and Suriname. It also extends through French Guiana, a territory of France. This forest is the world's largest tropical rainforest. Within this rainforest flows the world's longest river by discharge, which is the Amazon River. This river in 2011 was voted on the internet as one of the new seven wonders of the world.

The Amazon has more than thirty million people of which around one to two million are indigenous peoples. This magical forest has around four hundred billion trees. Did you know ten percent of the world's known wildlife is found in the Amazon Rainforest? The Amazon Rainforest is also home to the world's largest population of jaguars left on Earth.

The Amazon Rainforest is burning down at a fast rate. To protect the various types of trees, the wide variety of animals, and many other forms of life that scientists are still identifying, we must protect this miraculous rainforest. Let's everyone plant trees and not cut them down. Let's leave the animals to be safe and secured in their own homes. We can enjoy them from far away. By doing so, we let them know we do this because we love them.

Tonight, let me take you on a journey through the miraculous Amazon Rainforest in Brazil. There we had a brave warrior prince who was waiting for my beloved granddaughter, the girl with the lantern. Also, he awaited my other granddaughter Rietje, the brave warrioress, on her magical horse to appear as his last hope.

The two girls are accompanied always by the brave protectors of my ancestral home, Kasteel Vrederic, Theunis, the brave warrior, and Alexander, the brave knight. These young boys have joined hands with my two granddaughters to make the world a better and safer place for all humans and animals alike. I am Erasmus van Phillip, the proud grandfather of the girl with the lantern. I call this enchanted tale, "The Jaguar Prince Of The Amazon Rainforest."

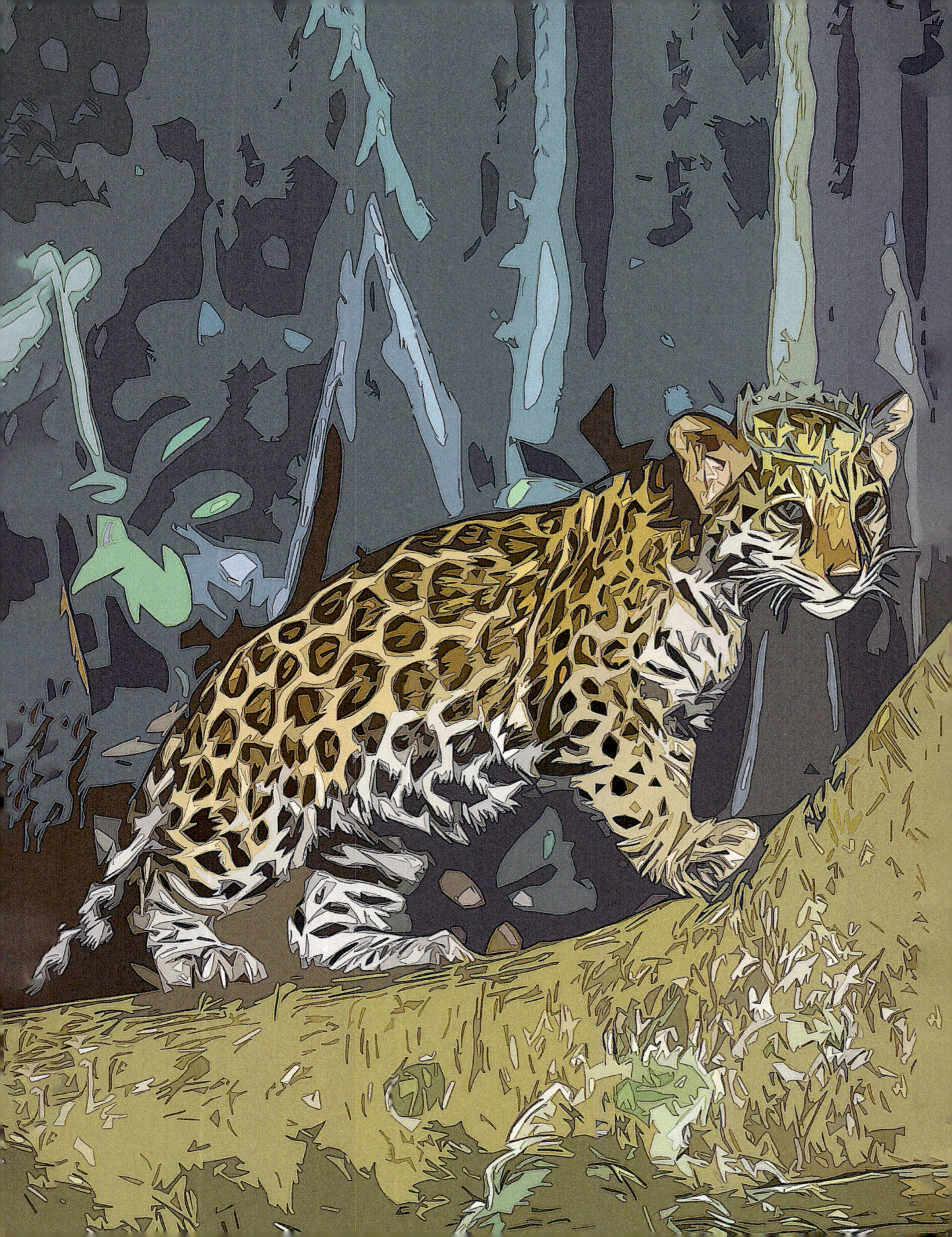

THE JAGUAR PRINCE OF THE AMAZON RAINFOREST

The flight to Rio de Janeiro was very nice as the weather held up for us on this trip. We flew from there to the city of Manaus right after my art exhibition in Rio de Janeiro. We planned on taking a cruise along the Amazon River. My son Jacobus had also rented a jungle lodge as his mother, my wife, wanted to stay in the jungle as an adventure. I wasn't worried about the weather as the climate in the Amazon Rainforest remains tropical basically all year round. It's nice to always have such amazing weather but I would miss the white snowfall of a cold winter.

The journey from Manaus to our jungle lodge was very adventurous as we cruised through the water. We found our lodge was like a tree house on top of the river, raised high enough so no animals could climb in. The boat captain and the guide went with us as they slept near our open lodge with machetes in their hands.

I watched my granddaughter Griet go to her Papa Jacobus and start to cry. She asked him, "Why does that man have a big knife like that?"

Jacobus told her, "It's for the bad animals, the huge jaguars. Because at night, sometimes bad animals come and attack the humans. That's when these guides protect us with their weapons, like the swords of Rietje, Alexander, and Theunis."

She then said, "No. Friend is scared of man. That's why he attacks. He said bad men have come and taken his family members away. He is lonely and is asking for help to save his family members from the burning fires."

I was worried if something happened in front of these men, then my Griet would be at risk. I only hoped if something did happen, then Aunt Marinda would be nearby somewhere to help us through this night. I reassured myself everything would be all right.

As the moon came out, we went outside to watch the amazing moonlight over the Amazon Rainforest. The women held on to the children as my three sons and I kept an eye out for the wild animals while we tried to enjoy the scenic beauty of the jungle life. It was then we heard the screams of the howling monkeys.

Everyone was shaken by the loud screams except Griet who smiled and said, "Friends are happy. They are asking for our help. They said the Prince is hurt and needs our assistance."

We then heard a strange sound like someone was sawing a tree. Then it sounded like a bark or a growl. Our tour guide started to scream like he was shaking in fear rather than warning anyone about anything.

Andries said, "Big Papa, there is something out there. Maybe we should get back into the lodge. Or maybe it's too late, because I think my sister Griet was not talking about them when she said her friends are calling her."

In the full moon's glorious glows, we watched Griet turn into a five-year-old girl as did Rietje. Alexander and Theunis looked a little older. I saw a flying horse had come with a woman who had a cloak on and somehow looked older. Then as she took off her cloak, we saw our time-traveling Aunt Marinda standing in front of us.

It was then Katelijne said, "Now I am scared as my daughter will be hunted down like a witch by humans. She is not a witch but just a normal girl with some miraculous powers. I must hide my child. Margriete, help."

I saw Margriete then said, "Katelijne, don't worry. The tour guide, the boat captain, and all the rest of the tourists are sleeping. You could thank Jacobus for these two, but the others you could say fainted as they saw the flying horse and Aunt Marinda fly in."

Aunt Marinda said, "Tsk, tsk, children. They won't remember anything by dawn. You all panic too much."

That's when we saw a huge jaguar come jumping in from behind the forest and drop in front of Griet. He had his mouth open and was in a hunting mood. I was positive he was going to bite my granddaughter. I don't know how but I think Andries jumped over to Griet first followed by the rest of us, yet Aunt Marinda just stood there like a glowing candle.

Griet said, "It's all right. Big Brother, don't bother him. He is trying to save my life."

That's when we all got over the shock of witnessing a real-life jaguar and saw that the huge jaguar was trying to move something from touching Griet's feet. There we saw a huge snake called Bothrops bilineatus. It is one of the most poisonous snakes in the Amazon Rainforest.

Then the jaguar introduced himself in a very human voice to Griet. He said, "Dear girl with the lantern, it is my pleasure to be able to do something for you at least once in my lifetime. I am known to all as the Jaguar Prince of the Amazon Rainforest. I am here, however, as my family members have been trapped by a human monster. They have fallen prey as his victims. He wants to take them as his trophy and has not even let the children go."

I realized he was talking about the poachers who were hunting down the animals of the amazing rainforest. I didn't know what to do as the talking Jaguar Prince was just standing there watching my little Griet for help.

It was then we saw in the river, a gondola came floating to us. Griet and the three kids flew over and waited for us to get into the gondola. The boat's captain was Aunt Marinda. As we got in, the jaguar followed us in the shallow water. We saw Griet stop at a point and we all went down there. We saw there was a huge camp, and a lot of people were sleeping. We could see the Amazon Rainforest fires glowing in the dark night. Griet then asked Andries to follow her.

Jacobus said, "It's the humans who have started this fire intentionally. As more and more lands are necessary, humans are not thinking about the endangered animals and their homes. On top of many other threats, the animals have two immediate threats which are the forest fires, and the poachers who are intentionally hunting the animals."

I told them, "Let's go and see what we can do."

My wife Anadhi, a dream psychic, said, "No, you won't go anywhere. These poachers are the real animals. They are the hunters and they won't stop at hurting you or anyone else."

I hugged my wife and told her, "We have the Prince of the Amazon Rainforest with us. I really don't think we have to worry about anything."

The Jaguar Prince then said, "I can handle it from here as I have my buddies Griet and her team with me."

We watched the four kids fly over to different parts of the camp and set free the jaguars. Then they saw there was a small wildfire that the group of hunters had started. It was getting bigger and going out of hand. The children with Andries and Aunt Marinda somehow got the fire under control.

The huge jaguars all came and stood in front of Griet as the Jaguar Prince then said, "Dear Griet, would you please try to heal my father, the King of the Amazon Rainforest? He is hurt and his feet are bleeding. They shot him there. Please help him."

It was then I saw a human doctor, Jacobus, help the wounded jaguar who too could speak in human words.

He said, "Dear friend, I know you all are afraid of us as we do hurt so many of you. Yet please know we only hunt because we too are afraid otherwise, we will be the hunted. It seems like we are with one another, always the hunters or the hunted, never as friends. Griet and her family members, however, will always be our friends."

That night as we all came back to our lodge, we saw everyone else there was oblivious to the events of the night. The only thing we heard was that there was a poacher who lost all of his jaguars. It was so sad as we watched what was fun and games to some had become a matter of extinction for a group of rare and endangered animals. Somehow, they all escaped alive and unhurt in the middle of the night. Our tour guide assured us we were safe as he was there to watch over us.

We knew we were safe as Griet's friend was watching over the Kasteel Vrederic family and all of you, who know we need to save all the endangered animals like the Jaguar Prince of the Amazon Rainforest.

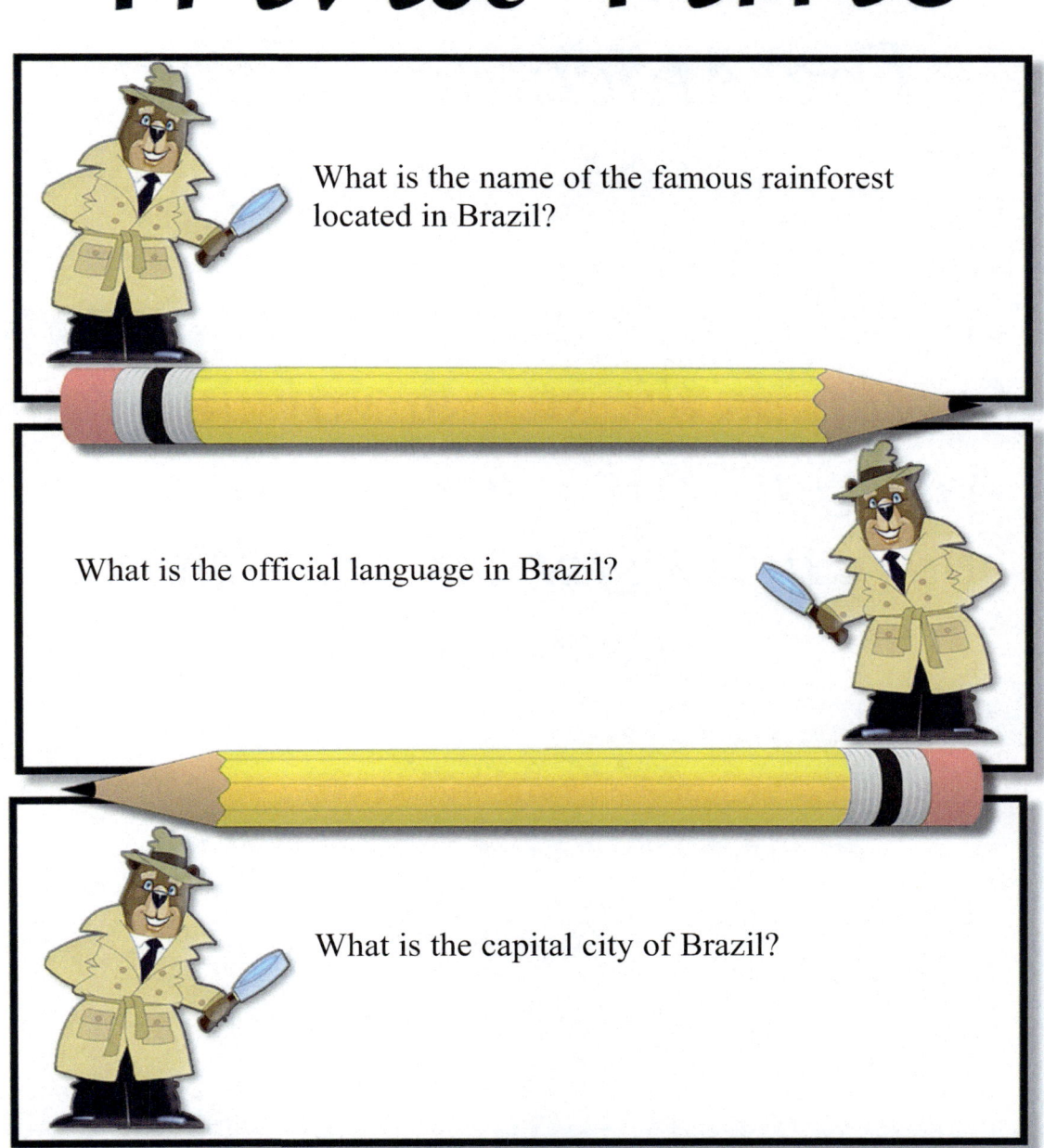

ENCHANTED TALES: A KASTEEL VREDERIC STORYBOOK FOR CHILDREN

Brazil Trivia Time

What is the name of the famous rainforest located in Brazil?

What is the official language in Brazil?

What is the capital city of Brazil?

CHILE

The Magical Star Girl Of The Atacama Desert

"Remember to wish upon the first star of night, as the star too awaits your wish, for that's how you and the miraculous star become friends eternally."

ENCHANTED TALES: A KASTEEL VREDERIC STORYBOOK FOR CHILDREN

Chile

Mirage, or misperception, is what drove through the minds of all the witnesses of this story. This time we were traveling through Chile's Atacama Desert. This is a desert in South America. In Spanish, it is called Desierto de Atacama. Three countries had fought over this desert during the War of the Pacific from 1879 to 1884. All the countries wanted to control the desert's sodium nitrate mines. Chile had eventually won the battle. So today, the Atacama Desert belongs to Chile.

Did you know, the world's oldest mummy and its mummified remains were found in the Atacama Desert? So, how could we skip this mystical desert as we traveled through South America? The Atacama Desert will always be one of Chile's most thrilling places to visit. This desert has it all, like the geysers, the volcanoes, the lunar rock formations, and it is the driest desert in the world.

Did you know this place is dry for 300 days out of the 365 days in a year? So, I hear it is the perfect place for stargazing. People from around the globe go there to stargaze. The desert's soil is also compared to the soil on Mars. This land is somehow similar to Mars, so maybe you could feel like you are in Mars. Maybe that's why there are so many mystical stories looming around this place.

One story is of the Atacama Giant which is a 390-foot-tall sculpture. Scientists believe it was created to predict the movement of the moon and the seasonal changes. Yet some also believe it actually represents aliens from outer space. You must travel to the desert to decide for yourself what you think it is. If you do, then don't miss the giant hand facing the skies as it is said, the hand represents the human feelings.

My family had visited a secretive red lagoon called Laguna Roja, or Mar Rojo. This lagoon's water is red and there are two more lagoons nearby which are yellow and green. The scientific reasons given for the water being another color are algae and sediments.

Yet the legend retold by the Aymara people is the lagoon belonged to the devil and he wanted people to stay away from it. Another legend says three virgins were sacrificed there, and each had wept a different colored tear. So, the lagoons are of three different colors.

Also do go and visit the Moon Valley in the Atacama Desert, for there you will see rock formations of the three Marías. These rock formations are called Las Tres Marías, or some say Los Vigilantes. Some believe the rock formations depict the Virgin Mary.

ENCHANTED TALES: A KASTEEL VREDERIC STORYBOOK FOR CHILDREN

Now you are wondering how people survive in this desert, or does anyone even live here? The answer is yes, roughly around one million people call this place home. They grow vegetables that are easy to grow in the desert.

Why my family and I went to the Atacama Desert is a question I had asked myself. Yet the answer is my wife, Anadhi Newhouse van Phillip. She was insistent on visiting this desert as she had a dream, we must visit this miraculous desert. There were no reasons given other than one that we must go there for there was another miracle waiting for us.

Tonight, let me take you on a journey through the Atacama Desert of Chile, where we know was waiting for us my granddaughters' friend who to you and me is known as the magical Atacama Girl. I am Erasmus van Phillip, and I call this enchanted tale, "The Magical Star Girl Of The Atacama Desert."

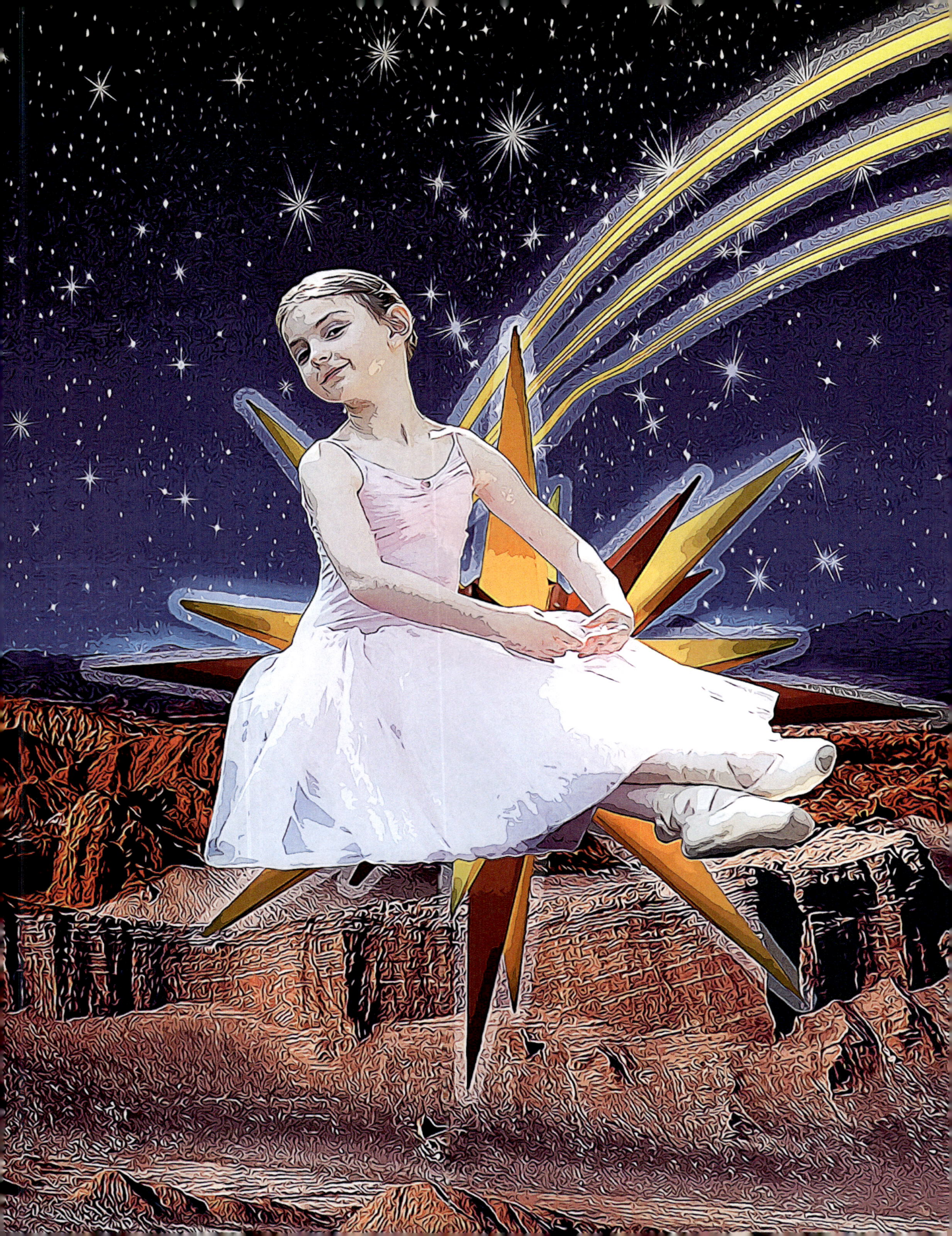

THE MAGICAL STAR GIRL OF THE ATACAMA DESERT

Santiago is the capital city of Chile. After a small art exhibition in Santiago, my family and I went on a two-hour flight to El Loa Airport in Calama. From there, we went to San Pedro de Atacama. We rented a campervan and had a tour guide to take us around the magical Atacama Desert. We also planned to camp in the desert overnight to get the best view for stargazing.

As we reached the campground, we found out some of the world's best observatories are in the Atacama Desert. We settled into our tents and were ready to get the perfect astronomic experience of our life. Andries was playing with his little sister Griet.

That's when he said, "Little Sister, maybe we will get to see some extraterritorial existence tonight. Or at the very least, we will get to see the stars above the skies and maybe make some new friends."

Griet watched her brother and said, "Brother Bear, I want to sleep on your lap. I am worried for the girl."

Every one of our family members knew when Griet wants her brother bear and wants to be with him, something is wrong or is about to be wrong. When Griet is needed, she wants to help yet I see my granddaughter's frightened little soul. Even though she is scared, she somehow knows what she has to do when she receives a call from a friend in need.

I watched my precious granddaughter kept looking at the empty desert sand as if she was searching for someone or something. Jacobus and Antonius both went and sat next to her as they wanted to be close to her for the unknown danger that loomed around us.

I walked with Anadhi as we held on to one another, worried for our granddaughters as we saw our little Rietje walk to Griet and hold her hands. Both now sat on Andries's lap. He was dancing with both girls in his arms.

Andries saw us and said, "Big Papa, I have the two best dancers with me. Please take some pictures of us."

Griet said, "No pictures as she is scared. She is about to fall Opa. She will need our help. She is worried she will turn into a rock if she falls on Earth."

I saw Margriete had a telescope as she said, "Something is wrong. There is a whirlwind or a storm of some kind over there."

I saw in front of us, Griet turned into her five-year-old form as did Rietje and the two boys too were older boys. All four children jumped on top of Rietje's magical horse that had appeared from the desert dust. I thought somehow the clear skies had us not just stargazing, but we were experiencing the mysteries of the galaxies.

On a quiet and clear night, there in front of our eyes a certain star was falling. I thought make a wish, yet before I could say anything, I watched my brave wife go and stand in between the fallen star and her granddaughters.

Griet said, "Oma, it's all right. The magical girl of the Atacama Desert is scared. She is standing over there."

It was then we saw in front of us, a child around ten years old was standing like she was lost. She had green hair, yellow skin, and red eyes. Her body was glowing like a star, and I wondered if she was made out of a star. She watched us and I didn't know what she needed. That's when she spoke to Griet.

She said, "I believe you are the girl with the lantern. I really need your help. My name is Star and I need to find my way back home as the evil woman of the Mar Rojo has pulled me to her. She does this frequently as she turns some into a red liquid and places them into the lagoon, where she also converts some into rock formations and imprisons all eternally. I need your help so I can go back home. I have been protecting this desert for a long time but tonight she somehow pulled me toward the desert."

Griet asked her, "How does she do this? There is no tunnel for her to do this, right?"

The magical girl said, "There is a tunnel here. From Mars to Earth, there is an invisible tunnel. The soil and the rock formation are similar to that of the planet Mars. So, she can make a tunnel and do evil acts. Throughout time, my family members have used this tunnel to help the humans in their time of need, without being noticed or being visible for humans don't take well things that are not known to them. We just want to help you in your time of need as we know you are our neighbors even though you don't know."

I watched Andries walk back and forth as he said to Griet, "Little Sister, just say what you want us to do, and we will try to help and get the child back home before she is seen by others or turns into something and becomes imprisoned on Earth."

Griet said to the magical girl, "Dear Star, my magical friend, please get on Rietje's horse as the horse will become a flying boat. Remember, whatever happens, don't get off this horse boat. We will do the rest."

That's when we saw there in the desert appeared a red woman who had long blue hair and was walking toward the child. Griet shined her lantern on the woman who screamed in pain as if she was burning from the light of the magical lantern. I saw then the magical returning boomerang swords of Rietje, Theunis, and Alexander flew toward the evil woman who wanted to capture Star as her own treasure of the red liquid waters. It was then the evil woman became dust and was just a part of the desert. I saw the magical girl of Mars fly on top of Rietje's horse directly into the vast skies.

We all heard a voice from the skies say, "Dear Griet, the girl with the lantern, thank you for your help. I belong in the skies where the greatest lantern, the sun, is. Yet your small lantern on Earth today saved a star girl's life. Forever, I, Star, shall watch over the Atacama Desert as the magical girl of the Atacama Desert."

That's when our children again became little. There was no sign of anything that had happened that night. Our tour guide said he fell asleep and thought he saw a shooting star. We told him we did see a falling star and it was magical. We all looked upon the skies and kept stargazing upon the clear night's skies. The amazing starry night actually reminded me of our famous Dutch painter Vincent van Gogh, and his phenomenal painting called *Starry Night*. Maybe he too was inspired by some kind of miracles he had seen upon the star-filled skies.

If you ever get to visit the Atacama Desert, do take some time to make a wish upon the stars from this amazing desert where you can see the magical stars almost every night of the year. Maybe you too will get to see the magical girl of the Atacama Desert.

This magical girl named Star comes through the tunnel that connects Earth and the skies in the Atacama Desert. She is always seen there. Maybe you too can wish upon her and get to see some magical mysteries when you visit the Atacama Desert. Through the magical gifts of the blessed daughter of Kasteel Vrederic, Griet, who is also the girl with the lantern, we have now collected another story for our book, the enchanted tale of the magical Star girl of the Atacama Desert.

Chile Trivia Time

What planet's soil is compared to the soil in the Atacama Desert?

What is the height of the Atacama Giant?

Why is the Atacama Desert a popular destination for stargazing?

MESSAGE FROM ERASMUS VAN PHILLIP

As we leave the continent of South America, let's go to the continent of North America. As we all travel to this amazing continent, I would like to introduce you to my beloved wife, Anadhi. Through her ancestors, she is half-American and half-Indian. So, she will take you on a journey through her father's land. This land is very special to me as this land gifted me my beloved wife.

This is a land where diversity is an incredible blessing. I know this land has made my beloved wife into who she is today. A wife, a mother, a grandmother, and a mother-in-law who refuses to be a mother-in-law but accepts her daughters-in-law as her daughters. Kasteel Vrederic for me in the sixteenth century was a stone castle without any heartbeats as my beloved wife had never entered the cold castle. Yet as she entered the castle in the twenty-first century, our cold castle became a miraculous home, where love and blessings became one.

Today from this miraculous castle, we have introduced you to the *Enchanted Tales: A Storybook For Children*, through which you too can embark upon the magical journeys through this one world. So now, why don't you get yourself acquainted with my beloved wife Anadhi? She will now take you on another enchanted journey through the third-largest continent, North America.

CHAPTER FIVE:

CONTINENT OF NORTH AMERICA

Storyteller:
Anadhi Newhouse van Phillip

"I am the third-largest continent. Before I became known as North America, I was known as Laurentia."

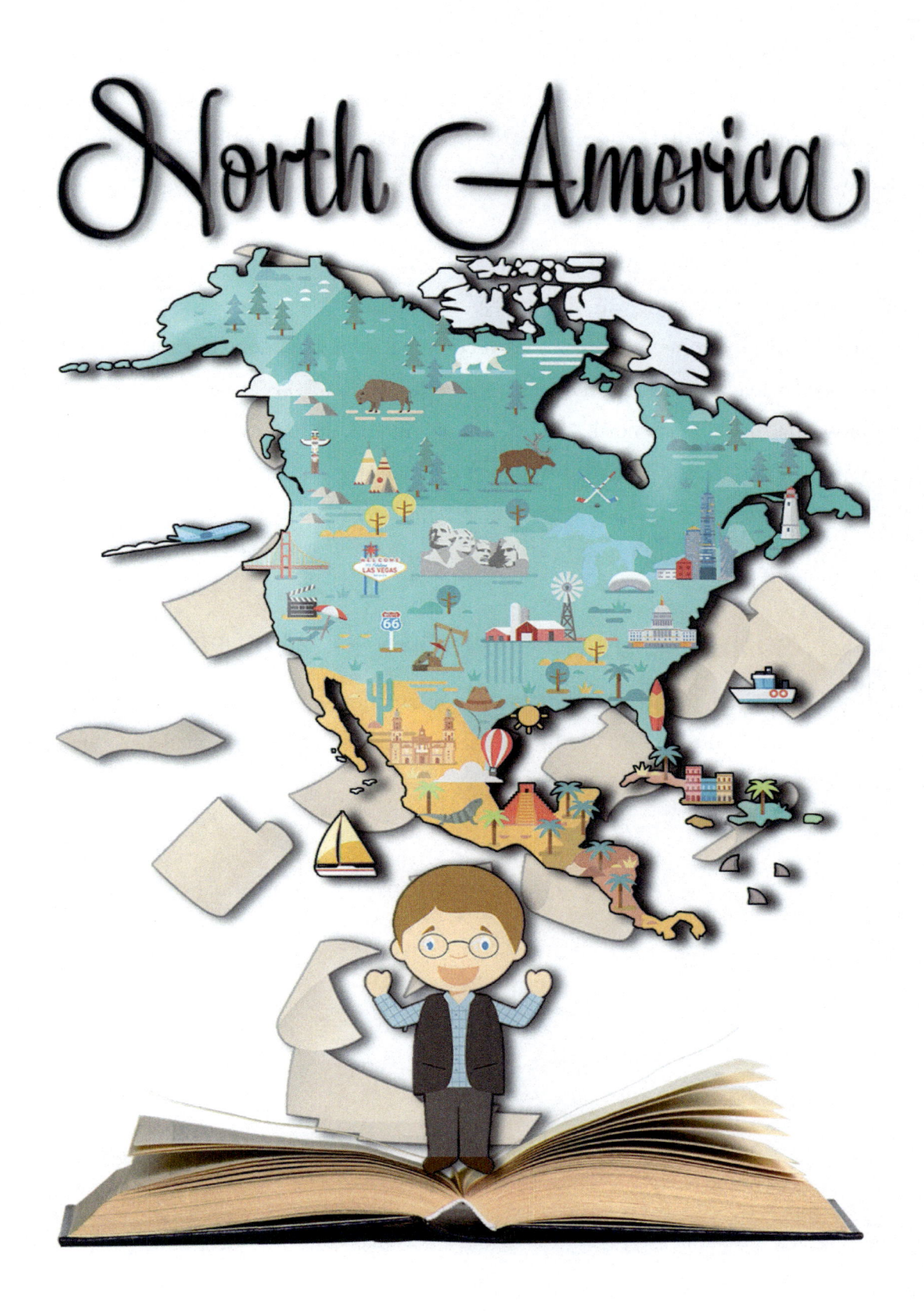

North America

North America is the third-largest continent in the world. The first time I entered this continent, I actually entered the great state of California in the United States of America, the land of my forefathers. North America is located in both the Northern and Western Hemispheres. North America is surrounded by three oceans, the Pacific, Arctic, and Atlantic. Don't miss the oceans as you fly into this continent. I love watching the aerial views from the plane.

Afterward, I actually lived with my paternal grandmother in Washington State. My grandmother now lives with me in the Netherlands, in our home Kasteel Vrederic. My grandmother taught me some facts of this great continent. Did you know the largest country in this continent is Canada and the second-largest country is the USA? North America has three subregions with Canada in the north, the USA in the middle, and Mexico in the south.

My grandmother and I bonded with one another at our kitchen table. She taught me it is always easy to share one's inner thoughts and feelings over a meal. So why don't we get to know one another over some of North America's famous foods?

SOME OF NORTH AMERICA'S FAMOUS FOODS

North America introduces to her table new international foods every day. Yet here my dear children, are some of the famous North American foods for you to try out when you visit this continent.

Burgers – *USA* *USA* – **Apple Pie**
Pecan Pie – *USA* *Dominica* – **Callaloo**
Cou-Cou – *Barbados* *Mexico* – **Chilaquiles**
Catrachas – *Honduras* *Haiti* – **Soupe Joumou**
Mole Poblano – *Mexico* *Costa Rica* – **Gallo Pinto**
Ackee and Saltfish – *Jamaica* *Canada* – **Maple Syrup**
Fried Flying Fish – *Barbados*

· Menu ·

COUNTRIES OF NORTH AMERICA

North America has twenty-three independent countries. Here is a list of the countries. I hope you get acquainted with them all, so when you come to visit this continent, you will be able to guide your parents and friends through all of the countries.

North America

Antigua and Barbuda

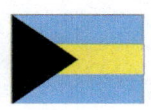

Bahamas

Barbados

Belize

Canada

Costa Rica

Cuba

Dominica

Dominican Republic

El Salvador

Grenada

Guatemala

Haiti

Honduras

Jamaica

Mexico

Nicaragua

Panama

Saint Kitts and Nevis

Saint Lucia

Saint Vincent and the Grenadines

Trinidad and Tobago

United States of America

ENCHANTED TALES: A KASTEEL VREDERIC STORYBOOK FOR CHILDREN

LANDMARK QUIZ

Which landmark is this and where is it located?

A. Statue of Liberty, USA
B. CN Tower, Canada
C. Washington Monument, USA
D. Old Havana, Cuba

SOME OF NORTH AMERICA'S LANDMARKS

When you visit one of these countries in North America, stop by at some of the amazing and famous landmarks of North America.

Landmarks

Statue of Liberty – *USA*

Golden Gate Bridge – *USA*

Mount Rushmore National Memorial – *USA*

Washington Monument – *USA*

Yellowstone National Park – *USA*

Niagara Falls State Park – *USA/Canada*

CN Tower – *Canada*

Teotihuacan – *Mexico*

Old Havana – *Cuba*

Great Blue Hole – *Belize*

Chichen Itza – *Mexico*

STORY TIME WITH ANADHI NEWHOUSE VAN PHILLIP

North America is a continent that is so vast with so many different foods, cultures, religions, and languages within her chest. My family members speak Hindi, Bengali, English, and Dutch. The three primary languages spoken here, however, are English, Spanish, and French.

Now let's go and hear some stories from this continent. I am Anadhi Newhouse van Phillip, a wife, mother, and a grandmother of the famous Kasteel Vrederic family. I will take you through the stories of North America. You have met my sons Andries and Antonius, my daughter Katelijne, and my husband Erasmus. I know all of you know my eldest son Jacobus.

Soon you will get to meet both Jacobus and Margriete as they too will take you around the globe through some enchanting tales. We will take you around the globe on a magical journey as we unite our home and your home through the enchanted tales of this world's seven continents. This united storybook we call, *Enchanted Tales: A Kasteel Vrederic Storybook For Children*.

UNITED STATES OF AMERICA

The Magical Eagle Of The USA And His Warriors

"From the land of the free, a magical eagle rises and awakens three brave souls to guard their land of the free."

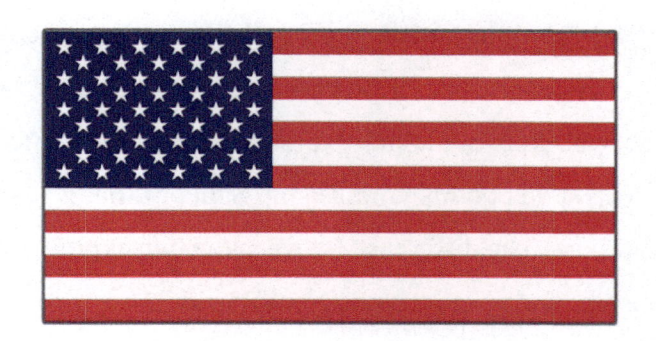

United States of America

The United States of America was declared by the Continental Congress on September 9, 1776, as the official name of the new nation. Its government is a constitutional federal republic. There are different theories as to how the country was named and who discovered the country. The widely accepted theory is that America actually found its name from the well-known Italian explorer Amerigo Vespucci. The Italian explorer Christopher Columbus, who sailed on his famous ship Santa María, is known for his discovery of the New World of the Americas. The difference between the two explorers is Columbus discovered the "New World" and Vespucci verified it as a "New World."

The USA has fifty states and one federal district, which is Washington, D.C., the capital city of the USA. There are five main territories and numerous minor islands. How many states have you visited in this country? Each state has something different to offer, so if you live in the USA or are visiting this country, do take some time and visit as many states as you can. Did you know this is the only country in the world which has all five climate zones of Earth?

The USA is very rich in its history, diversity, culture, film industry, music industry, politics, economy as a world power, and above all, its love for all humans around the globe to be safe in their own homes and abroad.

My family and I had traveled in a caravan for seven days as we traveled coast to coast from New York City, New York to Los Angeles, California. In New York City, we saw the Statue of Liberty. Then we headed toward Pennsylvania where we stayed one night and visited the historic town of Gettysburg in Pennsylvania. From there, we drove into the windy city Chicago in Illinois where we stayed another night.

We headed toward South Dakota where in the Black Hills, you can see the famous faces of four American presidents. It's called the Mount Rushmore National Monument. From there, we traveled to Denver in Colorado where we saw the famous "One Mile Above Sea Level" sign as Denver is one mile above sea level. Then, we visited the famous Rocky Mountains in Colorado. From the Rockies, we went straight to the Grand Canyon in Arizona. This stretches along a path carved by the Colorado River.

If you do come to the USA, do visit this natural formation. From the Arizona desert, we went straight to our last destination in the USA, the Golden State California. Our destination was near Los Angeles, the City of Angels. The distance from coast to coast was roughly about 2,900 miles, yet we did stop for sightseeing, so it was a bit more for us.

The driving was fun as my husband and my sons took turns driving. I got to enjoy the scenery as Katelijne and Margriete took charge of cooking. I had the best job ever, babysitting my adorable grandchildren. Traveling in our own caravan was wonderful as we did not have to be in hotels or look for any hotels.

Finally, we arrived at our destination where for us was waiting a magical bird, the national bird. The American national bird is the bald eagle. This bird stands for power and salvation. According to different scholars, this bird was always on the side of good.

Tonight, I will retell a story about one such brave bird where the brave bird calls upon a brave girl, when he finds himself in danger. He only comes out of his invisible hiding place as he calls her. You all know this brave girl, as the girl with the lantern. For me, she is my beloved granddaughter, Griet Vrederic van Phillip.

Let me now take you on a journey through the birthland of my forefathers known to all of you as the USA. Come hold my hands and enjoy your time with me. I will now take you through this night's enchanted tale. I am Anadhi Newhouse van Phillip and I call this enchanted tale, "The Magical Eagle Of The USA And His Warriors."

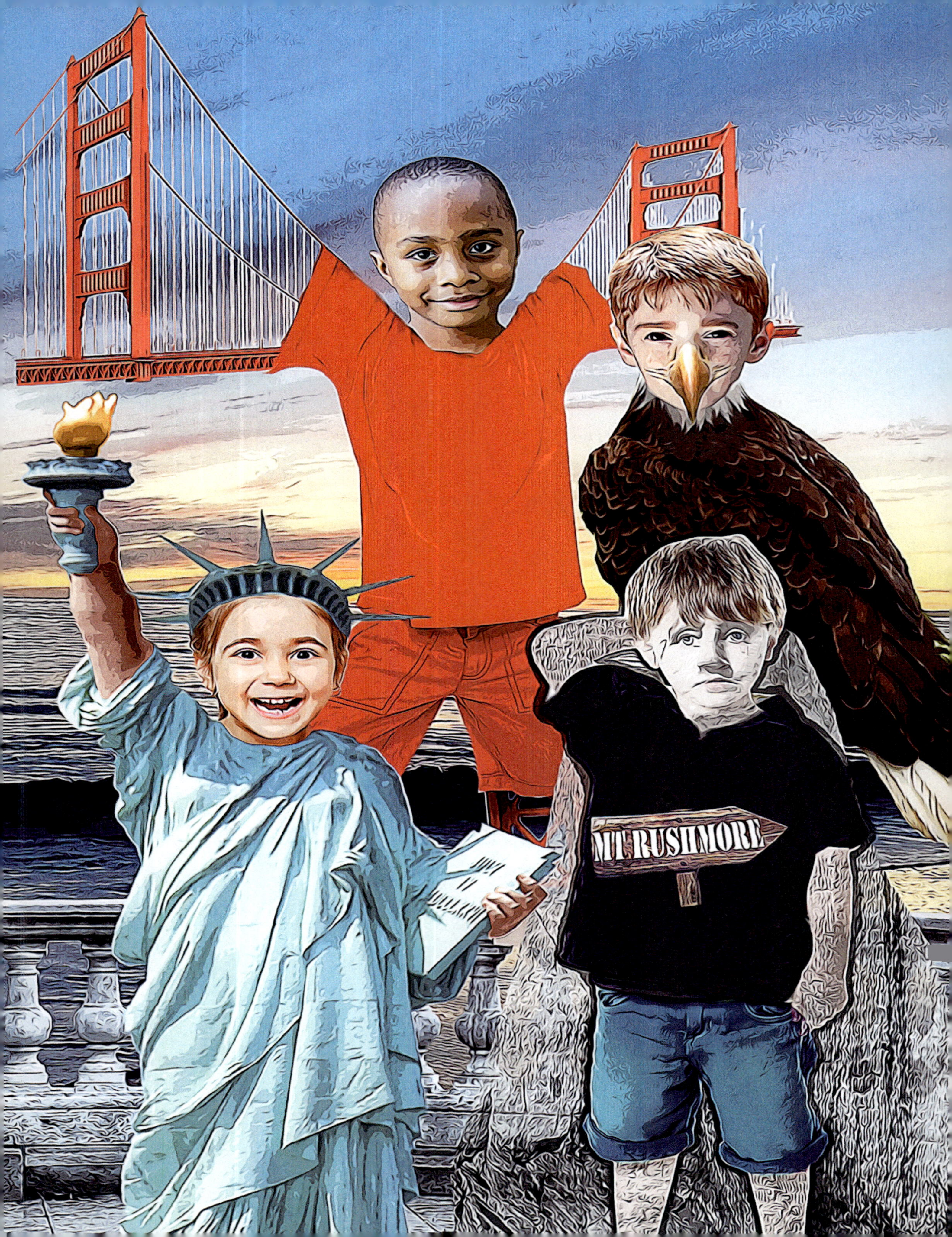
MT RUSHMORE

THE MAGICAL EAGLE OF THE USA AND HIS WARRIORS

Los Angeles, California is the second-most populous city in the USA. We arrived at sunset and parked our caravan in front of our vacation rental in Malibu, California. The Pacific Ocean gave us an amazing gift, as we got to see the joyful dolphins swimming in the Pacific Ocean at sunset.

We rented a beachfront cottage for a week as we had driven for a long time, driving coast to coast in the USA. As we arrived, we opened the back patio doors which had an amazing view of the ocean. The white drapes blew in the evening wind. The skies became red as the sun was setting above the Pacific Ocean. It was then for the first time in a week, my precious granddaughter Griet began to cry.

She started to hide her face in my chest as I stood with her on the back porch of our Malibu rental home. I wondered if she could still smell the fires of Malibu. I heard California was burning more wildly than any normal wildfire. It was as if there was something hiding in the air.

Griet started to cry as she said to me, "Oma, where is Big Brother? I go to Brother Bear Andries now. I am scared of Bigfoot. He is trying to harm my family as he calls for the spirits of Malibu."

I think I screamed my husband's name or maybe I said it quietly like a normal grandmother would do. Yet as I saw my family members jump up and come near me, I knew either I screamed or maybe they read my mind.

Erasmus asked, "Sweetheart, are you all right?"

My son Jacobus said, "Mama, what is it? Are you tired? You need to rest. I will take Griet and you can go over there and watch the dolphins and rest."

It was then Antonius and Andries came over as everyone saw I was frozen in fear.

Antonius took his daughter as Andries said, "Big Mama, did Griet say something? I thought we were having a normal vacation like normal people through the USA. This is our last stop. What did she say now?"

I told him, "She said they are coming. Bigfoot and some kind of evil are after us. I was hoping for a normal vacation, yet I'm not scared. We will do what we have to do. She asked for you Andries."

Andries went to his sister and she said, "Brother Bear, they will harm the USA as they will place poison in the water. They come down from the mountains and climb into the waters at night.

They are Bigfoots, yet they have huge tongues like poisonous snakes. A friend has been following us from New York. He is right there in front of you."

It was then we saw over our heads were flying some bald eagles. One of the huge birds came and stood in front of us. The bird converted to a bird boy. He had the body of a bird and the face of a boy. He watched us and he then started to speak.

He said, "Dear girl with the lantern, we need your help. For thousands of years, these mountains have been threatened by some unknown bears that look like humans. You call them Sasquatch or Bigfoot of the mountains. You also call the same monster the Loch Ness monster, as they swim in the water and become huge snakes. They are known as the ocean serpents, the mythical creatures who are trying to spread poison through the waters of the USA."

I watched Griet become older as she was a five-year-old girl standing in front of us with a lantern in her hand. The other children of the Vrederic household also turned older and stood next to her.

Theunis stood close to Griet as he said, "Please say if you are friend or foe as you seem to be scaring Griet. I am here as Griet's defender and will guard her eternally."

The bald eagle then said, "I am Bald Eagle. I have come from Heaven as I stand for salvation and power. I stand with good and will eternally protect this great nation. I fly over this land as I watch over this land and her waters and her people. I need Griet's intercession as I know she too has some kind of powers. If we unite for good, we could defeat this mythical creature that hides in the Pacific Ocean by the Malibu Beach."

I watched Theunis and Alexander both sit on top of Rietje's horse as did Griet. All four children very bravely got on top of the magical horse as they were prepared for yet another battle. Jacobus, Antonius, Erasmus, and Andries walked by the flying horse. Margriete, Katelijne, and I joined our family members as we watched the bald eagles multiplied and in front of us there were more children standing.

Next to Bald Eagle with a human face was a girl who looked like the Statue of Liberty. There was a boy who looked like a huge mountain with the face of a young boy but had on his chest a sign which read MT Rushmore. Another boy looked like he was made to represent the Golden Gate Bridge. He looked like a human boy, yet his two hands were like the bridge. They were all standing in front of us as the girl spoke first.

She said, "Please know I am the girl Liberty, and these are my friends — the mountain boy MT Rushmore, and the bridge boy Golden Gate. We have come to give our national bird, Bald Eagle, a helping hand as we know you too will help us as a friend."

Then we all saw in the Pacific Ocean, a huge monster appeared. The monster was a mix of a Bigfoot-looking body, with a snakelike head, and the eyes of a monster.

He spoke very loudly as he said, "I will churn poison all over the ocean. I will take over the ocean and the land as no one can defeat me!"

Griet then touched her lantern as it glowed when the night fell, and darkness had evolved around the land. I saw the glowing lantern was so bright that the monster was having a hard time keeping eye contact.

Rietje had her team fly directly over to the monster, keeping a safe distance. I watched Liberty go to the ocean as Golden Gate created a bridge for her to stand on. Then MT Rushmore stood on the ocean water as he guarded Liberty.

It was then Bald Eagle flew over to Griet and said, "Now brave girl with the lantern!"

Griet glowed her lantern as Alexander, Theunis, and Rietje threw their swords into the great ocean monster. The monster was still fighting as Griet lowered her lantern and it glowed in the Pacific Ocean. It was then the monster became water. Liberty got a bucket and filled her bucket with the melted monster water. She passed it to Golden Gate as he gave it to MT Rushmore. The flying eagle led all of them to Mount Rushmore in South Dakota, and the monster disappeared.

With that, I heard Bald Eagle reappear in front of us as he told Griet, "I am glad you were here at the time of our need. Remember Griet to let the world know, I will forever protect the land of the brave."

Like a mist, Bald Eagle disappeared. We took our four brave children back inside to our vacation rental. I knew there was a fearful feeling that had been in all of our hearts as we kept on hearing the sounds of Bigfoot coming from the mountains. Yet it was then our princess came over and opened the drapes as she observed over the mountains.

I asked her, "Griet, what are you looking for?"

She pointed her little fingers toward the skies as we all heard Bald Eagle say, "Don't fear Bigfoot, or the monsters of the ocean, as I will always fly over this land and protect her eternally. Enjoy the vacation dear girl with the lantern. This message is from I, Bald Eagle, and my warriors."

That night we had seen the most beautiful glow of the moon shining over the Pacific Ocean. I knew this land would always be safe as there in the magical night, the land was being protected by the magical eagle of the USA and his warriors.

United States of America Trivia Time

What state is the Statue of Liberty in?

What is the national bird of the USA?

What is Los Angeles known as?

COSTA RICA

The Warrior Monkey Boy, The Turtle Boy, And The Macaws

"Dreams guide us like a lantern through the dark nights, yet don't ignore the warnings from a dream if you don't want them to become your reality."

ENCHANTED TALES: A KASTEEL VREDERIC STORYBOOK FOR CHILDREN

Costa Rica

Dream Seekers' Convention. A first-time event for myself. As an author and a guide of dreams and the spiritual aspects of dreams, I have traveled around the globe. Yet for the first time, I had gone to Costa Rica where a few of my friends had gathered. This convention was very relaxing as spiritual gurus from around the globe had come to give their input on dreams. I left with my family after one day of participating. I didn't want anyone questioning my family or Griet on or about dreams.

We had traveled from Los Angeles International Airport (LAX) to Juan Santamaría International Airport (SJO). Costa Rica is in the Central American region as its heritage is Latin American even though the country geographically is in the continent of North America. This dreamlike land is bordered by Panama to the south and east, and also by Nicaragua to the north.

Coastlines are the Caribbean Sea and the Pacific Ocean. The capital city is San José. Costa Rica is famous for its Pre-Columbian Gold Museum. The country is also famous for its beaches, volcanoes, and wildlife reserves. The official language here is Spanish, even though other languages such as English and native indigenous languages are also spoken here.

We visited a reserve as our dreams had guided us to this reserve. We will be traveling to the Punta Islita Wild Macaw Reserve to get acquainted with some wild macaws, and maybe they will let us know why my little granddaughter was dreaming about them ever since our trip through the USA. In particular, my granddaughter and I both had seen the Punta Islita Wild Macaw Reserve in our dreams.

Tonight, let me take you on a journey through Punta Islita Wild Macaw Reserve. I am Anadhi Newhouse van Phillip and I call this enchanted tale, "The Warrior Monkey Boy, The Turtle Boy, And The Macaws."

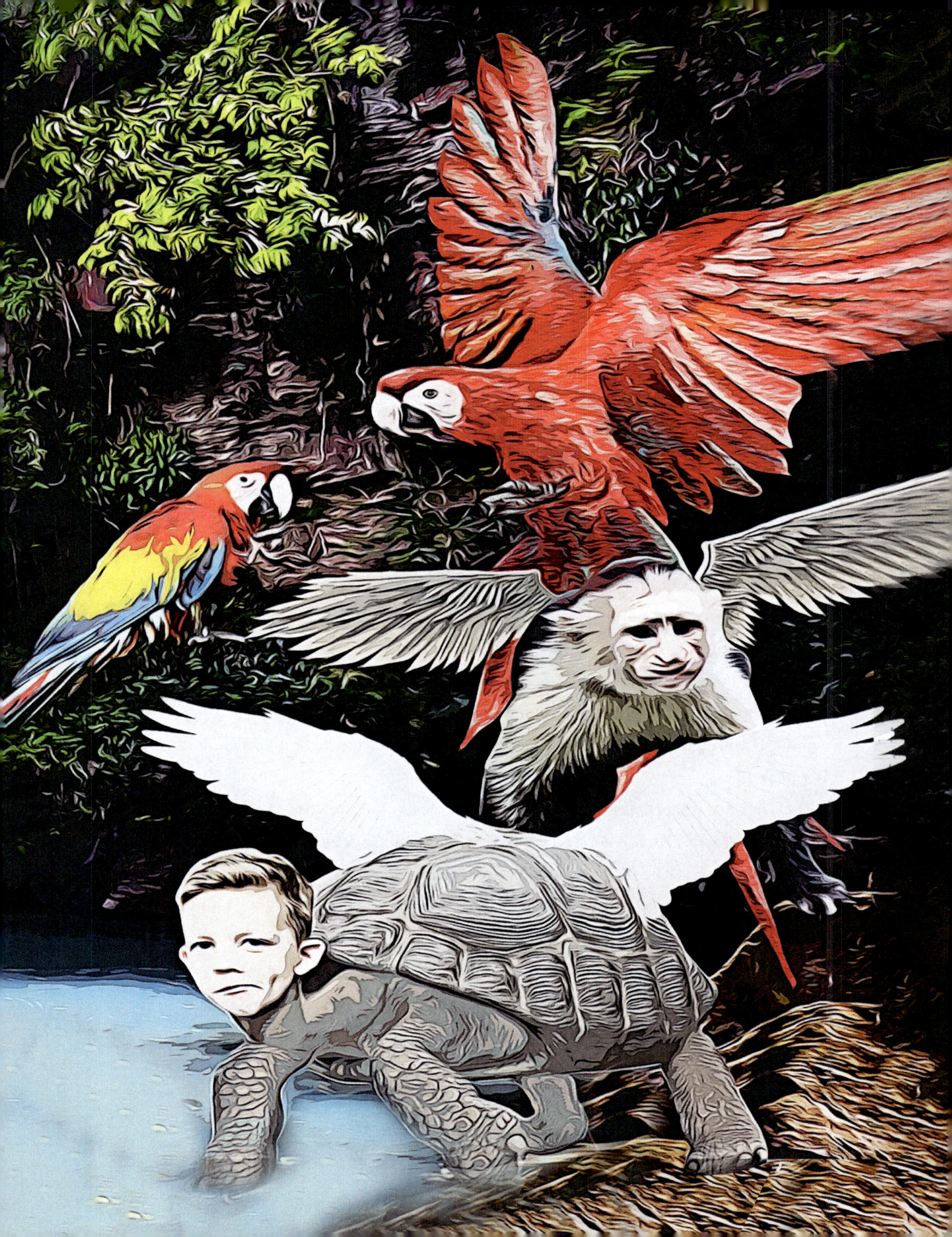

THE WARRIOR MONKEY BOY, THE TURTLE BOY, AND THE MACAWS

A magical dawn greeted us as we reached the Juan Santamaría International Airport (SJO). When my husband Erasmus van Phillip flies the plane, I actually feel relaxed. We watched the first sunrise in Costa Rica after we landed. Instead of flying again for a short one-hour flight to the local airport near Punta Islita, we drove for four hours. That way, we were able to see more of the country and enjoy the adventurous car ride through the adventurous roads of Costa Rica.

Punita Islita's Macaw Reserve and the surrounding area is like a dream haven on Earth where Costa Rica's pristine beaches, the magical rainforest, monkeys jumping around, and magical turtles come into view. We had rented a beachfront cottage and anticipated this trip to be as dreamlike as the enchanted land for our dreams had pulled us to this magical wonderland. As we entered our cabin, we saw there in front of our cabin was a huge tree. On top of the tree were some beautiful macaws. They were all watching us.

I watched Andries had at that time lifted Griet in his arms. She hid her head in his chest as Jacobus held on to Theunis, and Erasmus held on to Alexander. Antonius had Rietje hidden in his chest. I wondered why our brave children were frightened by the exotic birds.

Katelijne and Margriete were watching something like they were mesmerized or drained out of their bodies. Griet screamed and called her birthmother Katelijne.

She said, "Mama! Don't leave me! I need you!"

Then she looked at Margriete and said, "Mama Margriete, don't separate from me in this life please."

Jacobus jumped and took Griet from Andries as he said, "Hey baby girl, don't say these things. Never will I let you go. You are always safe within our embrace."

Griet said, "The old women is trying to harm Mama and Mama Margriete. She is really invisible but can be seen through the eyes of mothers who love their children more than themselves. I think Mama and Mama Margriete love us, double trouble."

Griet was talking more and more, and I felt like a proud grandmother. I was glad one of my boys got over the invisible trance quickly. I watched Andries go and stand in front of his mother Katelijne and Margriete, and with the help of Jacobus and Antonius, carried them both inside.

They were both still staring at the same direction as they were outside. It was then we saw a small monkey jump off the tree near our cottage and come inside of our cabin. He called upon something as we saw three macaws come flying into the cabin.

There in front of our eyes, Griet became older as did Rietje, Alexander, and Theunis. I watched the two boys cover the girls as did Andries. The monkey then in front of us became a human boy. He then in clear English spoke to us.

He said, "I am Gael the monkey boy, and this is my home. I live in the Punta Islita Wild Macaw Reserve. I am a mythical shape-shifting boy who converts into different animals to save my land. These three are my mythical macaws. They too are shape shifters, yet they only shift to different birds. Not everyone can see us or our magic as we only show ourselves to people who we know will keep our secrets."

The colorful macaws too spoke in clear English as they said, "Dear Griet, we need your help. There is a woman who had tortured little children during her lifetime. She had died and is still haunting little children as a spirit. She puts the parents to sleep and converts the children into different types of animals. She then places them in different reserves and rainforests. She, however, hides by the coastlines near the Punta Islita Wild Macaw Reserve as a spirit."

That's when Andries said, "Today as we were coming here and had stopped by a restaurant near our cabin, there was a bus full of children. They said they were coming for an overnight trip to the park."

That's when Gael the monkey boy said, "That's why we are here as before dawn, the children will all go missing. No one will ever find them. Yet they will all be here in front of everyone in animal form. Please we need your help Griet to put this invisible woman away. The only way we can do this if we can find a turtle who could swallow the woman in one piece and float away in the ocean with her. He would then turn her into a huge rock formation. The woman would be imprisoned under the ocean forever."

Griet then asked Gael, "Please help my Mama and my Margriete Mama. I don't want to ever let them go as I had to in my last life. In this life, I will keep them forever."

Then we saw a turtle entered our cabin. The turtle converted into a boy who looked half-boy and half-turtle. Erasmus went in front of our girls who were completely numb. I wondered how my girls were so frozen by the spirit woman, yet I was not.

Then Gael said, "You are the dream psychic, a dream caller, whom I called. Your granddaughter Griet too is a dream caller. We can call upon one other through dreams. Just like you, she too will guide everyone through her dreams. It's like dream traveling. That's why the evil woman could not touch you or your boys. Yet your daughters-in-law were easy targets for her."

I watched the turtle boy go in front of Margriete and Katelijne and place a kiss on their foreheads. It was then my two daughters woke up with a jerk.

They were both shaken up as Margriete told us, "We were in a place like a forest. There was a bus there and a lot of young kids. They were all hurt and were crying for their parents. We must help them, before it gets too late."

It was then Griet lit her lantern and said, "Let's go everyone, before dawn approaches. We have to imprison the evil spirit woman and set the children free from the Punta Islita Wild Macaw Reserve."

Rietje called her magical horse as she said, "Dear horse of mine, won't you come and help us on this magical night? We really need you as do forty-five other children who would all be lost otherwise."

Rietje's magical horse was there in front of us in the cabin's courtyard. The four children got on top of her as we walked by them. With our group, I watched the macaws were flying with Griet as Gail the monkey boy and the turtle boy flew with them. They both had wings on them, and it was such a magical sight. The sky was glimmering with bright stars.

As we entered a forest that looked more like a dreaded forest than a magical park near the ocean and a little further away from the reserve, we all heard shrieks from a woman. Griet had her lantern glow in the forest. As it shined so bright, we saw there were different birds flying near Griet.

The magical macaws, the turtle boy and the monkey boy, all blew kisses and converted the children as Griet's lantern kept glowing. The children then were being magically transported to their bus without any memories of the ordeal. Yet that's when we faced the evil spirit woman.

She shrieked and was trying to come to us head on. Yet I watched Rietje, Alexander and Theunis throw their returning swords at the evil woman. She froze in spot as the turtle boy swallowed her up in a gulp.

We watched the huge turtle then jump into the Pacific Ocean. He was nowhere in sight for a long time.

That's when suddenly a dolphin appeared in front of us as Gael then said, "That's our turtle boy. He has shape shifted into a dolphin."

The dolphin jumped up on land and became like a human boy as he said, "I must return your swords. Here they are. Yet I believe they would have flown back to you anyway as you are their owners."

I watched Gael and his macaws, and the turtle boy walk out into the deep forest.

As Gael said, "Dear Griet, I thank you and your family for helping us in your time of need. Also remember the macaws are dream givers. They can give you dreams and also can warn you through dreams if you are ever in danger. We will keep the door of dreams open for you and your family members eternally. As you have helped us, we shall always help you all through the door of dreams."

That's when we saw dawn was coming up in the vast skies as we saw the first arrival of dawn through the glimpse of the sun's amazing rays.

Griet fell asleep in her big brother bear's arms as she kept on saying, "Brother Bear, promise you shall never let me go."

Andries said to her, "Precious Sister Bear, never ever shall I let you go."

I watched my family members and knew they would all be protected through their magical dreams as promised by a magical dreamer and his group. You and I know them as the warrior monkey boy, the turtle boy, and the macaws.

Costa Rica Trivia Time

What is the official language of Costa Rica?

What continent is Costa Rica in?

What reserve did the Kasteel Vrederic family visit in Costa Rica?

MESSAGE FROM ANADHI NEWHOUSE VAN PHILLIP

Dear all, I know you have all been on a long journey through the world with us. It is so fun to meet and greet new people and cultures as well as new lands around the globe. You all can go around the world through these enchanted tales. Just keep reading the tales and travel along with us. You will learn about our one world through these magical enchanted tales.

We have ended our journey through the continent of North America. It's always hard to go back home after a trip, yet you wait until the next journey. Plan your next trip and be busy dreaming a little about your next trip abroad.

Here through the enchanted tales, you won't have to wait that long. Now I want you to turn the pages and travel along with the next storyteller from my home. She is my daughter-in-law, Jacobus Vrederic van Phillip's wife, Margriete Achthoven van Phillip. As you all know in my home, we consider all of our daughters-in-law as daughters. She will take you through the continent of Asia where her mother and my mother actually were from. My father was an American and her father was Dutch.

Now do turn the pages, and enjoy learning about this great continent, and meet some magical children from this continent.

Signing out now,

Anadhi Newhouse van Phillip

CHAPTER SIX:

CONTINENT OF ASIA

Storyteller:
Margriete Achthoven van Phillip

"I am the largest and the most diverse continent in the world. Within my chest, I have fifty countries. I also cover one-third of this world's surface."

ENCHANTED TALES: A KASTEEL VREDERIC STORYBOOK FOR CHILDREN

Asia

The land of the sunrise is referred to as the continent of Asia. Yet again there are so many different theories and conflicts, or you could say a difference of opinion where the name Asia came from. Some believe the name was derived from the word "Asu" which in the Phoenician language meant "east" and in the Akkadian language meant "to go out, to rise." They were referring to Asia as the land of the sunrise. That's how the largest continent of Asia found its name. The largest continent also covers thirty percent of the world's land area.

The continent of the fifty countries, is surrounded by the Arctic, Pacific, and Indian Oceans. The Suez Canal separates Asia from Africa. Asia is separated from Europe by mountains and waterways. Did you know the city of Istanbul is in Europe and Asia?

Asia also has sixty percent of the world's population, making it the most populous continent. It is home to over 4.6 billion people. This continent actually is also the birthplace to all of the world's major religions including Judaism, Christianity, Islam, Hinduism, Buddhism, and others. Different languages spoken around the globe is a treasure for this world's diversity. Within Asia, over 2,300 languages are spoken.

Have you ever visited Mount Everest, the world's highest point? If you have, then you too have been in this continent. If you have not, then you can look this great mountain up as there are people almost always climbing this mountain as a challenge. If you do get to visit this continent maybe you would like to also see the lowest point in Asia which is the Dead Sea.

Let's talk about some fun facts about Asia which you can share with your friends. Did you know there is a building in Singapore which was inspired by a Star Wars robot? Also, the Asian elephant is the largest mammal in this continent. Did you ever try to eat with chopsticks? If you have or not, maybe you will as China, a country in this continent, produces more than forty-five billion pairs of chopsticks each year.

SOME OF ASIA'S FAMOUS FOODS

Let's get familiarized with some of Asia's famous foods. So, my dear children why don't you and your parents get some or at least one of these foods from our table or maybe your kitchen as we get to know this continent? Here are some of the famous Asian foods for you to try out.

Sushi – *Japan*   *Nepal* – **Momo**
Pho – *Vietnam*   *Korea* – **Kimchi**
Samosa – *India*   *China* – **Spring Roll**
Haleem – *Pakistan*   *Thailand* – **Pad Thai**
Gulab Jamun – *India*   *Sri Lanka* – **Kottu Roti**
Roti Prata – *Singapore*   *Singapore* – **Chili Crab**
Tandoori Chicken – *India*   *Indonesia* – **Nasi Goreng**
Shorshe Ilish – *Bangladesh*
Bhuna Khichuri – *Bangladesh*

· Menu ·

COUNTRIES OF ASIA

Now let's get acquainted with all of the countries in Asia. Even though we won't be able to travel through all of them, we will get to learn all of their names here. Here are the names of the countries from the continent we all know as Asia.

ENCHANTED TALES: A KASTEEL VREDERIC STORYBOOK FOR CHILDREN

Afghanistan

Armenia

Azerbaijan

Bahrain

Bangladesh

Bhutan

Brunei

Cambodia

China

Cyprus

Georgia

India

Indonesia

Iran

Iraq	Israel
Japan	Jordan
Kazakhstan	Kuwait
Kyrgyzstan	Laos
Lebanon	Malaysia
Maldives	Mongolia
Myanmar	Nepal
North Korea	Oman
Pakistan	Palestine

ENCHANTED TALES: A KASTEEL VREDERIC STORYBOOK FOR CHILDREN

Philippines

Qatar

Russia

Saudi Arabia

Singapore

South Korea

Sri Lanka

Syria

Taiwan

Tajikistan

Thailand

Timor-Leste

Turkey

Turkmenistan

United Arab Emirates

Uzbekistan

Vietnam

Yemen

LANDMARK QUIZ

Which landmark is this and where is it located?

A. Ahsan Manzil, Bangladesh
B. Angkor Wat, Cambodia
C. Taj Mahal, India
D. Wat Arun, Thailand

SOME OF ASIA'S LANDMARKS

When you do visit one of these countries in Asia, do stop by some of these amazing and famous landmarks.

Landmarks

Taj Mahal – *India*

Mount Fuji – *Japan*

Great Wall of China – *China*

Dead Sea – *Israel*

Wat Arun – *Thailand*

Forbidden City – *China*

Hội An – *Vietnam*

Angkor Wat – *Cambodia*

Borobudur – *Indonesia*

Petronas Twin Towers – *Malaysia*

Mount Kinabalu – *Malaysia*

Chocolate Hills – *Philippines*

Ahsan Manzil – *Bangladesh*

Cox's Bazar – *Bangladesh*

STORY TIME WITH MARGRIETE ACHTHOVEN VAN PHILLIP

Now let's travel through the largest continent, Asia. In my eyes, this continent is the land of mysteries, dreams, and love. I am very familiar with this continent as my mother and my mother-in-law are both from there. As a daughter of a Dutchman, and as a medical doctor myself, I was able to travel through this continent a few times.

Tonight though, I will be taking you through a trip I had made with my Kasteel Vrederic family members through the mystical continent of Asia. Did you know I am Mama Margriete to Kasteel Vrederic's very blessed daughter, Griet Jacobus Vrederic van Phillip? I was her mother in the sixteenth century, yet I had to let her go to have her back in our home as this family's blessed daughter.

For all my love, I did let her go. As my love was proven and retested, I got her back as my niece. I am also the mother of Rietje Vrederic van Phillip, and we the Kasteel Vrederic family are the guardian caretakers of the mystical boys Theunis Peters and Alexander van der Bijl.

I am Margriete Achthoven van Phillip, wife of Jacobus Vrederic van Phillip, and a blessed daughter of the famous Kasteel Vrederic family. Tonight, I will take you through some enchanted tales of Asia. I hope you all have some of Asia's famous foods on your plate as we go and enjoy another night of storytelling from the *Enchanted Tales: A Kasteel Vrederic Storybook For Children*.

INDIA

The Classical Dancer, The Peacock Prince

"With grace, elegance, and love, he dances yet always keeps a moral eye out for all who need a helping hand."

India

ENCHANTED TALES: A KASTEEL VREDERIC STORYBOOK FOR CHILDREN

The land of mysteries, India, is officially known as the Republic of India, and is in the continent of Asia. The capital city is New Delhi. I have traveled to India all throughout my life. We traveled again as a family on a pure vacation and no-work trip. My Kasteel Vrederic family members were tied with this country for centuries through reincarnation.

My blessed in-laws, Big Mama and Big Papa, actually saw one another in the holy city of Varanasi during their time seeking one another. Varanasi is known to be the oldest living city of the world. This city gave birth to Ayurveda, yoga, and ancient healing powers.

India has been in our bucket list of places to visit as we could not see the whole country even during our numerous visits. Did you know India is one of the most-wanted-to-visit countries in the world? I know the diverse landscape, Indian cuisine, the colorful festivals, the amazing temples, and the amazing wonder of this world, the majestic white walls of the Taj Mahal, are enough reasons for this desire to visit. My family members, especially the children, loved visiting the Chenab Bridge, which is the highest rail bridge in the world.

You guys reading this tale also would love to know, India is the place where the popular game *Snakes and Ladders*, or *Chutes and Ladders*, originated from as *Moksha Patam*. India is where diamonds were originally found. From around the fourth century B.C. to 1,000 years later, India was the only source of the world's diamonds. The diamonds were found in the Krishna River Delta.

History is actually a fun lesson as it weaves a story and brings it to us in the present. History also told us Hinduism practiced in India is the world's oldest religion dating back to 5500 B.C. As most Hindu scriptures were written in Sanskrit, the books prove Sanskrit is one of the world's oldest languages. This language is thought to be the mother of all languages. In India, the official languages are Hindi and English; however, there are twenty-two recognized languages including Bengali, Tamil, Urdu, Gujarati, and Punjabi.

After our journey through Mumbai, India, we had gone on a short trip to Morachi Chincholi in Maharashtra, roughly about 124 miles away from Mumbai. Morachi Chincholi actually means the village of tamarind trees and dancing peacocks. Little did we know that aside from the dancing peacocks, we would actually get acquainted with a real-life Peacock Prince.

Come travel with me tonight to the land of mysteries as I take you through another enchanted tale. I am Margriete Achthoven van Phillip, and I call this enchanted tale, "The Classical Dancer, The Peacock Prince."

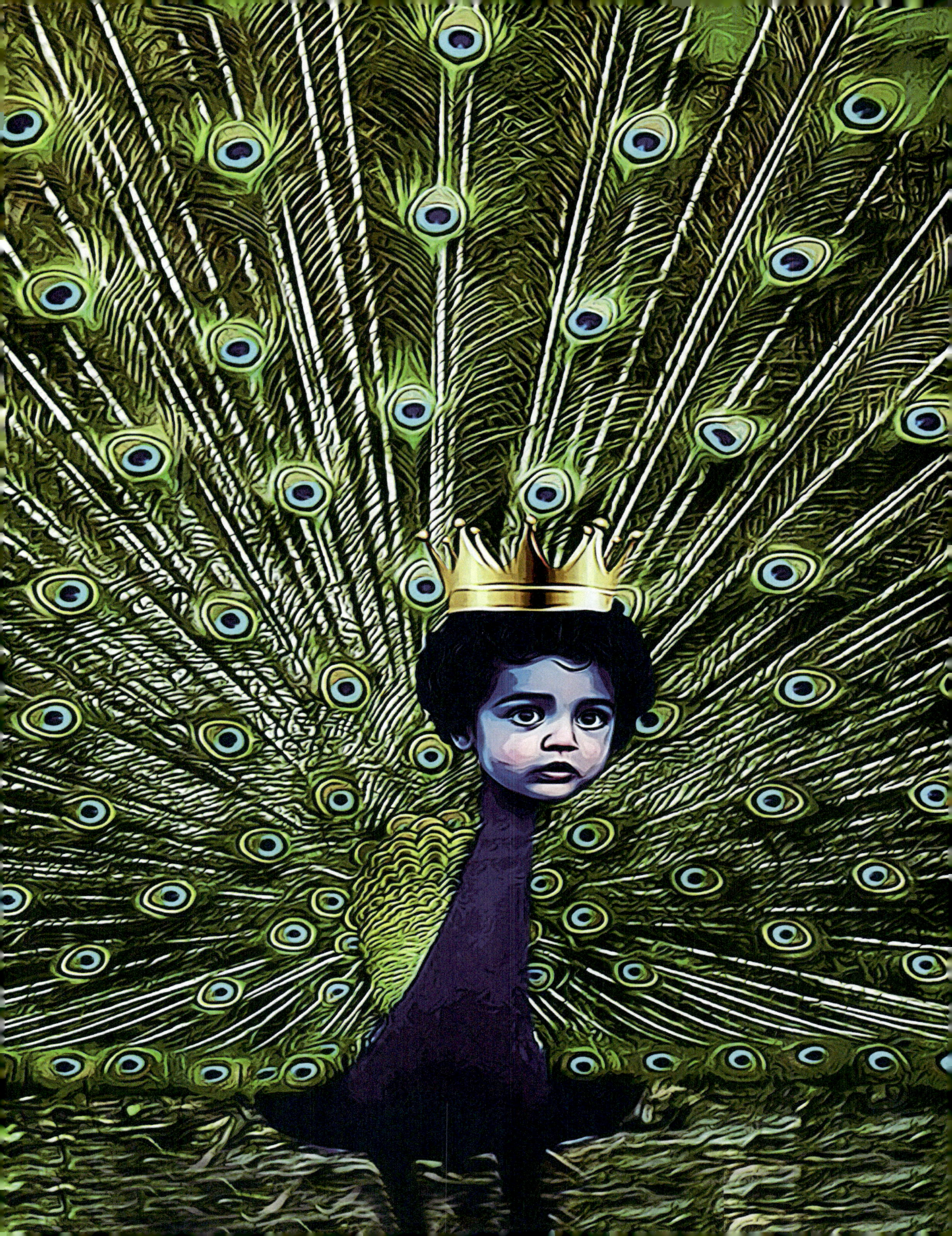

THE CLASSICAL DANCER, THE PEACOCK PRINCE

The sun was almost ready to set in the vast skies as we arrived in Morachi Chincholi. The city is located in the state of Maharashtra. It was monsoon season in India, and we got to see a very handsome peacock when we arrived in the village. The amazing peacock greeted us with his feathers spread. The most colorful and magical bird was dancing in the monsoon raindrops in front of our vacation bungalow. We watched him and drove to our vacation rental, a small bungalow in Morachi Chincholi, our next stop.

The magical bird somehow disappeared as the caretakers appeared. An elderly man named Vikram Joshi came and showed us around. An elderly woman walked in as she too introduced herself.

She said, "I am Ganga, like the river. I am blessed to have you here for even one night. I was actually expecting you."

She spoke in clear English and kept on looking outside at the moon over the monsoon night. I followed her gaze and saw the moon and clouds were playing hide and seek. She had gray hair and was wearing a white and blue saree. She had a red vermilion where her hair parted. I assumed they were husband and wife.

Ganga then said, "My husband and I also have a tent set up for you outside under the skies, so you can have a clear picture of the dancing peacocks as they come and dance under the tamarind trees. I believe the peacocks will dance for you as you come with clean and pure hearts. I hope you all enjoy this magical night. Remember you don't have to spend the whole night outside, but just a few hours to enjoy the sight."

She left as we settled in the amazingly cozy house. There was a fence made out of bricks. The house was constructed completely out of brick. There in the corner of the fenced property was a small guest house where the couple had stayed. They rented out the home for additional income. The property had so many different rose bushes, it felt like a rose haven.

Griet and the children settled in very nicely as they all played with Andries. Big Mama and Big Papa were walking down memory lane as they sat outside under the stars. Antonius, Jacobus, Katelijne, and I sat next to Big Papa and Big Mama as we loved listening to their love story.

Andries suddenly asked Griet, "Hey Baby Sister, what's wrong? Why are you crying again? Did you get hurt? Let Brother Bear kiss the boo-boo away."

Then we saw Rietje too came running to Andries as she said, "Cousin Bear, Cousin Sister Bear scared too."

We watched Andries try to take care of his sister and cousin. I walked over to our girls with Big Mama and Katelijne.

Big Mama asked the girls, "Okay, what is wrong with my grandbabies? Why are there sweet tears falling down your cute cheeks?"

Griet then in front of us became a five-year-old girl as she had in her hand the magical lantern. Rietje, Alexander, and Theunis all became older and had in their hands their magical swords. In the courtyard was also standing a magical horse, whom I hoped no one could see. Jacobus and Antonius both got on their feet ready to face whatever life would bring. Andries kept the girls in his embrace as if he was trying to hide them from whatever was outside.

Big Papa came in and said, "The caretaker is back and is asking for a doctor."

We all went outside where we saw the elderly couple were both staring at the moon which was brightly visible even on a monsoon night.

Vikram asked us, "I wanted to ask you a favor. Is there a doctor here amongst you all?"

Jacobus and I both stood up as Jacobus answered, "Yes, we are both doctors. Why do you ask? Is everything all right?"

Ganga who was frantically panicking said, "The monster is back and has bitten my daughter. This monster had bitten my very young child, my son a long time ago, and left us with a broken home."

She watched us and said, "We lost our son, and have our daughter who can never be a mother, so we don't have anyone taking care of us or will take care of her when she too needs help. Her husband, Vijay, is a bullock cart driver at the park. He takes people on a bullock cart rides for fun."

We found out the snake had bitten a few people at the fair that night. We watched in front of us appeared a huge peacock who had a human boy's face.

He stood in front of Griet and said in a clear human voice, "I am known as the classical dancer, as the Peacock Prince. As I was a classical dancer, I had been converted to a peacock because I wanted to stay near my parents and watch over them eternally. Yes, I am the son who had been bitten by the same monster snake years ago. Now I keep an eye out for all other children who are trying to dance with the peacocks and try to make sure the monster never bites anyone ever again. Yet I failed my own sister."

He watched his parents and said, "My younger sister who survived the snake bite years ago is fighting death today. The snake is out and wants to hurt many more children and adults. We must somehow stop this monster."

Jacobus said to the Peacock Prince, "We will help your sister. My wife and I are both doctors. We will be able to save your sister as we do have the antivenom with us. We must, however, administer it quickly."

After a few minutes, we had the young woman named Sita under control and safely tucked in bed. Yet we realized outside under the monsoon skies, the wild monstrous snake was out loose, and our young children were all hunting the snake as the snake was hunting for others.

I saw Griet was on Rietje's horse with Rietje, Alexander, and Theunis. Andries was walking by them as were Antonius and Big Papa. Big Mama, Katelijne, and I walked behind them. Jacobus stayed behind, closer to our patient. The Peacock Prince flew with Griet as they all landed at a very empty spot, near a huge banyan tree. We saw the monster snake was hissing and smiling with his very human face in front of us.

He saw the Peacock Prince and told him, "I finished your lineage today. Your sister too will be gone soon. I will take so many tonight as I am even more powerful during the monsoon season's full moon."

The Peacock Prince dropped tears on top of Rietje's sword as the lantern of Griet lit up the monsoon night. It was then the three magical returning swords flew into the snake's head and the Peacock Prince's teardrops were burning the snake. We watched the snake burn down in the powerful lantern's light and the magical tall swords that were covered with heartfelt and loving teardrops of the Peacock Prince. The Peacock Prince then started to do a classical Indian dance as he had brought joy to all his audience.

He flew high and then said something to the new dawn that was approaching us. The sun was breaking through the dark night's skies. We then saw the snake fly into the mouth of the burning sun. The sun smiled at all of us as we saw the sun wink at us.

Griet said, "Dear Prince, your classical dances have pleased so many throughout the years. You are famous as the classical dancer, the Peacock Prince, yet why are you always so sad? The snake monster will be gone forever, and all visitors or citizens of this land will be in peace. What is it that is still upsetting you?"

The Peacock Prince said, "My parents are getting old, and my sister too won't have any children of her own, so I wonder who will take care of them. I must go now as I have completed my job of protecting the people of my village from the monstrous snake."

Griet called Andries for help as she asked, "Brother Bear, what could we do for him now?"

It was Big Mama who answered and said, "Oh I am not worried really as you are in the land of reincarnation. Here, everything is possible. I got my son Andries back as my grandson. Jacobus and Margriete got their daughter Griet back as their niece."

Big Mama looked at Rietje and said, "We all have our favorite baby Rietje back, as we knew no one could separate Jacobus and Rietje. No, not even time. Through the power of love and belief, you too will come back as your mother's grandson and your sister's son, just watch."

As she finished speaking, we saw a star fall onto Earth from the skies. The star went directly toward the small cottage near our vacation house. Jacobus walked out from the house after he missed everything that had taken place. He just smiled.

I asked Jacobus, "What happened? Why are you smiling?"

He said, "Sita, the daughter of Vikram and Ganga Joshi, and the wife of the bullock cart driver Vijay is pregnant and doing so much better. I know when our little bears, Griet, Rietje, Alexander, and Theunis are involved, this is just another miracle of the night."

Rietje asked Jacobus, "Papa, did a shooting star just enter the house?"

He smiled and told her, "Yes, it did and if I have my theories right, that star has a name. He is the classical dancer called the Peacock Prince."

Yes, in a few months a letter did arrive at Kasteel Vrederic. It was from Vikram and in the letter, he and his wife announced the blessed birth of Mayur, his handsome grandson, the classical dancer, the Peacock Prince.

India Trivia Time

What is the capital city of India?

What popular children's game originated from India?

What is the highest rail bridge in the world?

BANGLADESH

Padma River's Youngest Ferry Boy

"A mystical river and a magical canoe unite in the hands of a courageous young ferry boy."

Bangladesh

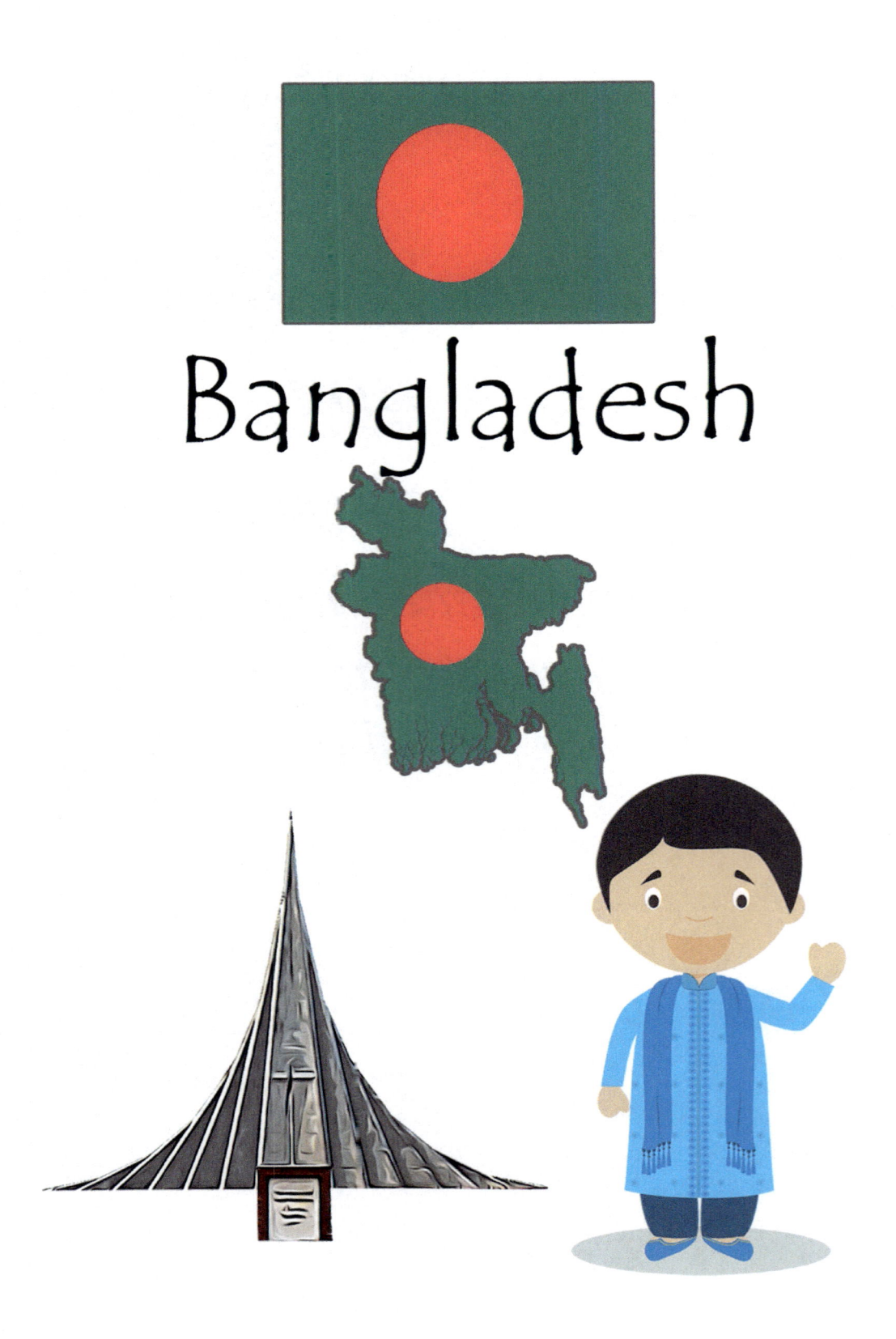

Rajshahi is a city in the division of Rajshahi of Bangladesh where our tale will take place. It's a fifty-minute flight from the capital city of Bangladesh, which is Dhaka. My family members and I had come to this country for the first time. Before my husband and I joined a colleague to help with some pediatric surgeries in Rajshahi, we had taken a trip around the country with our family. Like a miracle, all the pediatric surgeries were complete successes.

Bangladesh is a neighboring country of India, on the Bay of Bengal. The official language is Bengali. This is a lush green country and is known for its many rivers. Traveling through the great rivers Padma, Meghna, and Jamuna is very common and most people do it regularly.

Bangladesh is also famous for roaming Royal Bengal Tigers in the world-famous mangrove called Sundarbans. We stayed overnight in this famous place. Then, we traveled to the world's longest, natural, and uninterrupted sea beach. If you would like to see this amazing beach, you must travel to Cox's Bazar Beach in Cox's Bazar. Some of the other places we had visited are Old Dhaka, Jaflong, Sylhet, and St. Martin's Island. We also did go over the newly constructed bridge, the Padma Multipurpose Bridge, also locally known as the Padma Bridge. This is the longest bridge in Bangladesh and a pride of Bangladesh.

Now let's go and travel to where our story takes place. We had stayed one night with our colleague in his bungalow in Rajshahi. So now come with me as I take you through another enchanted tale within a magical country that is not known to all around the globe. Yet tonight, why don't you get yourself acquainted with a very young ferry boy of Bangladesh? I call this enchanted tale, "Padma River's Youngest Ferry Boy."

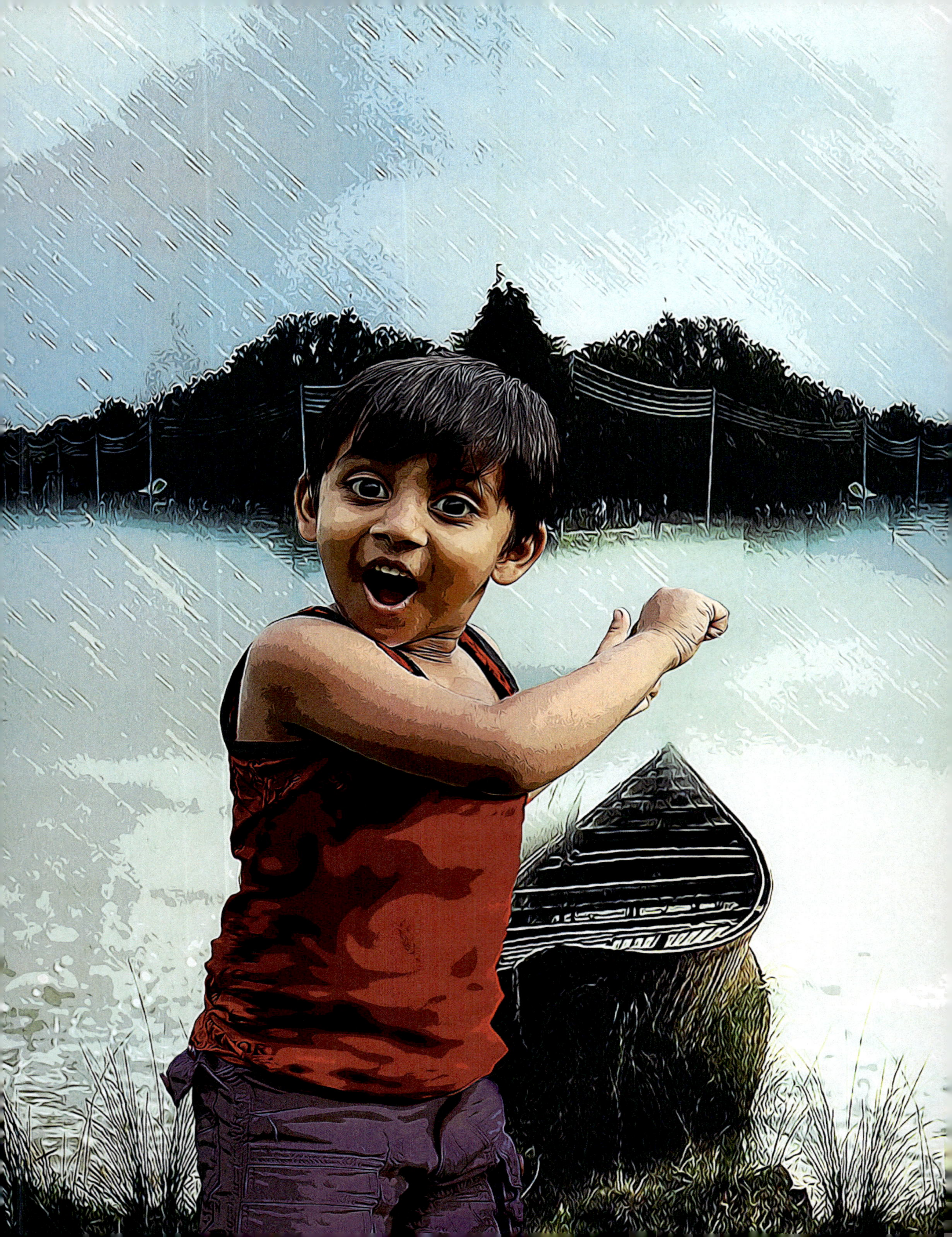

PADMA RIVER'S YOUNGEST FERRY BOY

Very late in the afternoon, we had arrived at our colleague Dr. Willem van Janssen's temporary bungalow. It was a short flight from the Hazrat Shahjalal International Airport (DAC) in Dhaka to Shah Makhdum Airport (RJH) in Rajshahi. Then, we drove to Willem's home on the bank of the Padma River. The Padma River is the main distributary of the Ganges River flowing from India. As the Ganges River enters Bangladesh, the river changes its name and becomes the Padma River. The amazing river actually divides Bangladesh and India as it flows magically into the Bay of Bengal.

At sunset, we all walked to Willem's veranda to enjoy our evening tea and biscuits with Willem, a single man of seventy years of age. He had devoted his entire life to medicine and humanity.

He said, "Did you know the Padma name is derived from Sanskrit? It means the sacred lotus flower, which symbolizes purity and growth. This river is seen to the local people similarly to a person's mood, sometimes happy, yet at times angry and at other times all giving or the one who takes away everything, as it's constantly everchanging."

It was then we saw after a long time of traveling, my niece Griet started to cry.

She ran outside to the veranda and asked for her brother, as she said, "Mama Margriete, where is Big Brother? Sister Bear needs Brother Bear now."

Katelijne and Jacobus both ran to her as we were worried what was wrong with our precious child. It was then we saw Antonius, Big Papa, and Big Mama walking outside with Andries. Everyone knew something was wrong as Griet ran toward Andries.

She hugged him and said, "Brother Bear, I was scared. Where were you? Remember the promise made, you will never leave me alone. I need you to be with me now as the ferry boy needs you now. Otherwise, he too will be gobbled up."

In front of Willem, Griet became a five-year-old child as did Rietje, and the boys turned into older boys too. I watched Doctor Willem faint and as he was falling backward, Big Papa caught him. With Jacobus's help, they placed him on the sofa in his living room.

We were lucky all the helpers and the drivers who come with the house were out for the day. It was then we saw there was a storm in the river. The waves were high, and the dark skies had lightning bolts ripping through. The thunders roared as did the winds. In the roads by the riverbank, we watched people run toward their homes. A man driving a rickshaw was announcing something on a megaphone in Bengali.

Big Mama came and told us, "He is saying there is a cyclone in the river. The crocodile monster is coming back for more fishermen tonight. It's weird. He is asking people to go inside their homes and keep the windows and curtains down. He asked everyone to not look at the crocodile monster of the Padma River."

I knew Big Mama knew some of the Indian languages as Bengali, or as some say Bangla, is also one of the languages spoken in Bangladesh and in India. Actually, the Indian national anthem and the Bangladeshi national anthem both were written by Rabindranath Tagore, a Nobel laureate. He was a Bengali Indian who spoke Bengali.

I asked Big Mama, "What else did he say?"

I knew all of Big Mama's boys understood Hindi but did not know they too understood a lot of Bengali.

Big Mama said, "He is saying to get inside over and over again."

Griet then spoke from her big brother's arms. He was carrying his little sister in his arms and tried to calm her down.

Griet said, "We must help Sagar, the ferry boy. He is alone rowing his ferryboat in the river."

Before she could finish her words, we saw there on the riverbank was a small child who was running toward our home. He came to the veranda and started to talk in broken English and in Bengali.

He said, "I am the Padma River's youngest ferry boy. I have come with my ferryboat to rescue my father and his buddies. They are all fisherman and ferrymen. They are fishermen and ferry taxi drivers. Yet there is a monster crocodile the fisherman had caught recently. The crocodile then swallowed up the men in one gulp. From then, the monster crocodile has been swallowing all the fishermen, ferrymen, and even other water travelers."

He watched Griet and said, "You are the girl with the lantern, and these are your team members. I have been having dreams about you. I knew you would arrive by the time we have another river cyclone. I need your help. Please tell me you can do something."

He then watched everyone with his sharp eyes. I saw he was about seven years old. He had big black eyes and black hair. He was so bright and sharp. I knew there was some kind of magic in him. Griet just watched him as he nodded and told him with her understanding eyes to continue.

Sagar then said, "I am not afraid of anything. I will save the men lost in the Padma River as I have courage. The river too will help me as I can talk to her. My boat too talks to me as my boat was a gift from my grandfather. Before he left this world, he told me this boat would always provide for me."

Griet spoke for the first time as she said, "We will help you. We will need you to get in your boat and take us to the middle of the river. We will take a magical mirror with us. Then we will show you how we will fool the monster crocodile in his own game. I believe all the men are still alive as they were all swallowed in one gulp. The monster crocodile is greedy. We will teach him how being greedy, he too will fall prey to his own greed."

Then we watched how the young ferry boy rowed his boat, which spoke in front of everyone and said, "Friends, welcome to the Padma River."

Even more shocking was how we then saw a woman appear in the Padma River and say, "Dear friends, I am Padma, and I will also help you capture this monster and take him away from my chest. Also, Sagar is our brave boy and is known to all as Padma River's bravest and youngest ferry boy."

The water began to rise as the storm was getting really bad. We watched there in the great Padma River was a beautiful woman named Padma. She was like a water maiden and pointed a finger toward a certain spot. The magical boat of the young and brave boy floated with him toward the same spot.

My brave Griet then said, "Papa, Opa, Papa Jacobus, help Big Brother take the mirror to the riverbank."

I saw Andries was holding a huge mirror which other men had rolled on a wheel to the riverbank.

Rietje called her magical horse as she said, "My dear friend, come as we need you now. We need you to carry us to the middle of the river and help Sagar the ferry boy."

We watched in front of us our four brave children got on Rietje's brave horse. They flew to the middle of the river as Andries with the help of the men took the mirror to the edge of the riverbank.

Griet then shined her lantern into the river. In front of us the huge crocodile that had a head like a sea monster came up roaring like a wild monster. It was then Griet told Sagar to do his part.

Sagar told the monster crocodile, "I have so many new men for you. It's going to be a feast. Just open your mouth and you will see all of them in front of you. You just need to keep your mouth open for a while. All the men I have brought for only you."

The crocodile monster opened his mouth as he looked directly into the mirror. He could see the men that were inside of him coming out from his belly. Yet he did not understand they were the men from his belly but thought they were men brought for him. With Griet's lantern glowing into the mirror, there was an illusion that even to us seemed like men were walking into the monster.

It was then the young ferry boy said, "All out now Griet."

The mirror became like a tunnel and the crocodile monster went into the mirror. Then I watched Theunis, Alexander, and Rietje throw their magical returning swords into the mirror. Like a magical star, the mirror flew into the sky and became a night star. It was reverse tonight. We did not see a falling star from the skies but saw a flying star that flew from the river to the skies. All the storms became calm as the children came back to the bungalow.

Griet then told everyone including Sagar, "Remember not to share or retell anyone about the magical night. Every single one of the men including your father will go back to their own homes. All they will remember is that they had a very busy night at work. You too must always keep the secret and never share it for all good things are given to those who are willing to sacrifice for others, not to those who are greedy."

I watched the night was almost over as we all walked inside and saw Willem wake up from his sleep and retell us about a dream he had. He called the dream, "Padma River's Youngest Ferry Boy." We did not say anything but heard his tale. He will never know this actually was a true tale, not a dream.

You too remember if you are ever visiting Bangladesh, you might just encounter the little boy named Sagar. The brave and courageous boy is known to all as Padma River's youngest ferry boy.

Bangladesh Trivia Time

What river does the Ganges River become in Bangladesh?

What is the capital city of Bangladesh?

Who wrote Bangladesh's national anthem?

MESSAGE FROM MARGRIETE ACHTHOVEN VAN PHILLIP

I hope you all had a wonderful time traveling with us through Asia. After I return home from a place I enjoyed visiting, I do tend to get sad. Yet I remind myself I still have the memories of my trip with me. These memories will be yours forever.

In this book, we have gathered all of our memories into a book format for you to enjoy eternally, for this journey will never end. If you miss any of the countries, all you have to do is open the pages of the book.

Now as I end my chapter, I would like to introduce you to my husband Jacobus Vrederic van Phillip, the reincarnated form of the sixteenth-century famous diarist, Jacobus van Vrederic. It was his diaries that had begun the journey through Kasteel Vrederic. He believed if he could keep all of his life stories in a diary then the stories of our lives would be eternal throughout time. Forever through you the reader, they would be eternal.

So now, Jacobus Vrederic van Phillip will take you on an adventure through the continent of Africa. With him, you will again meet the family members of Kasteel Vrederic, Antonius, Katelijne, Andries, Big Papa, Big Mama, and the blessed children of Kasteel Vrederic, Rietje, Alexander, Theunis, and Griet, our girl with the lantern.

It's time now we get acquainted with the seventh continent of this world, Africa.

CHAPTER SEVEN:

CONTINENT OF AFRICA

Storyteller:
Jacobus Vrederic van Phillip

"I am the world's second-largest continent and within my chest runs one of the world's longest rivers, the Nile."

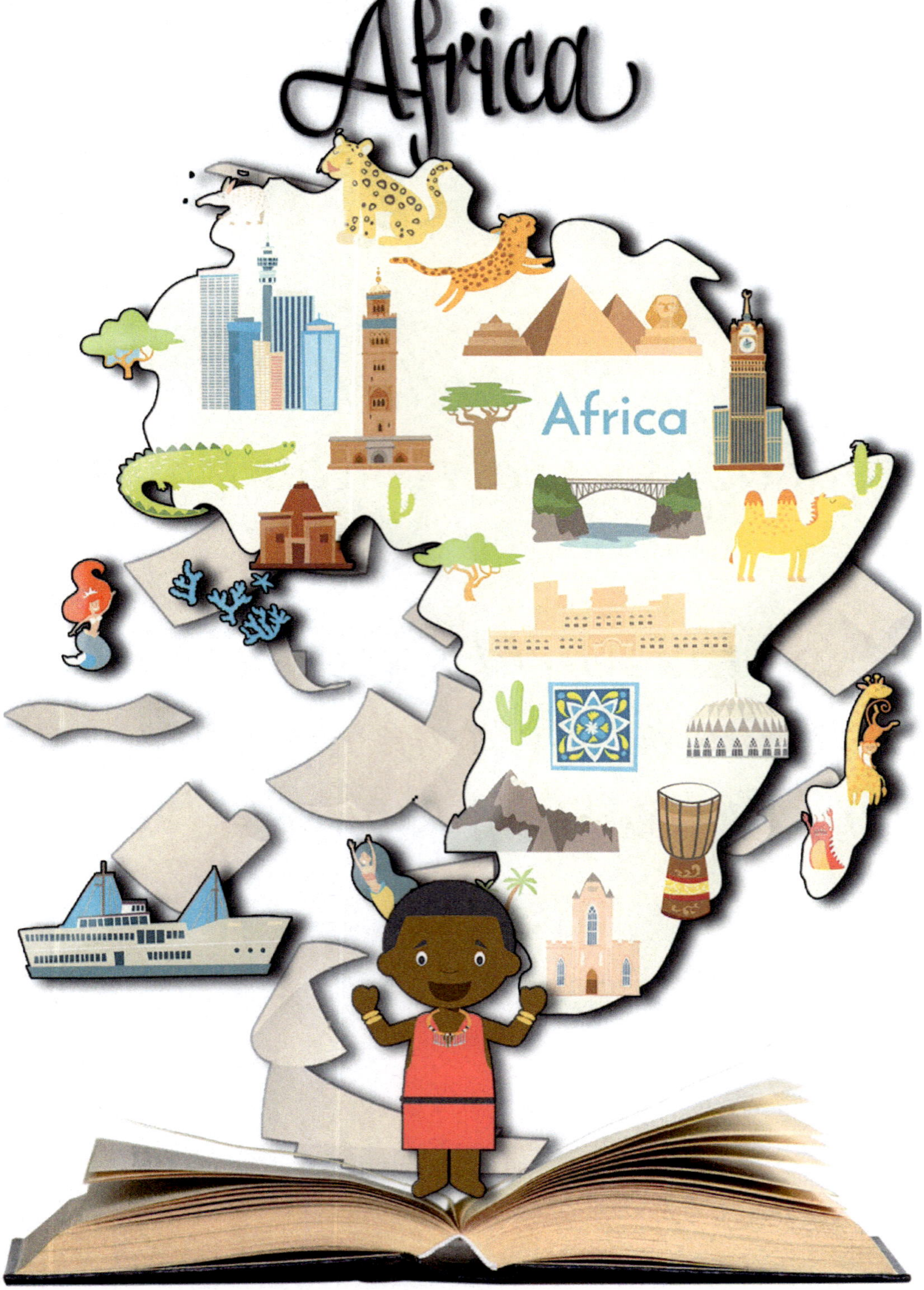
Africa
Africa

Welcome to Africa. This is a land which many scientists have thought to be the origin of mankind. Africa is the second-largest continent in this world. Fifty-four independent countries call this continent home. Algeria is the largest country in Africa. The mystical Nile River is the longest river flowing through this continent.

As the oldest inhabited place, this continent is also designated by some to be the Mother Continent. The Garden of Eden from the Abrahamic religions is believed by many to be in this continent.

An interesting and fun fact about this continent is the length and breadth of Africa are roughly the same. All of you who love geographical facts, the equator goes across this continent. The equator splits the continent into two nearly equal halves.

You should also try to learn a new language in your private time, so it will help you during your travels around the globe. Learning a new language is like having a friendship ring on your finger which says I am your friend. This language skill will be a true treasure box for you while you travel. Africa has around two thousand different languages spoken around the continent.

For jewelry collectors, did you know most of the world's diamonds actually come from Africa? If you all treasure chocolate like my brothers and I do, then know that Africa produces seventy percent of the world's cocoa beans.

My family and I had traveled to Africa to work with some nonprofit organizations. My wife and I were volunteering as doctors in mobile clinics in areas where there were no healthcare services. Sometimes these mobile clinics are dependent on international doctors.

Papa had again volunteered to fly us to Africa on his private plane. So, the Kasteel Vrederic family members all came along as volunteers. We would have private time after our needed work was complete.

Yet before we go to the enchanted tale of this night, let us get some food on our plates. You can ask your family to get you one of the following dishes from the famous foods of Africa.

SOME OF AFRICA'S FAMOUS FOODS

My dear children, here are some of the famous African foods for you to try out. My mother is a good cook and can whip up anything in no time as long as she gets to taste it at least once.

Cook with your parents and make it a family event. Aside from the fun of cooking, you too will have international cuisine on your dinner table all the time.

ENCHANTED TALES: A KASTEEL VREDERIC STORYBOOK FOR CHILDREN

Harira – *Morocco* *Cameroon* – **Koki**
Dumboy – *Liberia* *Nigeria* – **Jollof Rice**
Egusi Soup – *Nigeria* *Morocco* – **Couscous**
Ful Medames – *Egypt* *Côte d'Ivoire* – **Alloco**
Chambo with Nsima – *Malawi* *South Africa* – **Chakalaka**
Kapenta with Sadza – *Zimbabwe*

· Menu ·

COUNTRIES OF AFRICA

Now let's get introduced to the countries in Africa. So, when you see a child from one of the countries in Africa, you will know where exactly your friend is from. My father Erasmus van Phillip and my brother Antonius van Phillip are both amazing painters. They paint a portrait from all the places we visit as we then get to add the portraits as memories in our family library. You can just take a picture and add it to your library too. Here are the names of the countries from the continent we all know as Africa.

ENCHANTED TALES: A KASTEEL VREDERIC STORYBOOK FOR CHILDREN

Algeria

Angola

Benin

Botswana

Burkina Faso

Burundi

Cabo Verde

Cameroon

Central African Republic

Chad

Comoros

Congo

Côte d'Ivoire

Democratic Republic of the Congo

Djibouti

Egypt

Equatorial Guinea

Eritrea

Eswatini

Ethiopia

Gabon

Gambia

Ghana

Guinea

Guinea-Bissau

Kenya

Lesotho

Liberia

Libya

Madagascar

Malawi

ENCHANTED TALES: A KASTEEL VREDERIC STORYBOOK FOR CHILDREN

Mauritania	Mali
Morocco	Mauritius
Namibia	Mozambique
Nigeria	Niger
Sao Tome and Principe	Rwanda
Seychelles	Senegal
Somalia	Sierra Leone
South Sudan	South Africa
Tanzania	Sudan

Tunisia

Zambia

Togo

Uganda

Zimbabwe

LANDMARK QUIZ

Which landmark is this and where is it located?

A. Avenue of the Baobabs, Madagascar
B. Okavango Delta, Botswana
C. Pyramids of Giza, Egypt
D. Mount Kilimanjaro, Tanzania

SOME OF AFRICA'S LANDMARKS

Now let's see some of the famous landmarks of Africa. So, when you get to visit one of these countries, maybe you can preplan to stop by one of them.

Landmarks

Mount Kilimanjaro – *Tanzania*

Table Mountain – *South Africa*

Victoria Falls – *Zambia/Zimbabwe*

Okavango Delta – *Botswana*

Olduvai Gorge – *Tanzania*

Aloba Arch – *Chad*

Zuma Rock – *Nigeria*

Avenue of the Baobabs – *Madagascar*

Basilica of Our Lady of Peace – *Côte d'Ivoire*

Pyramids of Giza – *Egypt*

Namib-Naukluft National Park – *Namibia*

Black River Gorges National Park – *Mauritius*

STORY TIME WITH JACOBUS VREDERIC VAN PHILLIP

It was really fun going through some fun facts from the African countries. My personal favorite part is the food of each country. Every time I get to visit a new country, I try to get acquainted with some of their national dishes. Now let's go and hear some stories from this continent. As a child, my brothers Antonius, Andries, and I loved listening to different tales each night retold by our parents. We actually still gather by Mama and Papa as they still share stories with our children.

I am Jacobus Vrederic van Phillip, a son of the famous Kasteel Vrederic, and I will take you through the tales of the seventh continent, the last continent in this book, which is Africa. These are stories that are just not tales but things that actually happened to us during our travels. As I had promised in the beginning, my family members and I have taken you around the globe through the seven continents of this world. So now come with me as we travel through the last continent of Africa through *Enchanted Tales: A Kasteel Vrederic Storybook For Children.*

KENYA

The Mystical Princess And The Rhinos Of Maasai Mara

"What happens when you the predators become your own prey? It's then you need a lesson from life."

ENCHANTED TALES: A KASTEEL VREDERIC STORYBOOK FOR CHILDREN

Kenya

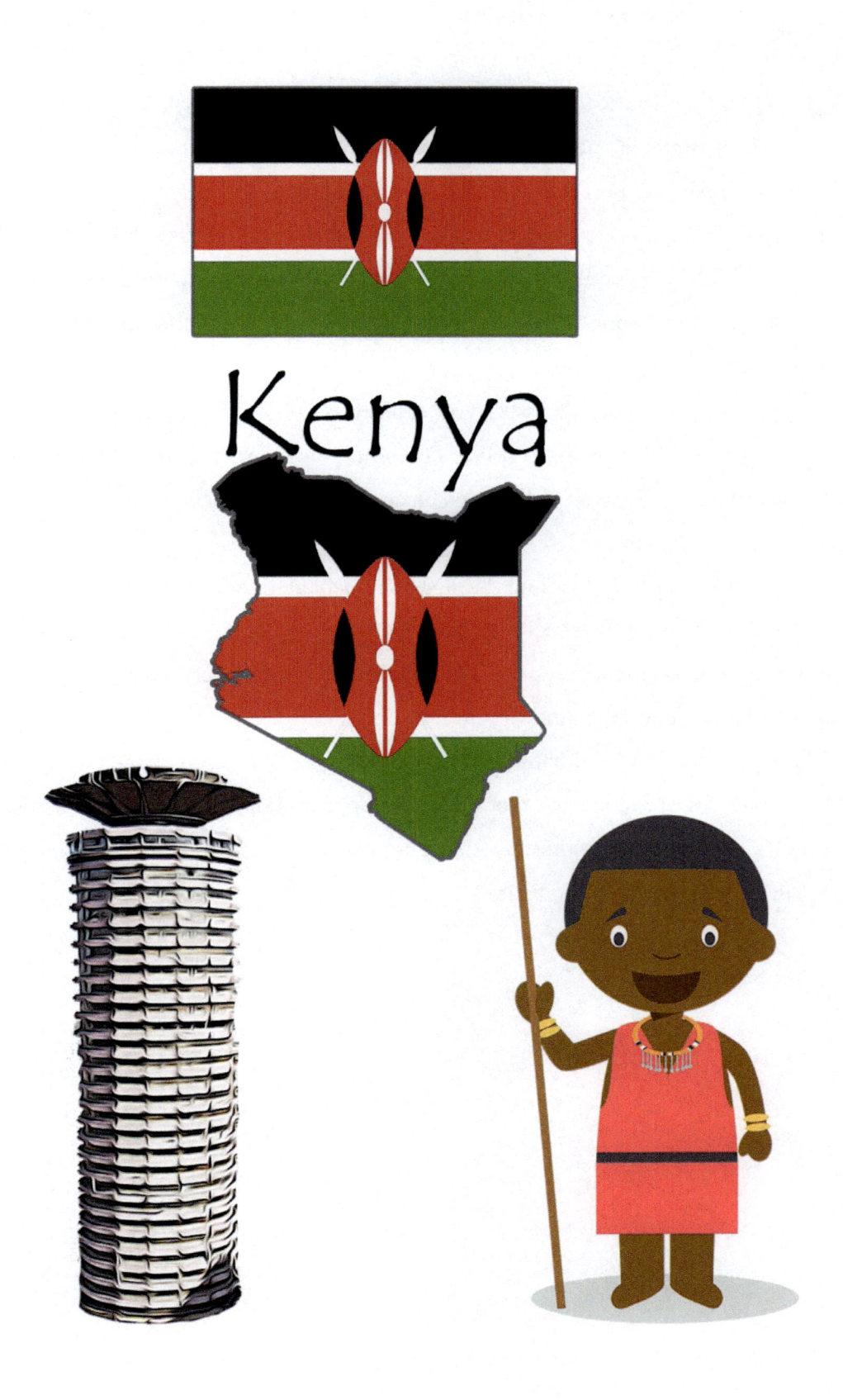

Maasai Mara National Reserve is a gigantic national game reserve in Narok, Kenya. This reserve is also spelled as Masai Mara, and sometimes locals refer to this as "The Mara." The name comes from the Maasai people. This globally renowned reserve is one of Africa's best known wildlife reserves.

This is one of the best places in the world to go on a safari as the Serengeti National Park of Tanzania is its neighbor, and together they have the world's best safari and wildlife reserves. Some of the wildlife you would see are lions, cheetahs, elephants, zebras, hippos, buffaloes, black and white rhinoceroses, spotted hyenas, hippopotamuses, African clawless otters, Masai giraffes, Nile crocodiles, and much more.

There are many species of birds you will see as you travel through this reserve, such as the Kenyan national bird lilac-breasted roller. Did you know Maasai Mara is the only protected area in Kenya where you will see an indigenous black rhino population? Also, the main leading role of our story is coming up soon.

Let us now travel to this land through our enchanted tale, as the mystical princess and the rhinos of Maasai Mara will take us on another magical journey. Yet first we must go and get Kasteel Vrederic's mystical princess. For remember all the stories had begun as our blessed daughter had landed upon the land for the first time.

All the stories only end happily ever after through the helping hands of Kasteel Vrederic's blessed daughter Griet Jacobus Vrederic van Phillip, also known to all of you as the girl with the lantern. Let's now all go on a journey through a country called Kenya. I call this enchanted tale, "The Mystical Princess And The Rhinos Of Maasai Mara."

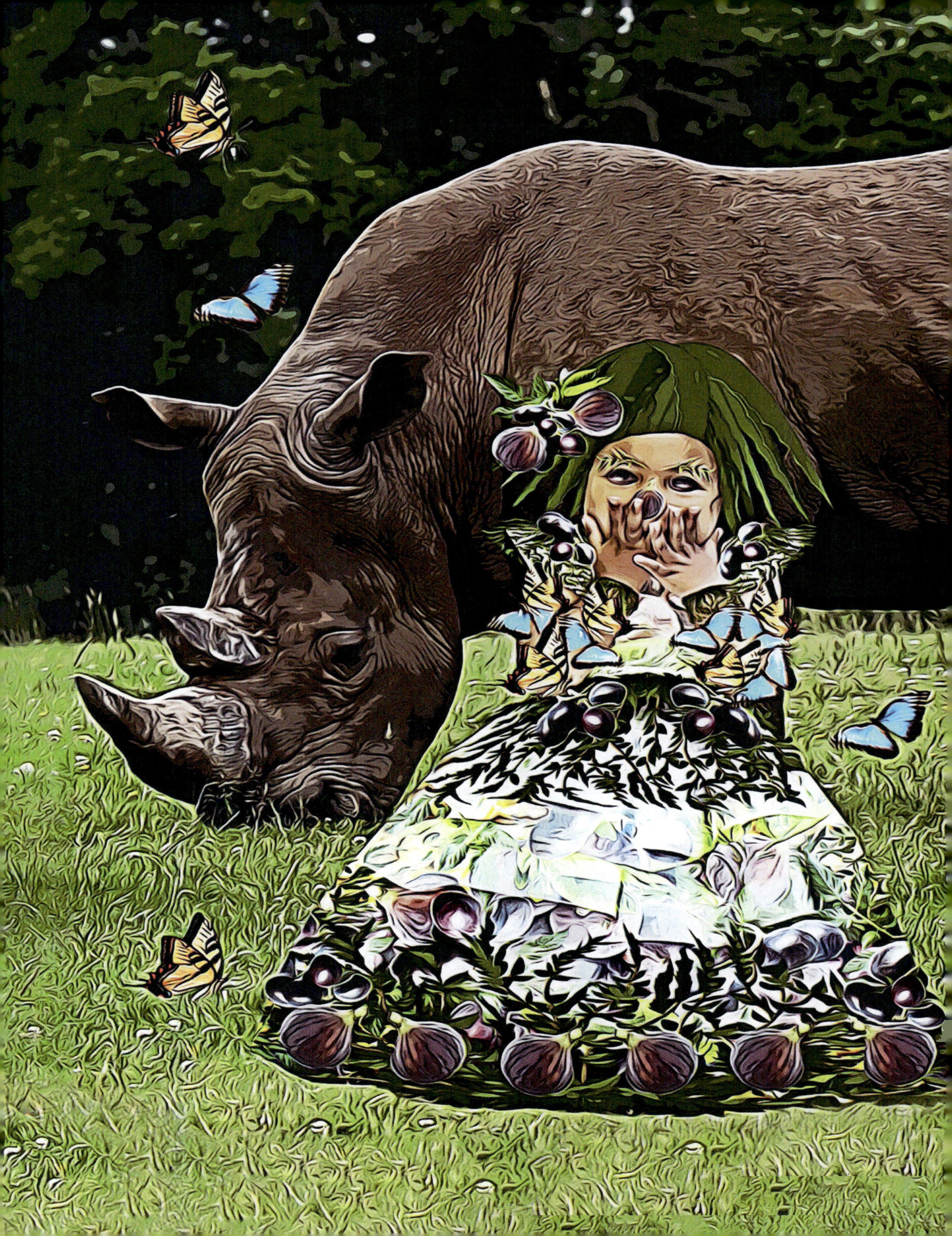

THE MYSTICAL PRINCESS AND THE RHINOS OF MAASAI MARA

An airstrip near Maasai Mara is where Papa landed our private plane. Then we had a short drive to our lodge which was handled by a tour company. A tour guide, cabins, private cook, and safari trips were all included in our all-inclusive travel deal.

The lodge actually looked like a movie set. We were in a cabin which had armchairs on the verandas. There were huge Persian rugs and cedar four-poster beds with mosquito nets. We walked to our lodge through a line of olive trees, ebony trees, and fig trees.

Griet and Rietje were not happy campers though. All the romantic sceneries were absolutely loved by the adults and our brave boys, Alexander and Theunis. The whole situation was so funny as Griet and Rietje refused to put their feet down on the floor. As soon as I placed Griet with her feet on the ground, she screamed and cried. At the same time when Antonius placed Rietje down with her feet on the ground, she also screamed and cried so loud it actually got the women in our lodge very unhappy.

Mama said, "Jacobus, carry Griet. Don't put her down. And Antonius, you don't want Big Mama to be upset on our vacation, so keep Rietje on your lap."

Andries could not stop being happy as he laughed and said, "Yes, Big Bro and Buddy, you two babysit as this is Big Mama and Andries's vacation."

I watched Papa, Margriete, and Katelijne just play around with the boys, trying to not get in the way. Yet I knew my mother the dream psychic and wondered why Mama was asking us to not let go of the girls. There was more into this as my mother never talks about her prophetic dreams. She believes everything has its time and place. Yet she will intervene if she has to at times.

Mama came to me and whispered in my ears, "Jacobus, a child will get hurt. I believe by a poacher. Keep the children within your arms. I will hold on to the boys. Don't share this with anyone as I could not see which child or if it was even here. I only know someone will get hurt."

At that time, we saw in front of our cabin some wild beasts were passing by us. The wild beasts were roaring but suddenly all of them stopped and watched our cabin. The skies were getting dark. I wondered though how we had planned a quiet family trip in between the wild animals. Yet my whole body froze in fear as I saw within my arms my beloved niece Griet had converted from a two-year-old to a five-year-old child. Antonius watched me as he grabbed on to the changing form of Rietje.

He said, "Okay dear niece, what's going on? Don't panic everyone! I have a strong grip on her. I won't ever let her go."

I realized no one was panicked but my brother who asked everyone not to panic, so I screamed for the bravest one amongst us, "Andries! Help!"

It was Griet who copied me and said, "Brother Bear! Hold me now! They will gobble me up. They will hurt me like they will hurt their own child."

Like a flying saucer, Griet jumped in air and went to Andries as did Rietje.

He grabbed both girls and asked, "Sister Bears, what's going on?"

Griet could not even utter a word, as we saw there in front of us was standing a beautiful young girl about Griet's age. She looked humanlike yet was completely made out of olives, figs, and butterflies. It was as if we had a combination of fruits on a human who was standing in front of us. Her hair was made out of aloe vera trees. In front of us was a medicinal human girl completely made out of plants.

She smiled and said, "Please don't be scared. I have been waiting for you for so long. My friends are in need of your help. They are being hunted down by monsters that hide amongst humans."

Griet asked her, "What kind of a monster do you talk about? Also, who are your friends and how are they in danger?"

She smiled and said, "I am the Mystical Princess of this reserve. I can keep all my friends hidden from even powerful lanterns and minds as I am an illusion and I try to keep my animal friends in a mystical illusion. Yet I have found out that the monsters wait and don't give up. They are hunting down all of the rhinos and now we only have a handful of rhinos left."

She saw something outside and said, "Dear girl with the lantern, please help us as they have taken a mother rhino away from a baby rhino. Now her neighbors, the wild beasts of the reserve, will hunt down the human monsters as our animal population actually call your kind animals. For remember you all come to our home, and we love it as you provide our food, health, and sustenance. Yet as you are taking away more and more of us, the animals now will hunt down the human predators."

She watched the wild beasts' procession behind us and said, "They all have teamed up, the cheetahs, elephants, zebras, hippos, and the lions. They all go with intention to hurt the three men who has the mother rhino. She is the mother of two rhinos. The rhinos who give me a ride are her sons."

Griet then told the Mystical Princess, "Follow me as you must cause an illusion and let the men see there are a herd of wild beasts running toward them. I will with my group free your friend. Yet please ask your friends not to hurt the human children and the women, who accompany the men."

The Mystical Princess said, "I will try and ask my friends. Yet they too want to know if you the human are hunting the animal, then how is it we are still the monster and not you the human?"

No one had an answer for the question as then in front of us we heard animals shriek in fear and pain as the Mystical Princess flew over the reserve. I watched Griet, Rietje, Alexander, and Theunis get on their magical horse and follow the princess. We followed on foot.

We saw a few men were hunting and running to get their wild catch. Yet there came a dense fog. In the fog, we could only see olives and figs were falling from the skies. The hunters got busy picking up the olives as I watched my brave kids go and throw their swords into the cages opening and letting go of the mother rhino and her friends.

All of the rhinos left as they found freedom. I saw there were lions watching the hunters. Then we saw a child run out from a camp and get in front of the roaring lion. The lion leaped forward to gobble him up as my Griet lit her lantern on to the lion's face. The lion walked backward as he sat down watching Griet's lantern, and like a good boy, he started to wag his tail.

The hunters got out and tried to shoot arrows toward the lion and take him as their trophy. I watched the flying arrows go and miss the lion. Yet one hit the child who was trying to protect the animals from his own family. The fog disappeared as did the lions and all the animals. Yet the Mystical Princess and the rhinos stayed behind. She came forward and spoke with Griet.

She said, "Sometimes, we try to do miracles yet the beast in humans and animals come in between. I can help heal the child with your help Griet. If you ask the parents to stay back and not come in front of us, or maybe I will create an illusion afterward if you could erase their memories."

The Mystical Princess thought for a while and said, "You see humans are nice, yet some are just human monsters. They will hunt you down and search everywhere for me too. Even though today they will appreciate the gesture, tomorrow they will become the predators again."

That's when I jumped in and told the hunters, "I am a doctor. Please allow me to give your child emergency medical care."

Andries carried the child into our cabin as I saw the Mystical Princess was there. My beloved wife Margriete, a doctor herself, jumped in when she saw there was a medical need. I told the child we will do our best and give emergency medical treatment.

Griet said, "Papa Jacobus, he needs more help than medicine can do for him now. He needs a miracle. Please allow the Mystical Princess to help and heal him."

I did, and as the Mystical Princess did her job, I watched the child wake up completely healed.

He sat up and cried as he said, "Dear Mystical Princess, I do believe in you and the rhinos. I am sorry for my father is unjust and mean. I tried to stop him, but he wouldn't listen. Please forgive us."

The Mystical Princess kissed the boy's head and said, "I know sweet child as you are as sweet as my friends the rhinos. I love you as much as I love the rhinos. You will be my new friend from now on. I only wait for you to grow up and be another friend of the Mystical Princess and the rhinos of Maasai Mara."

That night I had stayed awake with our little princesses and told them, "Precious ones, we could enjoy all the safaris and travel through the amazing jungles. Mankind could enjoy this world without hurting the animal kingdom if we just let them be alone. At all times, we too must take precautions so they too will let us be alone."

I watched the children and told them, "We could with care both the humans and the animals enjoy this one world together. I promise I will do my share and maybe plant a tree or just maybe adopt a puppy when we go back home. I will also be a little nicer to the animal kingdom as I realize they are just as scared of us as we are of them."

Rietje said, "Papa pinky promise we can have a puppy."

I told the children, "As long as Mama agrees, it's all right with me."

That's when we all saw in front of us a shooting star and shouted at once, "A shooting star! Make a wish!"

Griet said, "That's not a star silly Papa Jacobus."

As we all watched, Griet said, "That's friend! She is watching over her land. She is flying on top of the rhinos. There are two rhinos pulling a cart with the Mystical Princess on top of it. That's actually the Mystical Princess and the rhinos of Maasai Mara."

Kenya Trivia Time

What city is the Maasai Mara National Reserve in?

What is the Kenyan national bird?

What is one indigenous group of animals that is protected in the Maasai Mara National Reserve?

MADAGASCAR

The Lemur Girl Of Madagascar

"A mother and a child are never separated yet connected beyond time and place, through eternal love."

ENCHANTED TALES: A KASTEEL VREDERIC STORYBOOK FOR CHILDREN

Madagascar

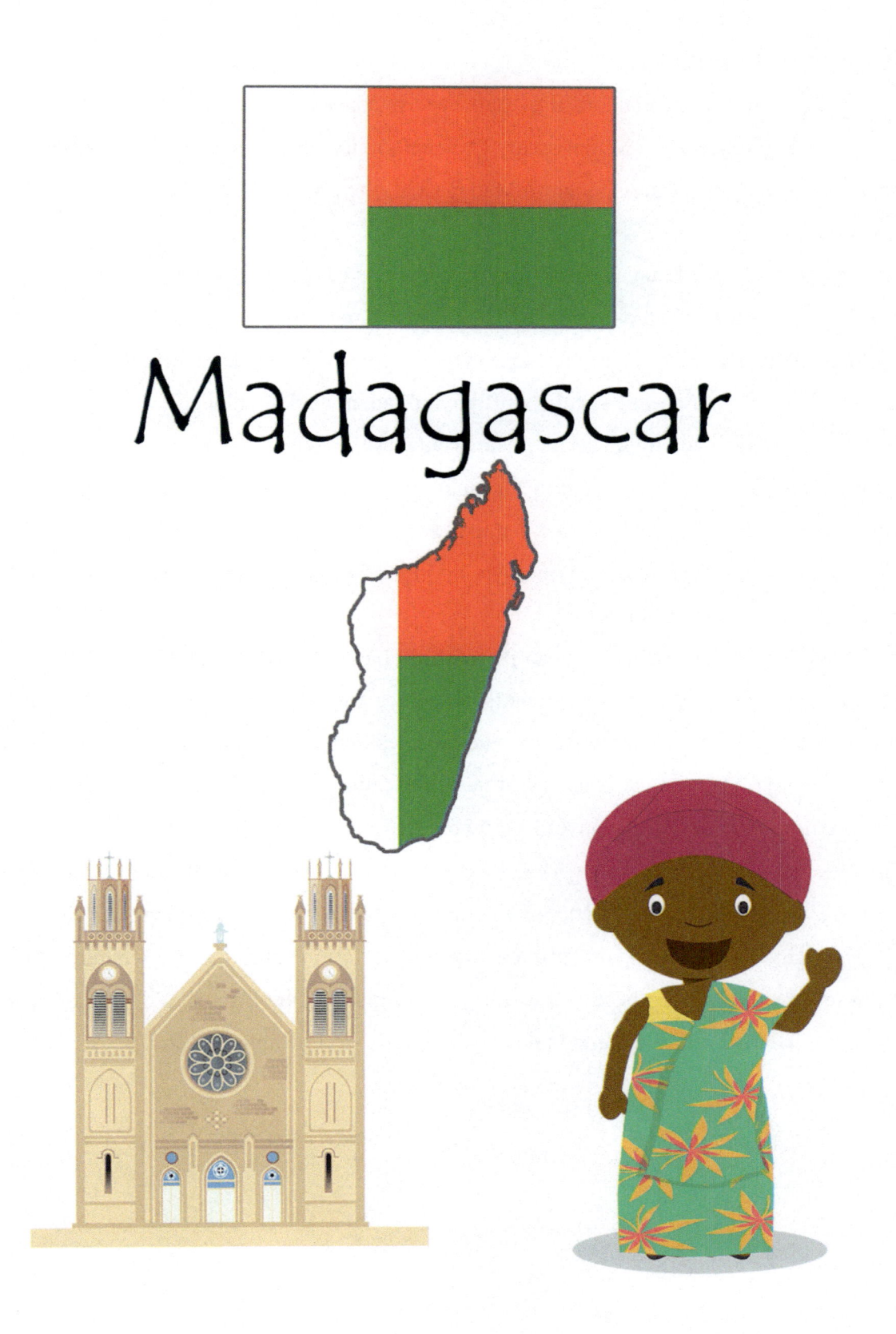

Madagascar, the world's fourth-largest island is also the second-largest island country. This country was not even discovered until 1500 A.D. It is located in the Indian Ocean off the southeastern coast of Africa. The official name is the Republic of Madagascar. The capital city of this country is Antananarivo. Even though various languages are spoken in Madagascar, the official languages spoken are Malagasy and French.

We arrived in Madagascar as we volunteered to help with some mobile clinics. It was fascinating to see the country in person. This land is considered paradise for wildlife as most of the wildlife found there is actually found nowhere else on the world. As this is an isolated island, because of its isolation, unique species of flora and fauna were developed.

Some wildlife you might see there are Madagascar owls, Madagascar cuckoos, and lemurs. The lemurs are sacred and protected in Madagascar as the belief is lemurs have souls and there is a connection between the human and lemur through our ancestry. There are roughly over one hundred species and subspecies of lemurs living in Madagascar. They have been specified as very rare, endangered, and vulnerable.

Madagascar, the country of beautiful orchids, baobab trees, colorful chameleons, and home of unique flora and fauna, was an adventurous place for a family safari. You too would enjoy traveling through this very popular family vacation destination. With it varied terrains and amazing wildlife, I believe Madagascar was a great family vacation.

Yet like my family always knows, where there is so much beauty, there always are some thorns. We too had encountered a very special friend when we traveled through Madagascar. This time, however, she did not need a helping hand yet came to give us a helping hand.

Tonight, let me take you through Madagascar's amazing safari adventure. As we had started our tour through the beautiful country, Griet made a new friend. We call her new friend, the Lemur Girl. I call this enchanted tale, "The Lemur Girl Of Madagascar."

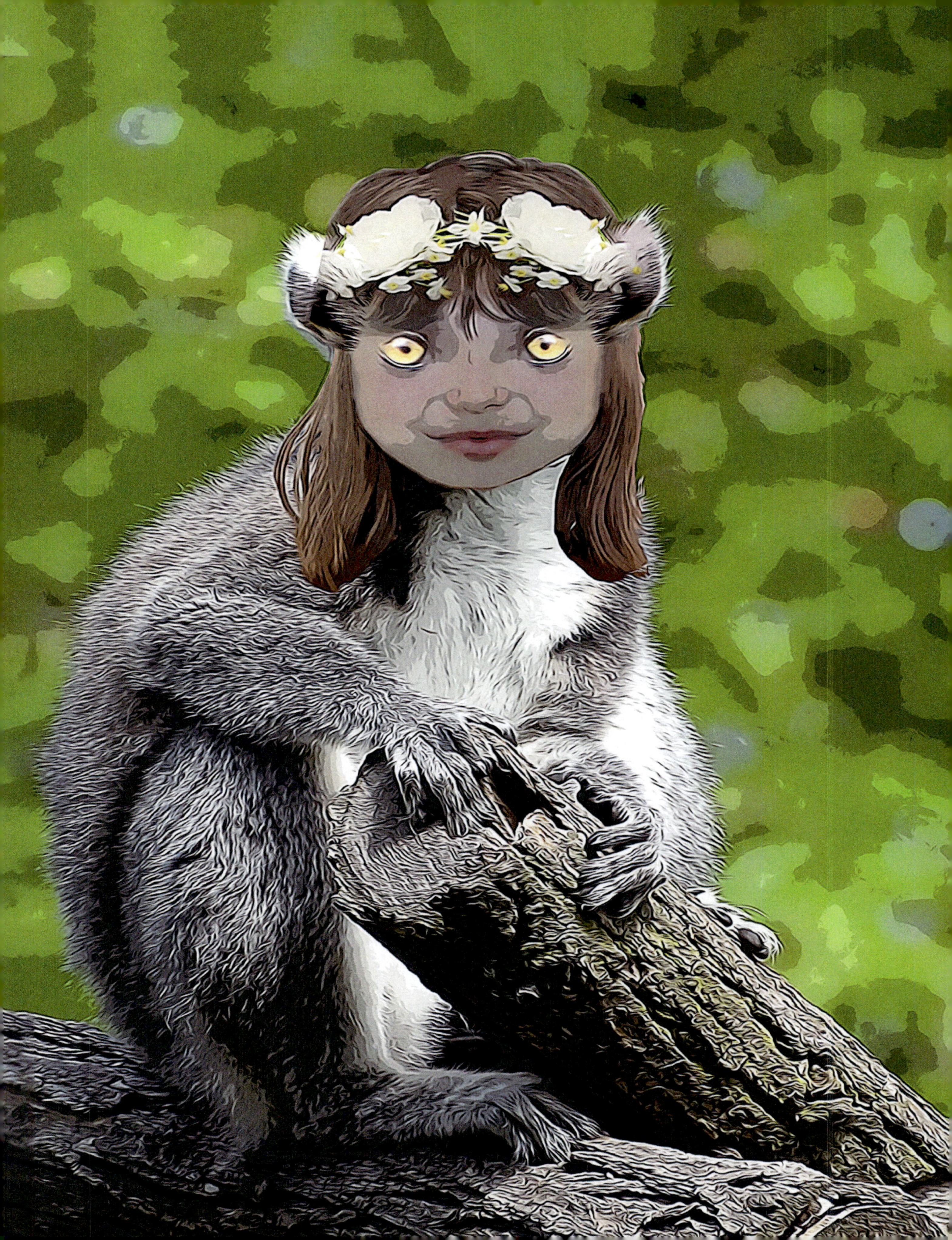

THE LEMUR GIRL OF MADAGASCAR

Traveling to Andasibe-Mantadia National Park was a very easy commute in Madagascar. We decided to drive there and just enjoy the vacation on our own. Papa had visited this park with Mama before. We stayed at a lodge close to the park's entrance. This lodge was actually owned by an Indian friend of Papa, named Mr. Deva Dutta.

The lodge was very welcoming even on a very cloudy moonless night. There was an open bar and restaurant with an open buffet for the guests. Our bungalow was set away from all the other bungalows which gave us our needed privacy. The beds were all covered with mosquito nettings. I watched my mother go around and spray everyone with an insect repellent.

She called the children as she said, "Griet, Rietje, Alexander, Theunis, come here to Oma and everyone close your eyes as I protect you from the monster mosquitoes."

They all ran toward her as they hugged her. Mama not only sprayed them but I watched Mama put pajamas on all of them. She always bathes the children and puts them to bed. I watched Antonius and Andries come next to me as they watched her too.

Andries said, "Big Mama, I feel tired. Maybe tonight we three can sleep in your cabin, just like old times. Your three boys get a sleepover with Mama and Papa."

Papa came and said, "Are we not all doing a sleepover? I thought the bungalow has only one bedroom and an open family room that has sleeping arrangement for ten. There are mosquito nets around the beds so the children can all sleep there. We can all take sleeping bags and mosquito nets fall off the ceiling for those too."

He watched the cabin and said, "Your mother and I had come here before as this bungalow belongs to my friend Deva. It's a nice memory. Jacobus and you two were very young."

I remember Mama ran after the three of us and was happy we tired off and slept like babies. Actually, we were babies. My brothers laughed as they too remembered our family vacation times.

As we turned all the lights off and tried to sleep under one mosquito net for men and one for the women, Griet walked in crying.

Katelijne jumped up and asked, "Baby girl, what is it? Why are you crying?"

Rietje and the boys joined in the crying group. It's like a competition in our home. If one child cries, then the whole team slowly joins in the concert. Yet as Griet did not say anything, I knew she needed Brother Bear.

Andries jumped up and carried her as she said, "Brother Bear, what is adopted or stepchild? Are they not real children? Are they fake children?"

I looked at Antonius and Katelijne as they watched their daughter and saw Mama walk up to Griet.

Mama said, "Why do you ask, because in our home there are no adopted or step or fake children. Remember we are all one family. I gave birth to your Papa Jacobus. I had adopted your Papa and brother Andries, but all three are my boys. Through love, we have united into one family."

Griet watched all of us and said, "The man in the next cabin is mean and he hurt his family. He said their child is missing because the stepmom lost her. The Lemur Girl told me. She said if I don't help her, then the girl will be gone far away before Oma comes to kiss me and wake me up."

I asked, "Griet, where is the Lemur Girl now? Can she talk to us? As I told you, you can help strangers only when they come in front of us and ask for our permission."

Then in the open courtyard of the bungalow like a glow of mystical lights, there stood a lemur who resembled a monkey or ape yet had a human girl's face. She had beautiful brown hair and big brown eyes. Her facial features were of a little girl, yet she had the body of a lemur.

We were staring at her very awkwardly as she broke the silence and said, "I am sorry for scaring you all like this. As I was told the girl with the lantern and her team have arrived, I could not stop myself but ask for her help."

Andries who was still holding Griet asked, "What is the problem here? Usually, we are asked to go somewhere but I hear something about adoption and stepchildren, what's going on?"

The Lemur Girl said, "It was about two weeks ago when the family next door had arrived. They visited the park and the animals, and even donated money to the park for its endangered animals. Yet there is a group of men who kidnapped the girl. The stepmom is being blamed for the situation as she had the child with her at the time of the disappearance. We must hurry as the father has left for he was told the child had fallen off a boat and will not be found anymore. The child, however, did not fall off the canoe. The mother was hit on her head and the kidnappers had taken the child for money."

She watched something outside as she nodded her head and I saw there were more lemurs walking in a crowd. Yet they all looked like monkeys. They spoke with her as she then nodded back to them.

The Lemur Girl said, "I am the princess of this jungle, and many others. I have promised to save the child who misses her mother and also protect the honor of a mother who loves her child, even though she is not the birth mother. The world must know a mother is one who raises a child, not the one who only gives birth."

Mama watched all of this and said, "I will help because I too believe a mother is one who raises a child. Also, I want to personally ask this world if you give birth to a child and don't want them, then send them to me. I shall raise them. Yet if you are a woman who is raising a child you did not give birth to, then it matters not what they say as your bond with the child will be eternal."

In the courtyard, there was an elegant young woman with her messy hair all out. She was dressed in very worn-out clothes said, "Please help a mother find her child. I believe my daughter is still out there. You see, I can hear her cries. She is asking for me. It's late and my daughter actually goes to bed early. She must be hungry as she has not had anything to eat for days."

I saw Griet, Rietje, Alexander, and Theunis were ready on Rietje's magical horse as the Lemur Princess climbed the trees and asked them to follow. Mama, Margriete, and Katelijne had stayed back with the woman. I knew they knew Griet and her team would be all right as long as they have Brother Bear with them.

The children flew above as Andries, Antonius, Papa and I walked right underneath them. We reached a cave in low water or a lake, where we saw were signs of humans. We walked into the cave and saw a huge crocodile sitting and guarding some men.

The crocodile spoke in English as he said, "Hello friends of Griet. I am the crocodile friend who had met her before. I travel from place to place trying to get rid of evil monsters. It seems like even humans have a lot of monsters in them. These men had kidnapped the child for money, yet we are holding them prisoners until Griet can come and intervene, as humans think we are all evil."

Griet spoke to her friend and said, "Dear friend, where is the child? I see you have these men under control. We have alerted the police and they will come and take the men. You can become invisible at the time. I will make sure they don't see you, yet we need the child."

The crocodile didn't say anything, yet the Lemur Girl said, "The child is fine. She is in my castle with my family members. We hid her there to save her from the kidnappers. No one human nor animal will get hurt here as long as I can keep an eye out for all of them."

That night, we brought the child back to the mother who refused to leave without her daughter. The father came back and apologized as he too learned his lesson. He realized a mother's love can save a child from all harm's way.

The men were arrested as they were simple thieves looking for money. Yet little did they know they would have become the treat for a crocodile who watches over all the children in distress. Not all crocodiles are bad as you see this friendly crocodile we will get to see again.

The lemurs had hidden the three-year-old child with them. They actually fed her and had taken good care of her. As soon as she saw her mother, she ran to her and kissed her as did the loving mother. I realized Griet had to do her miracles, so people only remember some parts of the night's story and not all of it.

The night went as dawn came to our cabin. Mama had all of her three sons in her embrace. As the morning sun glowed into our room, we saw Griet, Rietje, Alexander, and Theunis were all sleeping under the same mosquito net on top of Papa.

He woke up and said, "Best night ever. I have all of my children and grandchildren with me."

We all saw in the glowing morning's dawn, a princess had walked into our cabin and left us with a basket of fresh fruits. She waved at us for she was flying away to do something good for maybe another family as she said, "Have a great vacation and remember to call me if you need my help. I am the Lemur Girl of Madagascar."

Madagascar Trivia Time

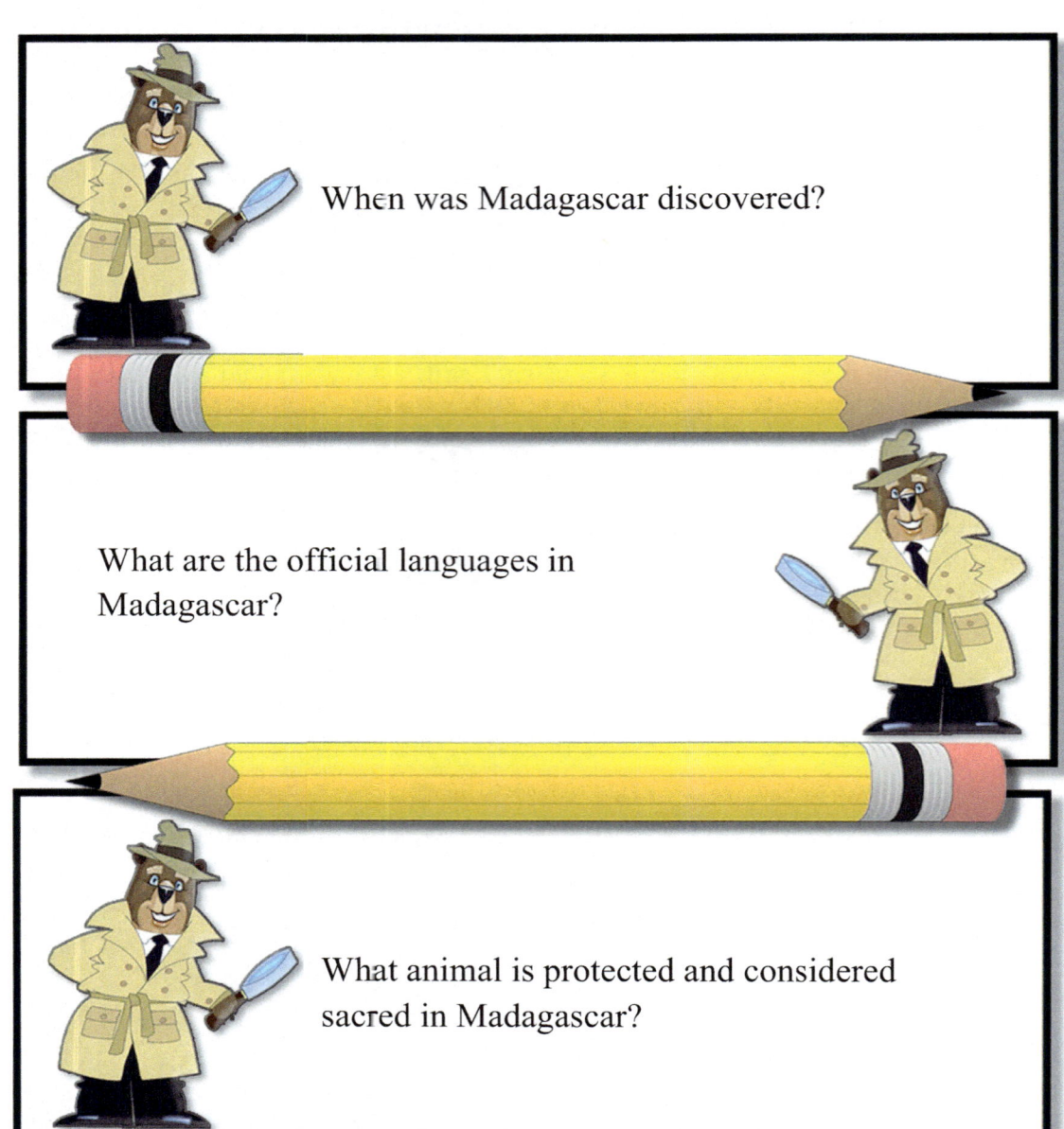

When was Madagascar discovered?

What are the official languages in Madagascar?

What animal is protected and considered sacred in Madagascar?

EGYPT

The Invisible Boy Of The Nile River

"Invisibility is a miracle if one wants to remain unseen, yet if one needs to be seen, you need to be visible first."

Egypt

Egypt is called by many as the "Gift of the Nile." Historically, the Nile River provided the source of water for farming and harvests which later was the main reason people started to settle along the river valley. Egypt links North Africa to the Middle East. The official name of Egypt is the Arab Republic of Egypt.

The official language is Arabic, and the capital city Cairo is set on the Nile River. As the river flows by the city, the Nile eventually empties herself into the Mediterranean Sea. I guess she connects people, land, and cultures to one another through her chest. The Nile River was once presumed to be the longest river in the world; however, some researchers have recently suggested the Amazon River might be slightly longer.

The largest Egyptian pyramid is the Great Pyramid of Giza which also is the tomb of Pharaoh Khufu. The pyramid dates back to the twenty-sixth century B.C. It took about twenty-seven years to be built. Moreover, even today, the pyramid is still almost intact. The Great Pyramid of Giza is the oldest amongst the Seven Wonders of the Ancient World. The Giza pyramid complex also includes the Pyramid of Khafre and the Pyramid of Menkaure.

Did you know all pyramids in Egypt were built next to the Nile River? It was easier to build them by the river as most of the stones would be brought to the site by boat. Every time the river flooded, they would create a manmade canal to the pyramids. That way, the boats would dock close to the job site.

Do go and hike on the historical Mount Sinai which might also be the Biblical Mount Sinai where Moses received the Ten Commandments. We will, however, go back to the Nile River as that's where our story of the night takes place.

As you are all now slightly more acquainted with Egypt and the Nile River, let me, Jacobus Vrederic van Phillip, take you on a journey through this great river of Egypt. Tonight, come with me on a magical journey through another real story that did happen to the Kasteel Vrederic family members. I call this enchanted tale, "The Invisible Boy Of The Nile River."

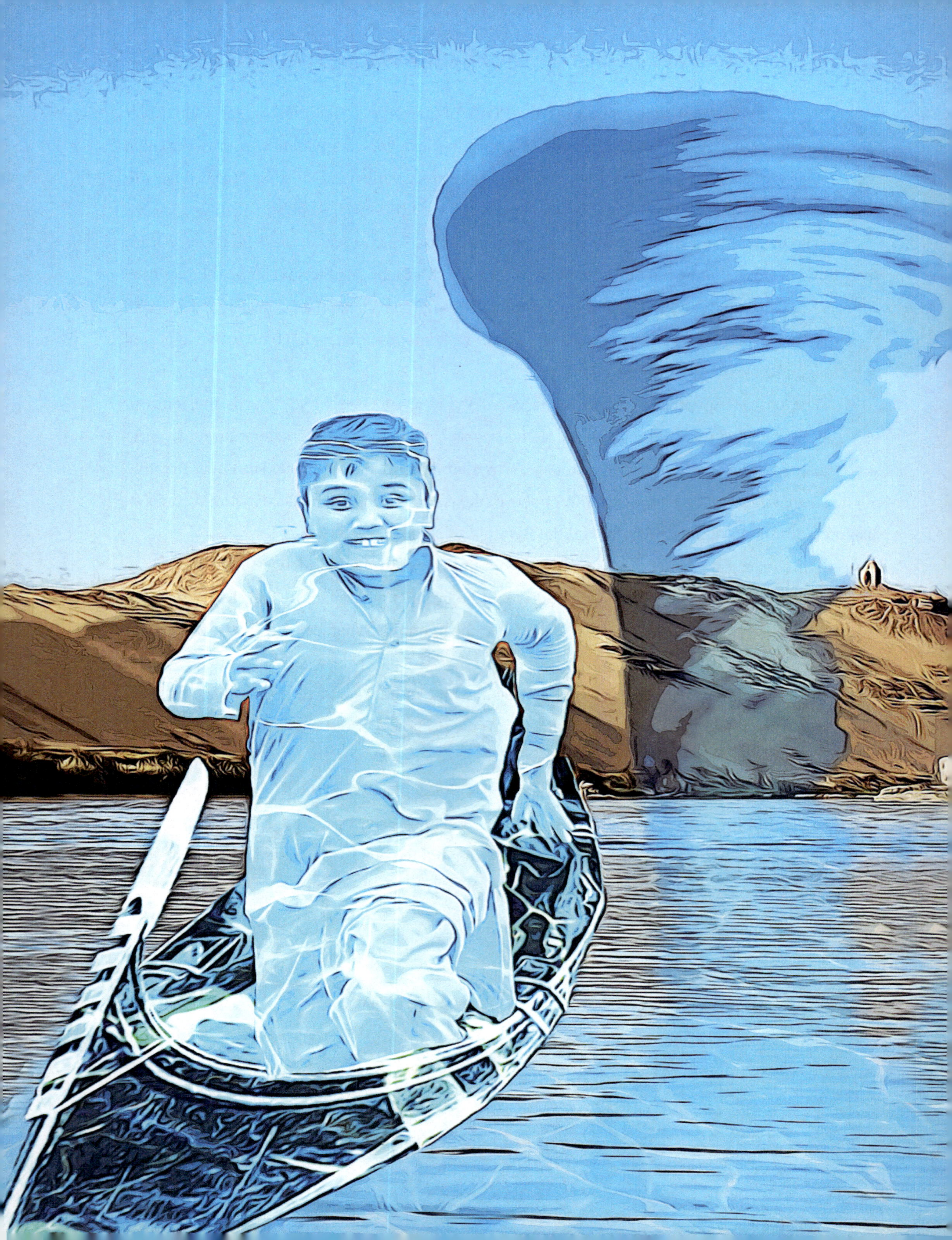

THE INVISIBLE BOY OF THE NILE RIVER

A rare and powerful cyclone hit Egypt while we were on board a Nile River cruise. A thirty-million-year-old river which is the lifeline of Egypt got hit by this cyclone. Andries had gifted us this vacation cruise after our medical expedition through Africa had finished.

The storm was getting very rough as we were in the middle of the river, far away from our final destination. The first two days had been amazing as we traveled through the longest African river, filled with history and memories. My family members did not seem scared or even stressed.

My mother who does panic very easily said, "The Nile River is the home of some of the oldest civilizations. They lived here and were just fine. We will all be fine. Everyone, we are all together in the same boat so whatever happens, we will all survive with even more memories."

She was watching the river as our cruise ship was tilting slightly toward the right. Then it went toward the left. Somehow it felt like a lightning bolt had banged on our cruise ship as it completely stopped sailing.

My brave mother panicked and screamed for Papa as she said, "Erasmus, hold me! I feel nauseous."

When Mama gets sick, all her boys start running toward her. There was no difference as the three of us ran and banged into one another.

We saw our little children were watching us and started to laugh at us as Theunis said in his young voice, "Jacobus is still very funny. A grumpy man you were and you are still grumpy but funny."

All the four kids were laughing together as Griet said, "Brother Bear funny too, and Papa funnier."

I was glad the children were enjoying themselves as I knew the women were not. They were frightened by what had happened to Mama as she never falls sick unless she senses some kind of paranormal activities happening around us.

My sister-in-law Katelijne who could never keep anything in her mind said, "Brother Jacobus, I am worried. There seems to be a huge crocodile over there blocking the other cruise ship. It seems like we might have stopped to see why there is another ship just stopped over there."

The storm was furious as the wind joined in the mystery night's musical theme. I kept an eye on Griet and Rietje as did Antonius and Andries. I watched Margriete had taken Mama to a sofa in our family wing and had given her the necessary medical help. I watched Mama and Papa walk over to Griet as they both were somehow worried about her.

That's when we saw the girls convert and become five-year-old girls. I knew the boys too would be a little older as there in the water I saw Rietje's magical horse was just floating and waiting for her.

Margriete said, "I have a weird feeling about letting my daughter go into the river where I don't know how many evil souls too float. I am worried about the deadly infections and parasites, especially Schistosomiasis, Jacobus. I am a doctor and it can be deadly if a person is exposed to dirty waters. They could be exposed to parasitic diseases. So please children, keep your body parts away from the water at all times. I speak as a doctor and as a Mama."

Griet came to Margriete and said, "Mama Margriete, your sacrifice is the reason I have my life and I will never let you go, I promise. I will not touch or drink any unclean waters of the Earth without my Mama cleaning it first. Pinky promise."

Margriete kissed all the children and Griet then said, "Watch the water boy. He is in the gondola made out of water too. He floats in this river trying to prevent people from drowning or getting gobbled up by the Nile River's monstrous Nile crocodiles. You can't see him as he is invisible. Yet I do give you permission to see him. So now, you shall all see him and his boat."

There in front of us was a young boy about seven years old. He was sitting in his gondola and tried to get our attention.

He said, "Dear girl with the lantern, please help me save the kids on that boat. They are all school children traveling with their teachers. Their boat was toppled by the Nile crocodiles that plan to gobble up the children. These spiritual monsters can cause river cyclones."

He saw the sinking ship and seemed worried as Griet asked, "Who are you and why is it we can see you? You look like a boy made out of water. How can we help you and why can't you help the sinking ship or warn them to get out before they all drown in the ship alive?"

He watched us and said, "I am living in a curse. I had wished upon a falling star millions of years ago to live eternally. I was told I could live eternally yet no one would see me. While I got immortality, I forgot the small detail that no one could see me."

He kept turning to see the sinking ship as he said, "So for millions of years, I have been living on my gondola and have tried to do some good to all whom I could help. In return maybe then I too would be visible and live a normal human life. What good is immortality if you are invisible and can't help anyone as they can't even see you or hear you, because you are invisible?"

Griet said, "Let's go and help them and see if we can get rid of the monstrous Nile crocodiles. Let's make sure they don't harm any more humans."

It was then the moon came out on top of the Nile River and we saw in front of us was a line of crocodiles. They had their mouths open and were looking for their nightly meals as they all proceeded to go closer to the sinking ship. Rietje had her horse stay at a distance as she remembered Margriete's warning about the dirty waters. Griet had her lantern shine just under the moon's glowing amber of light.

Then I was shocked as a crocodile spoke from beneath the waters and said, "So Griet, the girl with the lantern, finally comes to me. I have been waiting for you from the sixteenth century. You see, I tried to eat you up then, but your brave soldier Theunis Peters saved you from my harm's way. I hid in the North Sea as the greatest monster of the North Sea. Now I have yet another chance as we have both crossed time and I am back as the greatest monster of the Nile River. This is a diversion dear one, as I actually want your lantern and your spiritual strength."

I watched Andries walk over with his waterproof scuba diving clothes protecting him from all the dirty waters.

Andries jumped into the waters and he said, "No one shall touch my sister, not a beast nor an animal."

I watched myself jump into the water as did Margriete and Katelijne. Then as it was becoming hard to breath, I saw Antonius and Papa pull me on top of a rock.

Andries said, "If you are not wearing any protective gears, I suggest you all stay on the ship."

Then we watched the rock underneath us was moving as he said, "Don't fear me. I too am a crocodile, and I am actually one of the Nile crocodiles, feared by all. Yet I am not evil. We live in our separate worlds, but I will help you win the war over the monstrous Nile crocodile who has been shapeshifting for centuries."

As we all watched Griet and her team fly over to the sunken ship, a vulture flew over us and said, "Do not fear. I come as a friend and I shall help you all in this mission."

The water boy then walked up on top of the sunken ship and under the glowing light of the moon, we saw the vulture fly over him as the children from the boat all walked into the water boy's small gondola. He carried all twenty-five children and the three teachers to land on his invisible gondola that was very visible.

Then in front of us came Theunis, the brave warrior, as he said, "You foolish beast. What did you think? Griet would be reborn and I, her brave warrior, would not? I am back to protect her again."

It was then Andries who threw his two swords into the beast of the Nile River. Then the swords of Rietje, Alexander, and Theunis came one by one and lifted the beast out of the river as the flying desert vulture gobbled up the beast in one go.

The night ended with Margriete treating everyone who needed medical assistance. As dawn came by us, we saw there in the Nile River, a young boy was rowing his gondola. He saw us, smiled, and came closer to us.

He said, "Dear friends, now during the day everyone can see me as I just got an award for rescuing the school children from the Nile crocodiles. During the night, I have chosen to still be the invisible boy of the Nile River."

We did have a few miraculous nights cruising through the amazing Nile River. All along, Griet, the girl with the lantern, kept her magical lantern glowing for safety.

Do go and cruise the Nile with your family and friends. Be safe and carry all the important medical supplies with you. If you happen to need Griet, do call out as she does have her lantern lit waiting for you and all of the children of this world, to always guide you through another safe and adventurous storytelling night. Also, if you are cruising through the Nile River in Egypt, remember you just might get to see the invisible boy of the Nile River.

Egypt Trivia Time

What is Egypt called by many?

What is the name of Egypt's largest pyramid?

Which sea does the Nile River empty into?

MESSAGE FROM JACOBUS VREDERIC VAN PHILLIP

Traveling through Africa was an amazing journey. We got to see national parks, national reserves, the Nile River, and different pyramids while there. We also tasted different foods and made new friends. Each country we visit leaves an impact on our life as we too leave an impact on the lands we have visited. You too have acquired so much knowledge and maybe made some new friends today.

Africa was the last continent we had visited for our storybook of enchanted tales. I want all of you to come back and visit us in the future as we return and visit more countries around the globe. I know it's almost bedtime as the children in our home are all getting ready to go to bed. Now come and finish reading the conclusion chapter of this book with me before you go off to bed and dream about all of your amazing new friends and their lands.

CONCLUSION

By Jacobus Vrederic van Phillip

"I am a treasure box. In my chest, I have hidden all the riches of the past, the present, and the future. You the reader also live inside of my chest for I am your home, the Earth."

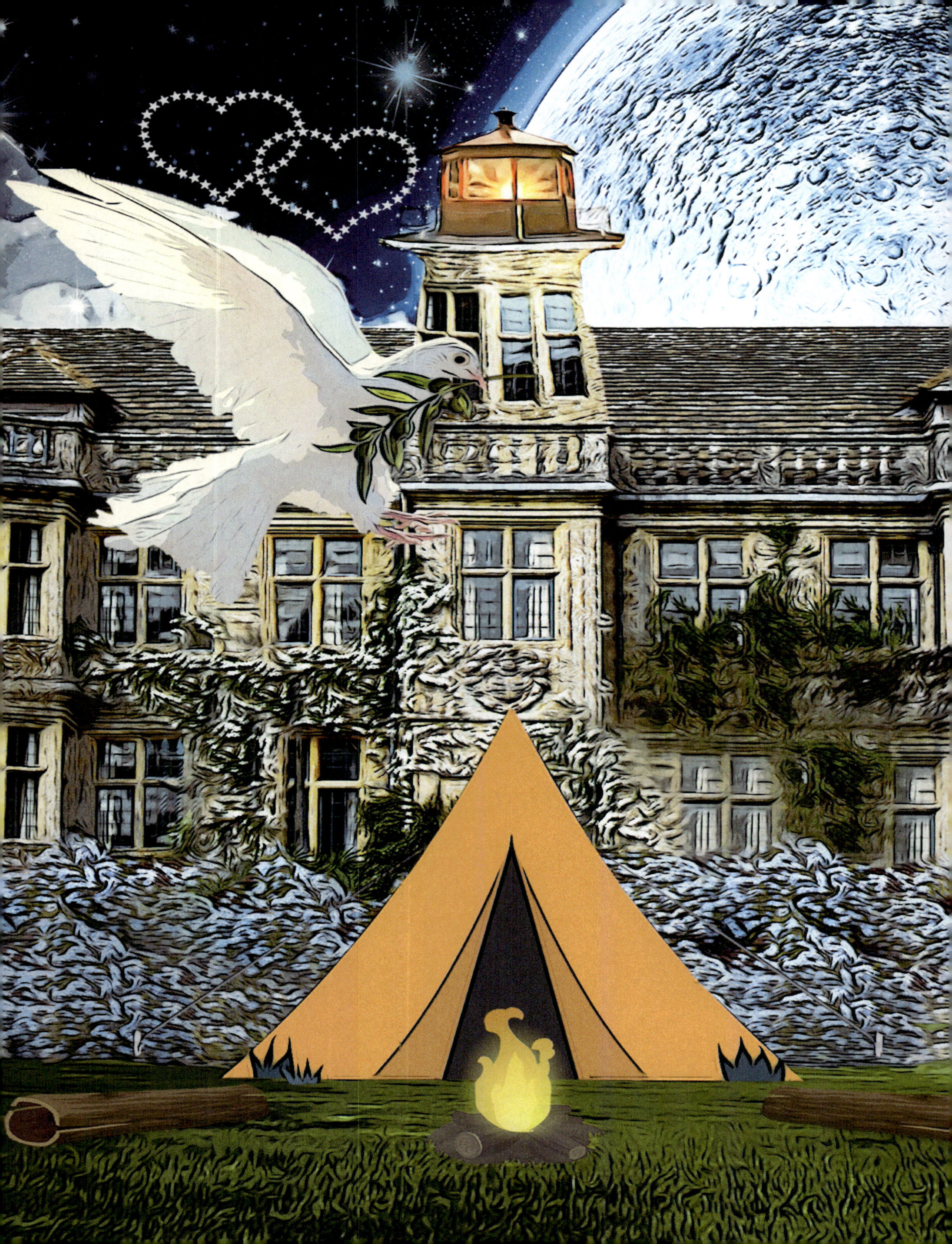

ENCHANTED TALES: A KASTEEL VREDERIC STORYBOOK FOR CHILDREN

Children are the future of this world as they were the past and are the present treasures this world has within her chest. While we the adults too were children once upon a time, like all fairy tales, we have grown up and found our own standing grounds. We realize after we travel time and land in our present, we have actually done well. We have gone to the moon. We have mobile phones, computers, bankers, nurses, teachers, artists, authors, scientists, inventors, and doctors like me, amongst us.

What led us to be so positive about life? How did we survive so many misfortunes of life? Why did we not give up through all the difficulties of life?

These questions had led my family members and me to write this book. My answer is holding on to the triangle of hope, we survived. So, keeping our own life as an example in each story, we have given examples of love, hope, and faith, the three angles of the triangle. With love, with hope, and with faith, all of you too can overcome any and all of the obstacles of life. Children learn fast and know as long as they can hold on to the triangle of hope, they too will be just all right.

Yes, like all fairy tales, in our life story too there are villains and heroes. Yet if we can guide the children from a very young age with wonderful fairy tales, teach them about conflicts, about human relationships, and about healthy lifestyles, positive and negative ones, we could actually make heroes out of all of the future kids. Through positive influences, we can have positive children.

How do we achieve this without creating fear, or pain and hurt in them? I believe the children of Kasteel Vrederic have done just that. They have held the lantern of hope in their hands and are teaching all the children of this world to live in the light, to be the lantern of hope for yourself and all others.

So, it is for our own children we have written *Enchanted Tales: A Kasteel Vrederic Storybook For Children*. As we traveled around the Earth, we realized our own stories needed to be collected and spread around the globe for all other children to enjoy and be guided through. We recognized tales actually support and guide children through psychological and physical stress. As they relate and connect these tales with their own life's struggles or problems, they become intellectually resilient and stronger.

These stories helped children I have visited as they realized they are not the only ones facing adversities. Yet as these tales resolved the troubles, they understood they too could resolve their problems without fear or anxiety.

We chose to travel around the globe as that's the only way we could teach our children to value and respect other cultures and customs. They learn to value all kids around the globe equally at a very young age. Cultures, settings, plots, places, and lands can teach children to value differences. They will appreciate differences as who would not like a princess or a prince from any country or the animal kingdom?

I actually value the languages our children have picked up. From a very young age, my mother, an Indian and American of mixed race, had taught all of us Hindi, Bengali, English, and Dutch. As my parents, Erasmus and Anadhi, adopted my two brothers who are of Italian and Dutch background, they too became fluent in all of the same languages. My mother never saw a difference in us as she says she carried me for nine months, but she carried my brothers for almost two years.

We have tried to teach our children about different cultures through stories from around the globe. As the children read about different countries and places at a very young age, they realize this world is not only about our own home. It's actually about all the countries unitedly living on one Earth. Their intellectual horizon actually includes all the different countries in one home.

I told my daughter Rietje, my niece Griet, and our wonder boys, Theunis and Alexander, to make a time capsule and bury it in the yard for the future generations to open. They made a globe and drew a picture of children from around the world holding hands. They told me when their children open the treasure box in the future, they will know the biggest treasure in this world is we the humans as one family working for one another, not against.

I know everyone reading this book is also a superhero as you can help the world be a better place to live in by planting a tree in your backyard. If you reside in an apartment, you can water the container garden in your kitchen or on your balcony. You know you can also keep all of your plastics and papers separate by recycling.

When you do go to the park and play with your friends, do include the child who sits alone because he or she is different. Then you too become a leader who will be known as a superhero. Make up a new fun game and talk it over with your parents as you teach others the same game. You will be the creator of a new fun game.

Tonight though, before you go to bed, write a superhero story. This superhero should be you and your activities from the day. As you keep a journal through your days, you will have a new superhero book written all by yourself.

Griet, Rietje, Theunis, and Alexander all have gone to bed as they wait for another dawn to come into our home. They know as we do that, there are so many more countries left to be explored around the seven continents that we have not visited yet. As we go around the seven continents of this world once again, we will include more of the countries we have missed in this diary.

I know some continents have more stories than other continents. The reason is we only wrote about the places we were able to visit. If you are from one of the countries we could not visit, remember we will be there soon. Maybe Griet and her team will come and tell you a tale in your dreams. Until then my sweet children of this one world, have a great night and sweet dreams.

We loved having all of you over here at Kasteel Vrederic for the *Enchanted Tales: A Kasteel Vrederic Storybook For Children.*

Signing off for today,
Jacobus Vrederic van Phillip,
On behalf of all the
Kasteel Vrederic Family Members

INHABITANTS OF KASTEEL VREDERIC

Dr. Jacobus Vrederic van Phillip — Medical doctor with multiple specialties, and one-of-a-kind specialist in never-done-before transplant surgeries. Son of Erasmus van Phillip and Anadhi Newhouse van Phillip, cousin of Antonius van Phillip and Andries van Phillip, uncle of reincarnated Andries van Phillip and Griet Vrederic van Phillip, twin flame and husband of Dr. Margriete van Achthoven, and father of Rietje Vrederic van Phillip. Reincarnated form of sixteenth and seventeenth-century Jacobus van Vrederic.

Dr. Margriete van Achthoven — Medical doctor, cardiologist, and pediatric cardiovascular surgeon. Co-owner of Agatha and Marinda's Orphanage. Twin flame and wife of Dr. Jacobus Vrederic van Phillip, and mother of Rietje Vrederic van Phillip. Reincarnated form of sixteenth and seventeenth-century Margriete van Wijck.

Anadhi Newhouse van Phillip — Author. Daughter of Dr. Andrew Newhouse and Dr. Gita Shankar Newhouse, granddaughter of Martin Newhouse and Miranda Newhouse, granddaughter of Hari Shankar and Parvati Shankar, twin flame and wife of Erasmus van Phillip, mother of Dr. Jacobus Vrederic van Phillip, aunt and adoptive mother of Antonius van Phillip and Andries van Phillip, grandmother of reincarnated Andries van Phillip, Griet Vrederic van Phillip, and Rietje Vrederic van Phillip. Reincarnated form of sixteenth-century Mahalt.

Erasmus van Phillip — World-renowned painter, and twenty-first-century owner of Kasteel Vrederic. Son of Greta van Phillip, descendant of the van Vrederic family, twin flame and husband of Anadhi Newhouse van Phillip, father of Dr. Jacobus Vrederic van Phillip, uncle and adoptive father of Antonius van Phillip and Andries van Phillip, and grandfather of reincarnated Andries van Phillip, Griet Vrederic van Phillip, and Rietje Vrederic van Phillip.

	Reincarnated form of sixteenth-century Johannes van Vrederic.
Antonius van Phillip	World-renowned painter. Son of Petrus van Phillip and Giada Berlusconi van Phillip, nephew and adopted son of Erasmus van Phillip and Anadhi Newhouse van Phillip, twin brother of Andries van Phillip, cousin and adoptive brother of Dr. Jacobus Vrederic van Phillip, twin flame and husband of Katelijne Snaaijer van Phillip, and father of reincarnated Andries van Phillip and Griet Vrederic van Phillip.
Katelijne Snaaijer van Phillip	Stepdaughter of Ghileyn Snaaijer, twin flame and wife of Antonius van Phillip, and mother of reincarnated Andries van Phillip and Griet Vrederic van Phillip.
Andries van Phillip	Deceased world-renowned pianist, son of Petrus van Phillip and Giada Berlusconi van Phillip, nephew and adopted son of Erasmus van Phillip and Anadhi Newhouse van Phillip, twin brother of Antonius van Phillip, and cousin and adoptive brother of Dr. Jacobus Vrederic van Phillip. Now reincarnated son of Antonius van Phillip and Katelijne Snaaijer van Phillip, grandson of Erasmus van Phillip and Anadhi Newhouse van Phillip, nephew of Dr. Jacobus Vrederic van Phillip and Dr. Margriete van Achthoven, brother of Griet Vrederic van Phillip, and cousin of Rietje Vrederic van Phillip.
Griet Vrederic van Phillip	Daughter of Antonius van Phillip and Katelijne Snaaijer van Phillip, granddaughter of Erasmus van Phillip and Anadhi Newhouse van Phillip, niece of Dr. Jacobus Vrederic van Phillip and Dr. Margriete Achthoven, sister of Andries van Phillip, and cousin of Rietje Vrederic van Phillip. Reincarnated form of sixteenth-century Griet van Jacobus.
Rietje Vrederic van Phillip	Daughter of Dr. Jacobus Vrederic van Phillip and Dr. Margriete van Achthoven, granddaughter of Erasmus van Phillip and Anadhi Newhouse van Phillip, and cousin of Andries van Phillip and Griet Vrederic van Phillip. Reincarnated form of sixteenth and seventeenth-century Margriete "Rietje" Jacobus Peters.

Theunis Peters	Adopted son of Aunt Marinda. Adoptive brother of Alexander. Reincarnated form of sixteenth-century Theunis Peters.
Alexander van der Bijl	Adopted son of Aunt Marinda. Adoptive brother of Theunis. Reincarnated form of sixteenth and seventeenth-century Sir Alexander van der Bijl.
Aunt Marinda	Time traveler, spiritual seer, nurse, and herbalist from the sixteenth century in the present day. Adoptive guardian of Theunis and Alexander.

GLOSSARY

Get acquainted with some of the global words, historical figures, and animals mentioned in this book.

Aboriginal	Indigenous group of people in Australia
Acropolis	High city, in Greek
Akkadian	Language that was spoken in ancient Mesopotamia
Amerigo Vespucci	Italian explorer who recognized the New World as not being Asia but a new land which became to be known as North America and South America
Antarktikos	Opposite to the Arctic, in Greek
Aotearoa	Name of New Zealand in the Māori language
Aymara	Indigenous group of people in South America
Ayurveda	Science of life, in Sanskrit, and is an alternative medicine system that came from India
Bel Paese	Nickname of Italy meaning beautiful country, in Italian
Christopher Columbus	Italian explorer who is known for his voyages across the Atlantic Ocean
Hendrik Willem Mesdag	Famous Dutch painter
Joey	Name for baby kangaroos in Australia
Johannes Vermeer	Famous Dutch painter
Kasteel Vrederic	Castle and home named after the ancestors of Jacobus van Phillip
Koolewong	One of the Aboriginal words for koala
Lac Léman	French name for Lake Geneva
Lemur	Sacred and protected animal endemic only to Madagascar

Lo Stivale	Nickname of Italy meaning the boot, in Italian
Loch	Lake, in Scots and Scottish Gaelic
Māori	Indigenous group of Polynesian people in New Zealand
Mayur	Peacock, in Hindi
Oma	Grandmother, in Dutch
Opa	Grandfather, in Dutch
Phoenician	Language that was spoken in ancient Mediterranean coastal areas and Lebanon
Pitohui	First known poisonous bird
Rabindranath Tagore	Bengali Nobel laureate from India
Rembrandt Harmenszoon van Rijn	Famous Dutch painter
Sasquatch	Native American name for Bigfoot
Starry Night	Famous painting by Vincent van Gogh
Vincent van Gogh	Famous Dutch painter
William Shakespeare	Famous English poet and playwright

ENCHANTED TALES: A KASTEEL VREDERIC STORYBOOK FOR CHILDREN

ANSWER KEY

EUROPE

Which landmark is this and where is it located?
Answer: C. Leaning Tower of Pisa, Italy

THE NETHERLANDS

What is the language spoken in this country?
Answer: Dutch

What is the political capital of the Netherlands?
Answer: The Hague

What sea connects the Netherlands to France, Germany, Sweden, Norway, Belgium, and Denmark?
Answer: North Sea

ITALY

What is Italy nicknamed because of its shape?
Answer: Lo Stivale or the boot

Where in Italy is the famous Trevi fountain located?
Answer: Rome

Who are the two famous Italian painters mentioned in this story?
Answer: Michelangelo di Lodovico Buonarroti Simoni, commonly known as Michelangelo, and Leonardo di ser Piero da Vinci, commonly known as Leonardo da Vinci

SWITZERLAND

What shape is Lake Geneva?
Answer: Crescent-shaped lake

What is Lake Geneva also known as?
Answer: Lac Léman

What are the four official languages in Switzerland?
Answer: German, French, Italian, and Romansh

GREECE

What sea did the Kasteel Vrederic family sail through in Greece?
Answer: Mediterranean Sea

When was the Parthenon in Athens dedicated to the Greek goddess Athena?
Answer: Fifth century B.C.

Where in Greece is the Temple of the Greek god Poseidon?
Answer: Cape Sounion

UNITED KINGDOM

What four individual countries are included in the United Kingdom?
Answer: Wales, England, Scotland, Northern Ireland

Where is the famous Loch Ness located?
Answer: Scotland

Who enforced the curfew law prohibiting everyone from going outside after 8 p.m.?
Answer: King William I

AUSTRALIA/OCEANIA

Which landmark is this and where is it located?
Answer: A. Sydney Opera House, Australia

AUSTRALIA

When does summer start in Australia?
Answer: December

What indigenous group of people does Willow belong to?
Answer: Aboriginal

What state is the Gold Coast in?
Answer: Queensland

NEW ZEALAND

What is the Māori name for New Zealand?
Answer: Aotearoa

ENCHANTED TALES: A KASTEEL VREDERIC STORYBOOK FOR CHILDREN

What are two famous movies that were filmed in New Zealand?
Answer: *The Lord of the Rings* and *The Hobbit* trilogy

What fruit shares the same name as the people born in New Zealand?
Answer: Kiwi

PAPUA NEW GUINEA

What is the capital city of Papua New Guinea?
Answer: Port Moresby

What is the world's first known poisonous bird?
Answer: Pitohui

What island did the snorkeling triplets come from?
Answer: Samarai Island

ANTARCTICA

Which landmark is this and where is it located?
Answer: B. Cierva Cove, Antarctic Peninsula

What months are months of darkness in Antarctica?
Answer: Antarctica's winter months

When was the Antarctic Treaty originally signed?
Answer: December 1, 1959

What continent do most people travel through to reach Antarctica?
Answer: South America

SOUTH AMERICA

Which landmark is this and where is it located?
Answer: B. Christ the Redeemer, Brazil

BRAZIL

What is the name of the famous rainforest located in Brazil?
Answer: Amazon Rainforest

What is the official language in Brazil?
Answer: Portuguese

What is the capital city of Brazil?
Answer: Brasília

CHILE

What planet's soil is compared to the soil in the Atacama Desert?
Answer: Mars

What is the height of the Atacama Giant?
Answer: 390 feet

Why is the Atacama Desert a popular destination for stargazing?
Answer: It is dry for 300 days out of the year

NORTH AMERICA

Which landmark is this and where is it located?
Answer: A. Statue of Liberty, USA

UNITED STATES OF AMERICA

What state is the Statue of Liberty in?
Answer: New York

What is the national bird of the USA?
Answer: Bald eagle

What is Los Angeles known as?
Answer: City of Angels

COSTA RICA

What is the official language of Costa Rica?
Answer: Spanish

What continent is Costa Rica in?
Answer: North America

What reserve did the Kasteel Vrederic family visit in Costa Rica?
Answer: Punta Islita Wild Macaw Reserve

ASIA

Which landmark is this and where is it located?
Answer: C. Taj Mahal, India

INDIA

What is the capital city of India?
Answer: New Delhi

What popular children's game originated from India?
Answer: *Snakes and Ladders*, or *Chutes and Ladders*, originated from *Moksha Patam*

What is the highest rail bridge in the world?
Answer: Chenab Bridge

BANGLADESH

What river does the Ganges River become in Bangladesh?
Answer: Padma

What is the capital city of Bangladesh?
Answer: Dhaka

Who wrote Bangladesh's national anthem?
Answer: Rabindranath Tagore

AFRICA

Which landmark is this and where is it located?
Answer: C. Pyramids of Giza, Egypt

KENYA

What city is the Maasai Mara National Reserve in?
Answer: Narok

What is the Kenyan national bird?
Answer: Lilac-breasted roller

What is one indigenous group of animals that is protected in the Maasai Mara National Reserve?
Answer: Black rhinoceros

MADAGASCAR

When was Madagascar discovered?
Answer: 1500 AD

What are the official languages in Madagascar?
Answer: Malagasy and French.

What animal is protected and considered sacred in Madagascar?
Answer: Lemur

EGYPT

What is Egypt called by many?
Answer: Gift of the Nile

What is the name of Egypt's largest pyramid?
Answer: Great Pyramid of Giza

Which sea does the Nile River empty into?
Answer: Mediterranean Sea

MESSAGE FROM THE AUTHOR

"Love for all humans and faith in humanity create this world's glowing lantern of hope."

Dear Readers,

Life is a miraculous journey where you are the traveler. On this journey, you can choose to pack within your luggage whatever your heart desires. I packed in my luggage, love, hope, and faith. My luggage is my magical treasure box, with what I call treasures from my chest.

I believe in the miracles of life for I am the traveler who walks upon the path of miracles. After a long, hard, and worn-out journey, we find ourselves on the path of miracles. Nothing in life comes easy as you the traveler must walk upon the path to reach your desired destination.

This world is a book where all around us there are so many inspirational stories taking birth each day. We don't get to hear about them, nor do we share them with one another. I wanted to share this magical Earth with you the reader. I wanted to share a meal with you. I also wanted to travel with you through the seven continents of this world. I wondered how I could pick up all the children from around the globe and go on a magical journey together, where we would meet up with some magical friends like the Jaguar Prince and the Lemur Girl.

We could make this world into our magical home through friendship. In this magical world, you could visit me, and I could visit you without any prior appointments. I know the pure miraculous love for humanity, the hope for all humans, and the faith in humanity would bind us all in an unbreakable friendship throughout eternity.

So, I created my book of tales from around the globe for all of you. I want you to keep this treasure within your chest with love eternally. Remember, this is my way of taking you all on a journey throughout this world with me. As I had a meal in a new land far away from my home, I wrote down what I had so I could share it with you through this book. When I stayed in a cottage under the blue skies, I wrote down the description of the cottages for you to travel with me through the pages of this book.

I do believe this world is a book. So, we can actually all travel around the globe without leaving our homes through this magical book. This book has a secret door to the seven continents of this world for this book unites all the continents and all their inhabitants with you.

Enchanted Tales: A Kasteel Vrederic Storybook For Children through its magical doors will eternally take you on a journey through the seven continents of this world whenever you decide to travel. You are the traveler who has now traveled around the globe through this magical book. All you had to do is open the pages of the book.

ENCHANTED TALES: A KASTEEL VREDERIC STORYBOOK FOR CHILDREN

Here each continent is a chapter, where you the traveler get to see the landscape, the landmarks, the culture, and food through the pages of this book. You also got to live and travel with a family. You made new magical friends who will forever be your friends.

I hope you now will always find a place in your heart for all of your little friends from around the globe. All the children mentioned in this book are students of the *Enchanted Tales* classroom, and so are you as you too have the book in your hands. Together as we hold hands around the globe, we could unite this world into one classroom, one school, one big family, and forever friends.

I hope you all enjoyed traveling with the Kasteel Vrederic family members. They have opened their door to all the children of this world. As they sit with the children of this world through a book, I hope my message finds a gentle and safe space in your magical chest.

Spread my message around the globe and know your neighboring countries are your neighbors. We all can live happily ever after if only we believe in one world, one family, and one love. All the countries and all the inhabitants, humans, and animal friends can love one another. May my love for you and your love for me spread throughout this world and may we all unite under the banner of love, hope, and faith, for one another.

My message to all of you is simple. I believe faith, love, and hope can make this one world see all of the world's inhabitants as one big family. The blue sky above our head is our roof and the Earth beyond our feet is our home. The walls we create to keep ourselves in and others out won't divide us but give us enough time away from one another to really appreciate one another.

Love your neighbors and do watch out for your neighbors. For maybe you too will get a visit from the girl with the lantern when you too need her. Until then, you can keep the candles of hope glowing in your home. You can become the friend of the girl with the lantern and spread love, faith, and hope around your neighborhood and slowly around the globe.

Let's be the candles of hope around the world as we love all the citizens of this world as one family and one race, the human race. I hope with complete faith and all my love, you will keep this book as a treasure in your chest. This treasure unites this one world through your love, your hope, and your faith.

My love, my hope, and my faith have created a magical book for you all. Here, you the travelers of this world will find the needed hope, and share this hope with all who need a magical house to gain hope. Through my faith, I shall bring all of you to my house of hope, my enchanted book where you the traveler will find all the other lonely travelers and show them the magical path to gain back their faith in humanity.

Through the magical stories, I send you all my unconditional love. Do spread this unconditional magical love with all who need a loving word or phrase to guide them back to believing in one world. Believe in the magical messages of this book. For in life, we all have a choice as to what we believe in or don't. I believe in miracles. All the stories in this book are made with pure miracles. The heart and soul of each story is simply love, hope, and faith.

Through the magical hands of humanity, I have united all the children of this world into one book. For more than all the glitter or gold or treasures of this world, I treasure all the children of this world. Every single one of you have made a spot for yourself in my chest. So, I give you from the bottom of my chest, the only treasure I have, which I have written and bound into a book for you the children of this world, my magical book of tales. I call this book *Enchanted Tales: A Kasteel Vrederic Storybook For Children*.

To all of the travelers who have joined us at our story time, this book is my gift to all the children of this world. To the readers of the *Kasteel Vrederic* series, you all had read in *Forbidden Daughter of Kasteel Vrederic: Vows From The Beyond*, our famous doctor and diarist, Jacobus Vrederic van Phillip, and his family members love sharing story time with children around the world. So here I have included a description of all the Kasteel Vrederic books released up to now.

BOOK ONE:

Eternally Beloved: I Shall Never Let You Go

This book introduces you to Kasteel Vrederic through the first diary of the famous diarist Jacobus van Vrederic. He walks you through his sad love story and goes through the love story of his daughter Griet van Jacobus and the brave soldier Theunis Peter. Based during the Dutch Eighty Years' War in the sixteenth century.

BOOK TWO:

Evermore Beloved: I Shall Never Let You Go

Here you walk through the amazing love story of Jacobus van Vrederic and his beloved wife Margriete van Wijck, where we get to meet Jacobus's beloved granddaughter, baby Rietje. Based during the witch trials and the Dutch Eighty Years' War in the sixteenth and seventeenth centuries.

BOOK THREE:

Be My Destiny: Vows From The Beyond

This book takes you through reincarnation and the blessed door of dreams. Here infinite twin flames Erasmus van Phillip, a twenty-first-century descendant of Jacobus van Vrederic and the reincarnated father of Jacobus van Vrederic, is reborn again to find and unite with his forever twin flame, Anadhi Newhouse, also the reincarnated mother of Jacobus van Vrederic. Find out how their son reunites them through the twenty-first century and takes them back to Kasteel Vrederic.

BOOK FOUR:

Heart Beats Your Name: Vows From The Beyond

Here you will get introduced to a blind son of the Kasteel Vrederic family, the nephew and adopted son of Erasmus van Phillip and Anadhi Newhouse van Phillip. In this paranormal thriller, you will see how Dr. Jacobus Vrederic van Phillip, the biological son of Erasmus and Anadhi, guides his brother to unite with his pronounced dead wife, while trying to solve her murder mystery. A paranormal book where everyone realizes family members are bound with one another throughout time.

BOOK FIVE:

Entranced Beloved: I Shall Never Let You Go

Twenty-first-century Dr. Jacobus Vrederic van Phillip must return to the seventeenth-century Kasteel Vrederic, as he realizes his beloved granddaughter is missing and must be rescued for the inhabitants of *Vows From The Beyond* to even exist. This can only be done through the miraculous hands of the famous twenty-first-century physician. So here we go, Dr. Jacobus must travel time and go back to the *I Shall Never Let You Go* diaries. Walk back and get reacquainted with the seventeenth-century Kasteel Vrederic family members with Dr. Jacobus as he meets his sixteenth-century self, Jacobus van Vrederic. Margriete "Rietje" Jacobus Peters and Sir Alexander van der Bijl's love story is written and retold by the twenty-first-century famous physician, Dr. Jacobus from the *Vows From The Beyond* diaries.

BOOK SIX:

Forbidden Daughter Of Kasteel Vrederic: Vows From The Beyond

Dr. Jacobus Vrederic van Phillip and Dr. Margriete van Achthoven through the door of reincarnation traveled time yet now must face the wagon of karma. The unborn child asks, "Why am I the forbidden daughter of Kasteel Vrederic?" With the answer, revolves the existence of the Kasteel Vrederic Lover's Lighthouse and the father of the lighthouse. Trying to find an answer to this question, Dr. Jacobus finds out his family is being terrorized by a murderer who hides within Kasteel Vrederic.

KASTEEL VREDERIC STORYBOOK FOR CHILDREN:

Enchanted Tales: A Kasteel Vrederic Storybook For Children

Kasteel Vrederic has for the first time not as the forbidden but as the beloved daughter, Griet, in her home. For centuries as a spirit, she protected the inhabitants of Kasteel Vrederic. Now as a beloved daughter, she travels with her family, solving mysteries with local superheroes around the globe.

-Ann Marie Ruby

ABOUT THE AUTHOR

"Meet Ann Marie Ruby from San Francisco, California. This is her story."

Ann Marie Ruby was born into a diplomatic family for which she had the privilege of traveling the world. This upbringing made the whole world her one family. She never saw a country as a foreign country yet as a neighbor who was there for her as she would be there for them. After all, isn't that what families do for one another?

Ann Marie became an author as she started to place her chosen words into the pages of her diaries. She knew she must collect all her thoughts and produce them into different diaries. Each diary became her different books.

Ann Marie's life goal is not to just write something but only what she believes in. So all her thoughts and words remained within the pages of her diaries until she realized it was time she must share them with you. Otherwise, she felt selfish and knew that was not her characteristic as she lives for everyone, not just for herself.

INTERNATIONAL #1 BESTSELLING AUTHOR:

Ann Marie became an international number-one bestselling author of nineteen books. Alongside being a full-time author, she loves to write articles on her website where she can have a better connection with all of you. Ann Marie, a dream psychic, became a blogger and a humanitarian only because she believes in you and herself as a complete, honest, and open family.

PERSONAL:

Ann Marie is an American who grew up in Brisbane, Australia. She resided in the Washington, D.C. area, later settled in Seattle, Washington, and currently lives in San Francisco, California. In her spare time when she is not writing books, she loves to meditate, pray, listen to music, cook, and write blog posts.

BESTSELLING:

Ann Marie's books have placed her on top 100 bestselling charts in various countries including the Netherlands, United States, United Kingdom, Canada, and Germany. In 2020, she became a household name as her books began to consistently rank #1 on multiple bestselling charts. *The Netherlands: Land Of My Dreams* and *Everblooming: Through The Twelve Provinces Of The Netherlands*, both became overnight number-one bestsellers in the United States.

In 2020, *The Netherlands: Land Of My Dreams* also became a bestseller in the Netherlands and Canada, consistently becoming #1 on various lists and one of the top selling books on Amazon NL. *Everblooming: Through The Twelve Provinces Of The Netherlands* became #37 on the Netherlands top 100 bestselling Amazon books chart which includes all books from all genres. Ann Marie's other books have also made various top 100 bestselling lists and received multiple accolades including *Eternal Truth: The Tunnel Of Light* which was named as one of eight thought-provoking books by women.

ROMANCE FICTION:

Ann Marie's *Kasteel Vrederic* series was written in a diary fashion. She has always kept a diary herself, so she thought her characters too could keep a diary. All of their diaries became individual books yet collectively, they are a part of a family, the Kasteel Vrederic family.

OTHER BOOKS:

All of Ann Marie's nonfiction and fiction books are available globally. You can take a look at short descriptions about the books at the end of this book.

THE NETHERLANDS:

Ann Marie revealed why many of her books revolve around the Netherlands, sharing that as a dream psychic, she had seen the historical past of a country in her dreams and was later able to place a name to the country. This is described in detail in *Spiritual Lighthouse: The Dream Diaries Of Ann Marie Ruby* and *The Netherlands: Land Of My Dreams* where she also wrote about her plans to eventually move to the Netherlands.

Ann Marie has received letters on behalf of His Majesty King Willem-Alexander and Her Majesty Queen Máxima of the Netherlands after they received her books *The Netherlands: Land Of My Dreams* and *Everblooming: Through The Twelve Provinces Of The Netherlands*. Additionally, Ann Marie has received letters on behalf of His Excellency Mark Rutte, the Prime Minister of the Netherlands for her books.

WRITING:

Ann Marie also is acclaimed globally as one of the top voices in the spiritual space, however, she is recognized for her writing abilities published across many genres namely spirituality, lifestyle, inspirational quotations, poetry, fiction, romance, history, travel, social awareness, and more. Her writing style is hailed by critics and readers alike as making readers feel as though they have made a friend.

FOLLOW THE AUTHOR:

Now as you have found her book, why don't you and Ann Marie become friends? Join her and become a part of her global family. Ann Marie shall always give you books which you will read and then find yourself as a part of her book family.

For more information about Ann Marie Ruby, any one of her books, or to read her blog posts and articles, subscribe to her website, www.annmarieruby.com.

Follow Ann Marie Ruby on Twitter, Facebook, Instagram, and Pinterest:

@TheAnnMarieRuby

BOOKS BY THE AUTHOR

INSPIRATIONAL QUOTATIONS SERIES:

This series includes four books of original quotations and one omnibus edition.

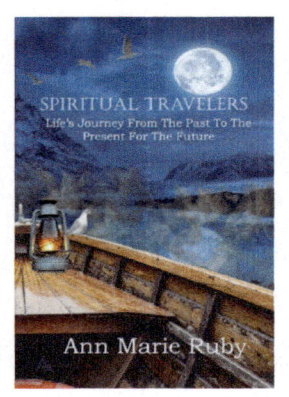

Spiritual Travelers:
Life's Journey From The Past
To The Present For The Future

Spiritual Messages:
From A Bottle

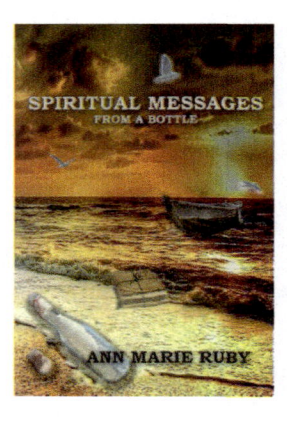

Spiritual Journey:
Life's Eternal Blessings

Spiritual Inspirations:
Sacred Words Of Wisdom

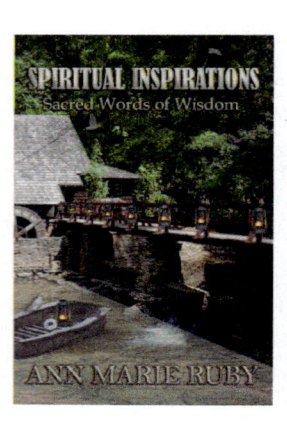

Omnibus edition contains all four books of original quotations.

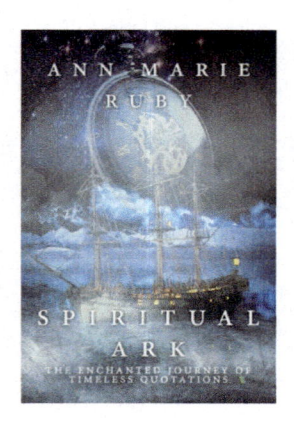

Spiritual Ark:
The Enchanted Journey Of Timeless Quotations

SPIRITUAL SONGS SERIES:

This series includes two original spiritual prayer books.

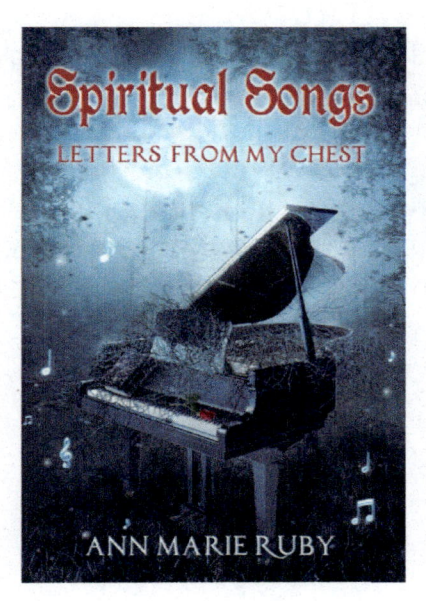

SPIRITUAL SONGS: LETTERS FROM MY CHEST

When there was no hope, I found hope within these sacred words of prayers, I but call songs. Within this book, I have for you, 100 very sacred prayers.

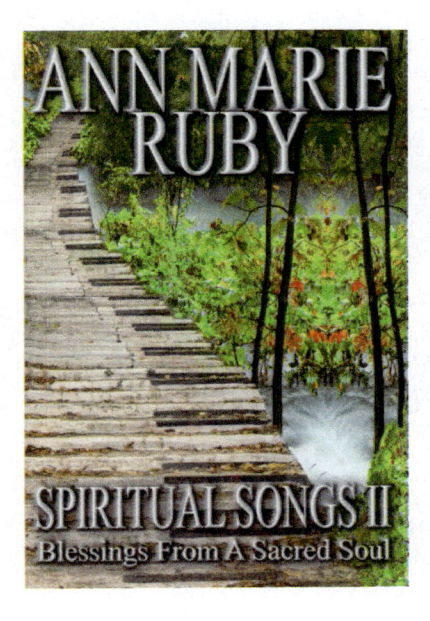

SPIRITUAL SONGS II: BLESSINGS FROM A SACRED SOUL

Prayers are but the sacred doors to an individual's enlightenment. This book has 123 prayers for all humans with humanity.

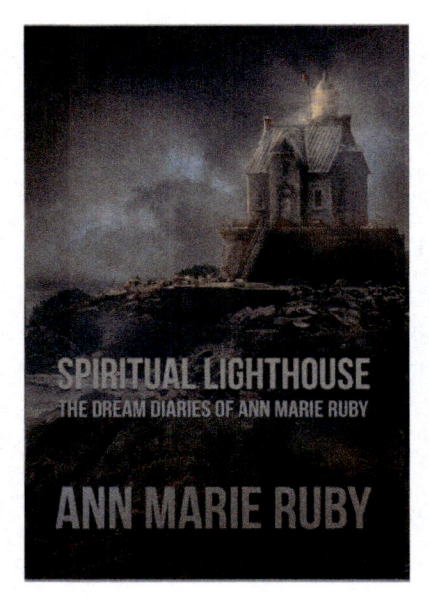

SPIRITUAL LIGHTHOUSE:
THE DREAM DIARIES OF ANN MARIE RUBY

Do you believe in dreams? For within each individual dream, there is a hidden message and a miracle interlinked. Learn the spiritual, scientific, religious, and philosophical aspects of dreams. Walk with me as you travel through forty nights, through the pages of my book.

THE WORLD HATE CRISIS:
THROUGH THE EYES OF A DREAM PSYCHIC

Humans have walked into an age where humanity now is being questioned as hate crimes have reached a catastrophic amount. Let us in union stop this crisis. Pick up my book and see if you too could join me in this fight.

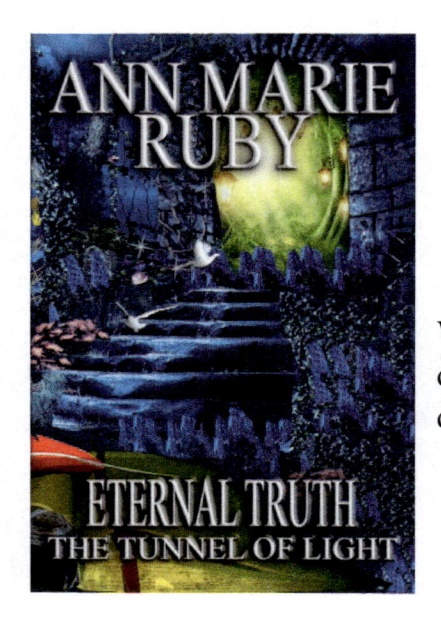

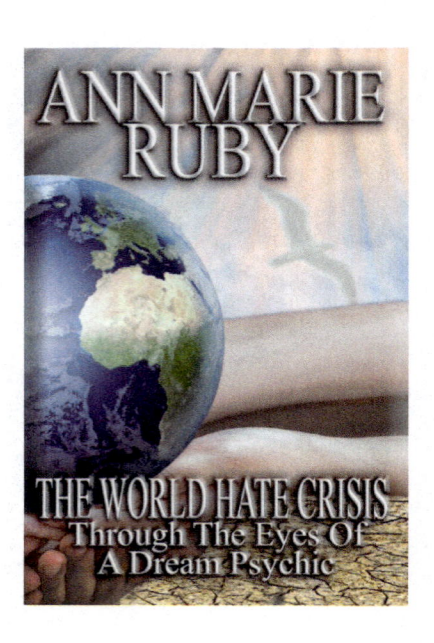

ETERNAL TRUTH:
THE TUNNEL OF LIGHT

Within this book, travel with me through the doors of birth, death, reincarnation, true soulmates and twin flames, dreams, miracles, and the end of time.

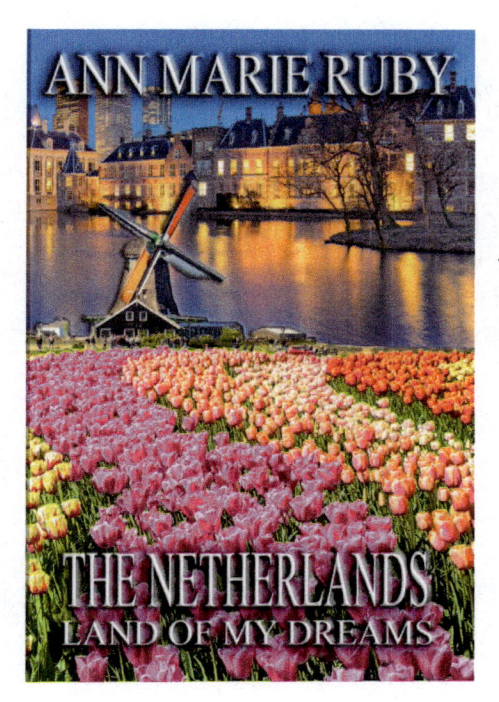

THE NETHERLANDS: LAND OF MY DREAMS

Oh the sacred travelers, be like the mystical river and journey through this blessed land through my book. Be the flying bird of wisdom and learn about a land I call, Heaven on Earth.

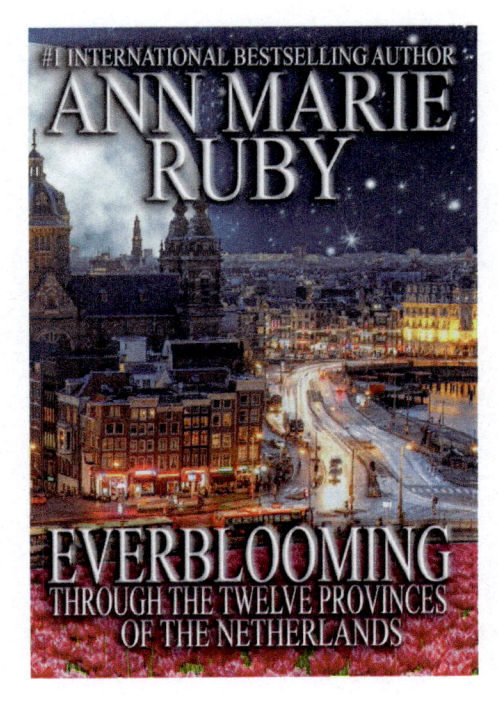

EVERBLOOMING: THROUGH THE TWELVE PROVINCES OF THE NETHERLANDS

Original poetry and hand-picked tales are bound together in this keepsake book. Come travel with me as I take you through the lives of the Dutch past.

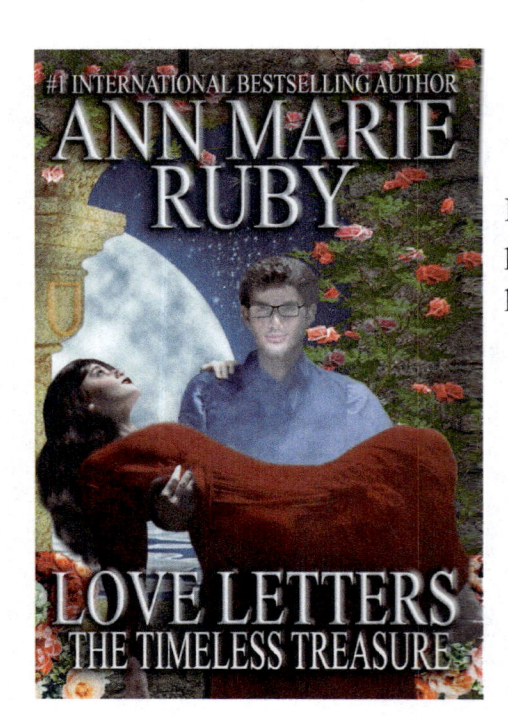

LOVE LETTERS:
THE TIMELESS TREASURE

Fifty original timeless treasured love poems are presented with individual illustrations describing each poem.

KASTEEL VREDERIC SERIES:

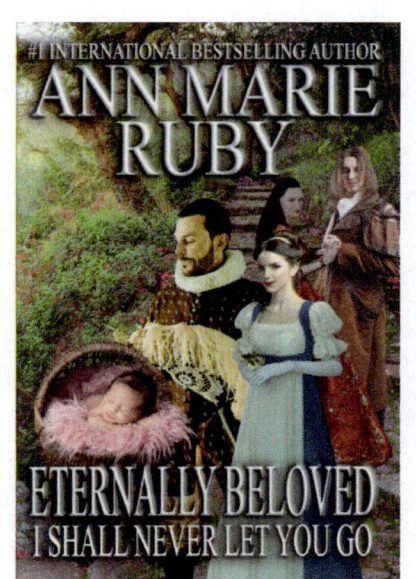

ETERNALLY BELOVED:
I SHALL NEVER LET YOU GO

Travel time to the sixteenth century where Jacobus van Vrederic, a beloved lover and father, surmounts time and tide to find the vanished love of his life. On his pursuit, Jacobus discovers secrets that will alter his life evermore. He travels through the Eighty Years' War-ravaged country, the Netherlands as he takes the vow, even if separated by a breath, "Eternally beloved, I shall never let you go."

EVERMORE BELOVED:
I SHALL NEVER LET YOU GO

Jacobus van Vrederic returns with the devoted spirits of Kasteel Vrederic. A knight and a seer also join him on a quest to find his lost evermore beloved. They journey through a war-ravaged country, the Netherlands, to stop another war which was brewing silently in his land, called the witch hunts. Time was his enemy as he must defeat time and tide to find his evermore beloved wife alive.

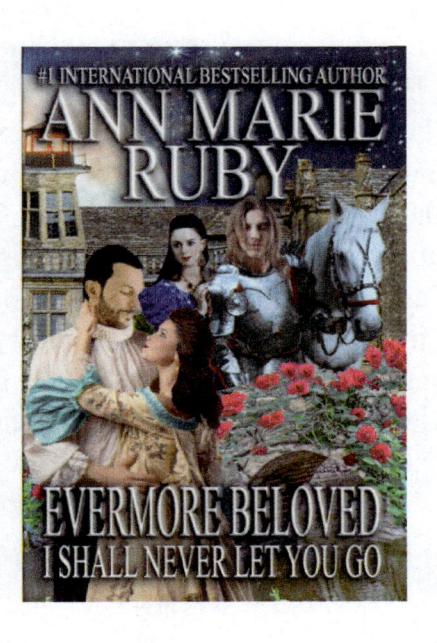

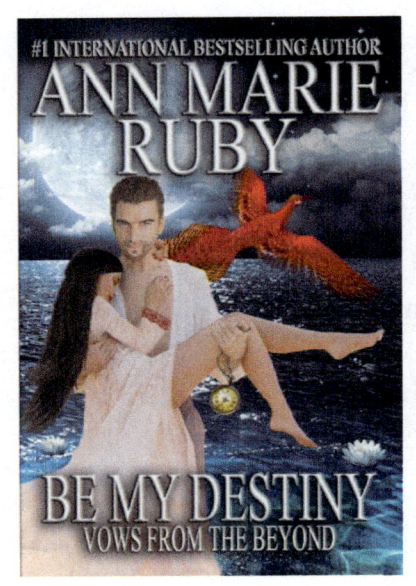

BE MY DESTINY:
VOWS FROM THE BEYOND

Fighting their biggest enemy destiny, twin flames Erasmus van Phillip and Anadhi Newhouse are reborn over and over again only to lose the battle to destiny. Find out if through the helping hands of sacred spirits of the sixteenth century, these eternal twin flames are finally able to unite in the twenty-first century, as they say, "Reincarnation is a blessing if only you are mine."

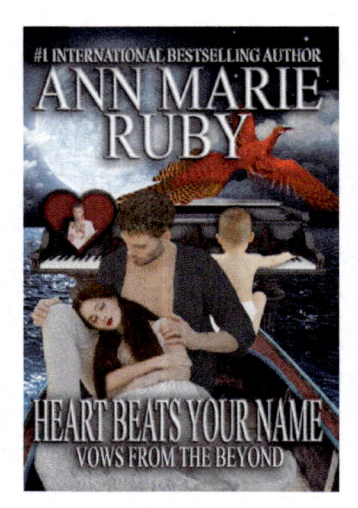

HEART BEATS YOUR NAME:
VOWS FROM THE BEYOND

While one is sleepless, the other twin flame is sleeping eternally. Now how does Antonius van Phillip awaken his twin flame Katelijne Snaaijer from beyond Earth, and solve a murder mystery, she is the only witness to yet also a victim of? Find out how the musical sound of heartbeats guide him to his sleeping beloved while he solves the mystery sleepless.

ENTRANCED BELOVED:
I SHALL NEVER LET YOU GO

The pages of Margriete "Rietje" Jacobus Peters's love story from her diary slowly go missing from the library of Kasteel Vrederic. The twenty-first-century descendants fighting death and time must travel back in time to save their ancestors and their beloved Kasteel Vrederic. Traveling through the tunnel of light, the family of the twenty-first century must save the seventeenth-century twin flames. Rietje and her beloved twin flame Sir Alexander van der Bijl must create another paranormal, magical, historical, romantic diary for the dynasty to even exist.

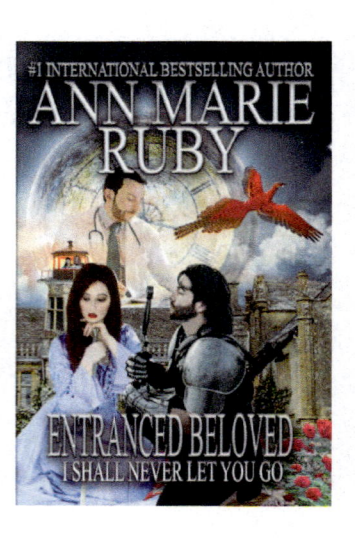

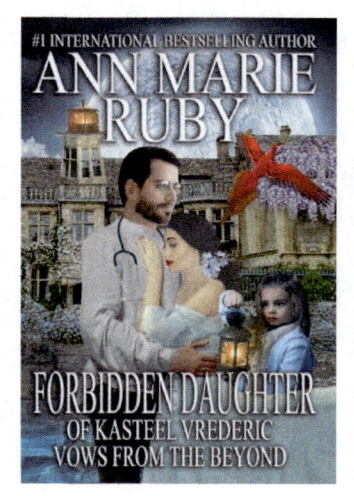

FORBIDDEN DAUGHTER OF KASTEEL VREDERIC:
VOWS FROM THE BEYOND

Jacobus Vrederic van Phillip stopped pouring tears and burning himself with memories of passion to become a stone, so he could live with memories and not recreate new ones. The Vrederic family members realize the curse of past life's karma will come and meet them in this life and erase the only child who kept the dynasty going, the child known to all as the forbidden daughter of Kasteel Vrederic. The man who has sacrificed his life for all members of his family and society now must find a way to awaken his sleeping soul, recognize his twin flame, and bring back as the beloved daughter the only child he had rejected. To this world she was known as the forbidden daughter of Kasteel Vrederic.

THE IMMORTALITY SERUM:
VOWS FROM THE BEYOND

The seventh book in this series is coming soon.

THE IMMORTALITY SERUM: VOWS FROM THE BEYOND

KASTEEL VREDERIC STORYBOOK FOR CHILDREN:

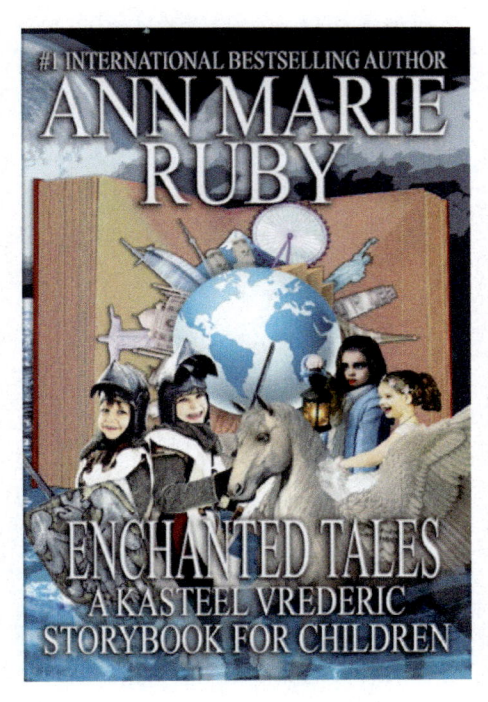

ENCHANTED TALES:
A KASTEEL VREDERIC STORYBOOK FOR CHILDREN

Travel around the world in seven nights. Through enchanted tales you will meet and assist superheroes from the seven continents of this world. While there, you will learn about different cultures and landmarks. Keep your magical lanterns glowing as you help the girl with the lantern solve mysteries around the globe.

Printed in Great Britain
by Amazon